VIRGINIA BLACK

CONSECRATED
GROUND

Bywater
BOOKS

2023

Bywater Books

Copyright © 2023 Virginia Black

All rights reserved. No part of this book may be
reproduced, stored in a retrieval system, or transmitted
in any form or by any means, without prior permission
in writing from the publisher.

Print ISBN: 978-1-61294-255-1

Bywater Books First Edition: February 2023

Printed in the United States of America on acid-free paper.

Cover designer: Ann McMan, TreeHouse Studio

Bywater Books
PO Box 3671
Ann Arbor MI 48106-3671

www.bywaterbooks.com

For Kate and Chase, always.
And for Nico.

CHAPTER 1

The gnarled oak greeted Joan like an old friend. Half a mile from the Calvert town limits, its lowest thickest limb marked the curve in the road just as she remembered, but she ignored the sign to slow down.

If she did, the three men blocking her side of the two-lane road would probably try to stab her tires.

One was armed with only a menacing look, but the others held a crowbar and a knife, respectively. One was Black like Joan but with short, thick matted natural hair, and shorter than her near six feet in height. Crowbar guy had a few inches on her. All three of them were too grimy and underfed to gauge their ages any better than between twenty-five and forty.

They stood in direct sunlight, so they weren't vampires. Even cocky new vampires who thought nothing could touch them avoided the sun. Ultraviolet rays made dead flesh decompose faster. These men were most likely vampire thralls, human minions under vampire control.

"Well, Luther," Joan said, her SUV ever the patient listener. "It's always somethin', right?"

Joan revved the biodiesel engine in warning, but they didn't budge. This wasn't the first time she regretted making the trip. Coming back to Calvert had never been part of her plan but circumstances had changed. Now a two-hour drive inland from the Oregon coast had somehow ballooned to five, and she wanted to be done already.

Maybe these losers would move, and she wouldn't have to clean anything from Luther's grille today. A behemoth of a Range Rover customized to travel through dangerous lands, Luther wouldn't stop a vampire horde, but it would protect her against one or two attackers—or all of these guys, who didn't look like much of a threat. Filthy clothes hung loose on their malnourished limbs, another sign of their dwindling humanity. Vampires never seemed to feed their humans well. The irony might have been funny under different circumstances.

Crowbar tried to knock out a headlight, but the cages on the grille prevented that sort of thing. The one with the knife fell over in an attempt to stab a tire, then rolled clear when she sped up.

Joan glanced in the rearview mirror. The short, unarmed guy helped his fallen comrade to his feet. Would they give up and leave, or lie in wait for the next traveler? This close to the county line marking the outskirts of her hometown, they were bound to run into the town watch.

She chalked the whole event down to a wide, boring miss. Today was a bad day for a fight anyway. Who knew what was waiting for her in Calvert after all this time?

Joan pressed on the gas pedal.

Then the dog showed up.

Even for a Siberian husky he was large, with black, gray, and white fur warring for dominance over his coat. He should have been lumbering down the highway, as big as he was, but all that muscle raced in spectacular symmetry.

The dog passed Joan as he ran in the opposite direction, bearing down on the enemy behind her.

In the rearview, he leapt for the neck of the human thrall with the knife and took the man down in one clean pounce. Crowbar raised his weapon with obvious intent.

Joan hit the brakes so hard, the tires screeched in protest.

She shifted into reverse.

A honk of the horn distracted them from the dog. She jacked the wheel to one side before parking Luther at an angle in the lane, then opened the door and leapt to the road without her gun. A ranged battle was always better, one where the enemy never got the chance to touch her, but if she shot her semiautomatic pistol into this mess, she might hit the dog.

Instead, she drew a six-inch black powder-coated Bowie from the worn leather sheath at her thigh.

Knife Guy lay on the ground wrestling with the dog, thankfully forgetful that he held a weapon. The amount of blood leaking from his neck suggested he was losing. Crowbar came at Joan, but she blocked his overhead swing with one arm. She swept her other elbow at his jaw. He grunted in pain and fell back but didn't drop the crowbar.

Shorty moved in, his fists raised like a boxer's, but without gloves one solid punch would break his hand. Joan tried not to roll her eyes in the middle of a fight.

She tapped her tongue twice against the roof of her mouth and puffed a burst of air in his direction. A small cloud of mist appeared in front of his face, and he pulled back in surprise. She almost felt bad for him. The chances these guys had ever faced a war witch were slim, and even basic battle maneuver spells—ones that didn't require incantations—would give her an advantage.

"It's okay if you want to forsake your masters," she said. "I swear I won't tell." Maybe she could end this without killing any of them. Human thralls deserved pity—no matter how they'd ended up in vampire clutches.

None of them had her level of training, but it was still three against one. Against two, if she counted the dog, who had scrambled away from the guy on the ground when he grabbed at an ear hard enough to make the dog yowl.

Crowbar had long greasy hair and a thick, filthy beard.

Thanks to her elbow hit, one of his lips was split and bleeding. He adjusted his grip and came at her again. Knife Guy moved more slowly, looking grislier by the second as the blood flowed down his front. Shorty lurched into any gap where he'd fit, even if he didn't seem to know what he was doing.

It was madness in close quarters as she hit them more than they managed to hit her. Despite the number of her hard-enough-to-debilitate blows, though, they kept coming back for more.

The dog joined the fight, but that only made things more complicated.

Especially when Joan tripped over him and landed flat on her back.

Her head slammed against the asphalt seconds before Crowbar threw himself over her. He tried to pin her to the ground with his hips. She bucked him half off her, enough to get a knee between his legs, but he landed a solid hit, his weight behind it, to her midsection.

She didn't yell or puke and counted herself lucky he'd missed her ribs. Joan shook her head to clear it.

"*Aere vacuum*," she said, the words conjuring an air-based spell of her own design. It sucked the air from his lungs, and while he sputtered to catch his breath, she broke free.

Joan blocked the hits from the other two as she rolled away. They hadn't tried to kick her, which would have incapacitated her, and instead tried to punch at her as she moved.

They weren't going to stop, and if she didn't end this, she'd tire and they'd gain an advantage. Sparing them was taking too much time. No way was she dying on a shit-country road in backwater nowhere at the hands of bloodsucker gophers.

The next time Shorty came at her, she slid her knife between his ribs right into his heart. He was dead before she pulled the knife free.

She was too busy staving off the other two to watch him fall.

Knife Guy came at her, his neck a macabre sheet of blood, but she kicked him hard enough in the stomach to shift him back. It gave her enough room to deal with Crowbar.

The dog had his teeth sunk into this guy's ankle and gave him a solid pull, but the man persisted. When he was close enough, Joan palmed his nose into his brain. His head snapped back and he collapsed.

The bloody one came at her again. She whispered an incantation to trip him, and by the time he'd recovered enough to charge at her again, she'd switched the grip on her knife.

"Last chance to change your mind." She eyed his clumsy approach and tasted her victory. He wasn't talking, which was weird. Human males in a fight? They always had something to say.

The arc of the autumn sunlight shifted and threw the road into shadow. The dog snarled at an empty patch of dirt across the road. A shiver of warning slid across the back of Joan's neck.

A fourth man leapt from a nearby tree to the ground.

He didn't look a day over twenty. Shirtless despite the chill, his skin gleamed a warm bronze. He wore his long black hair tied back in a ponytail, and completed the look with black utilitarian pants and hiking boots.

An unnatural golden light glinted in his honey-brown eyes, and sclera that should have been white gleamed yellow. When his malicious grin promised pain at best and violation at worst, Joan tasted nothing but danger.

The bloodling strolled towards her as if he had all the time in the world.

While vampires were consistently fast and strong, bloodlings were beyond human but not yet undead which made them more unpredictable. Some were stronger than humans. Some were damned near as indestructible as vampires but with half the sense of self-preservation since they still enjoyed some measure of human recovery and recuperation.

She had no way to tell what abilities this bloodling possessed. Some gained preternatural healing abilities, which meant they could take a ridiculous amount of damage without falling. She'd seen one absorb half a dozen bullets without stopping and only a point-blank shot to the frontal lobe had finally ended him.

Since when did her backwoods hometown merit this kind of attention?

This was a new game. Leaving the gun behind had been stupid. This fucking place messed up her judgment. Now, the only things standing between the monster and her own annihilation were six inches of carbonized steel and spellcraft.

Time to make them count. First, get the human out of the way to deal with the greater threat.

Joan licked the fingertips of her empty hand and muttered an incantation when she pressed her fingers against the skin of the bleeding man's arm.

"*Aere voltage.*" Another war witch spell of her own making. This time, a shocking pulse passed from her to her opponent. He shook with its power, and fell to the ground twitching.

Maybe he'd die, maybe he wouldn't, but she didn't have time to watch.

The dog moved with Joan as she backed up but snapped and growled at the newcomer. Joan didn't blame him. Most bloodlings were humans who'd chosen to become vampires, though the "how" was still a contested theory. Her fear warred with her hatred of the despicable creature, one who had chosen a way of life that would ultimately have him feed on humans for as long as his flesh held together.

Her head pounded from the hit on the ground, and she hadn't been completely unaffected by the hits from the thralls. She'd never best this new threat hand-to-hand, even with her knife.

Joan had only one long shot in her arsenal, but she needed earth energy to do it.

She backed off the asphalt toward the forest scrub and dropped to a crouch in the damp dirt. When her fingers touched the ground, she pushed back her fatigue by summoning energy from the earth itself.

"*Aere rampart.*"

For as long as she could stream breath from her lungs, the wind wall spell would manifest hurricane force winds in one direction. She blew the wall at the bloodling, grateful the dog was closer to her than to him.

The dog howled at the noise but didn't move toward their opponent. After all this bullshit, she'd hate to lose her ally.

The bloodling pushed against the gale force wind, his eyes intent on her. If he resisted much longer, she'd run out of air.

The flow of her power draw from the earth waned and the need for more air would soon force her to release the spell. He'd only need a second to overpower her.

The bloodling frowned and backed off. He sniffed at two of the men without bending over, prodding them with a boot, then lifted the blood-drenched one over one shoulder.

Guess that one had survived after all.

With unsurprising agility, the bloodling disappeared into the woods faster than deadweight might normally allow.

Joan sagged, relieved, and drew a long overdue deep breath.

She couldn't stay here.

She wiped the sweat from her brow with the back of her wrist, swiped her filthy blade across a nearby swatch of moss, and pushed herself to her feet.

Two men lay dead, and the dog sat in the dirt and panted, but the sudden lack of action didn't make Joan feel any safer. She'd alert the watch when she got into town, because no way in hell was she putting their stinking corpses in Luther. The last time she'd treated her ride like a meat wagon, the stench had lingered for weeks.

The fight was over and the sun would go down soon. That

bloodling might return with friends. Time to call it a day.

The toughest part of the journey still remained.

"I suppose you want a ride into town." Joan opened Luther's passenger side door and waved the dog inside.

He climbed into the seat like he'd been there many times, and sneezed. The blood on his muzzle dripped onto the floor mat. This was why Luther had an all-black interior.

Once she took her seat, she shifted into gear and guided her ride into the lane. "Just don't tell anyone I fell on my ass."

Mentioning how bad the dog smelled seemed rude.

A half a mile later, the road rose and fell before something once again obstructed her path. This time only one man blocked the highway. She might have passed him but stacked storage containers walled off the rest of the road. Joan couldn't ram her way through them or the trees.

Besides, judging by her passenger's whining and tail-twitching, she had to give the man back his dog.

Joan powered down the passenger side window as she came to a stop. The dog took full advantage of the invitation and leapt through the opening. She winced as his claws scratched the door. Bodywork was tedious and expensive.

The dog howled in greeting as he sauntered up to the man. The man was built like a bank vault door and had to be almost seven feet tall. He wore the regional uniform of heavy-duty canvas pants, a fleece-lined jacket over flannels, and well-worn work boots. Long dark brown hair with sun-bleached ends framed broad shoulders and a surprisingly peaceful, thickly bearded face with ruddy sepia skin.

He held an axe in one gloved hand, handled like a familiar afterthought while he petted the dog's ruff with his other hand. His manner suggested he wouldn't start a ruckus. Everything else said he'd damned sure end one.

Behind him, an orange and white barricade the length of her SUV stood between the storage containers. An old camp chair, a shotgun propped at the ready and a worn-out cooler completed the picture of a lone guard on duty.

He seemed in no hurry to initiate communication, but he wasn't moving either. His eyes lingered on Luther's mounted lights and armored grille. Maybe he thought he could take her vehicle single-handed.

Then again, maybe he could.

She leaned her head out of the car, wincing at the pull on her aching muscles. "This a toll road now?"

"Not exactly." He finished petting the dog and propped the axe against one shoulder. "Willy's not known for hitchhiking."

"Willy decided he could take out three thralls and a bloodling on his own. I saved his ass, but then he returned the favor. Least I could do was give him a ride."

The man looked back the way she'd come. "This road's a little small for that kind of attention. They follow you here?"

She bristled, but it was a fair question. Any newcomers were suspect, even if he didn't know Joan wasn't new to the area. "Blocking the road when I got here."

He glanced at her again, his question unspoken.

"One wounded," she said. "Two dead on the road about a half mile back. The bloodling disappeared with the still-breathing one, but it might come back."

He grunted and reached into his pocket. "You solo?"

Maybe the axe was a distraction, and he was reaching for a gun. "Who's asking?" She slid her hand from the gear shift to the pistol jacked into the center console.

He pulled out what looked like a small, thin flashlight. "This is the southern checkpoint into Calvert. I'm just making sure the only folks coming through are human." He didn't seem to think she'd refuse.

He was right. She relaxed. "Fair enough."

He raised the flashlight and angled it sideways at her eyes. A click, and purple light flared in her peripheral vision. She winced, even though she'd known what was about to happen. On rare occasions, freshly turned vampires sometimes looked human, but their eyes always gleamed in UV light.

Another click and the light was gone. The afterimages stained her vision for a few seconds.

He tucked the flashlight back into a pocket. "You'll need to check in at the fire station once you hit town."

Check-ins meant the watch was keeping track of who was coming and going. Probably a necessary precaution, but it was sad to think of what might have happened to cause such security measures. And if it had anything to do with the reason she was here.

"Will do," Joan said.

The man whistled, and the dog moved to the side of the road, tail wagging now that the alert had been called off. The man nudged the cooler to one side with his boot after moving the gun, the axe, and the chair. He lifted the barricade with a sustained grunt, shifted it to one side of the road, and set it down to wave her through.

Those things weren't light. For as calm and matter-of-fact as this guy was acting, he was no one to be underestimated.

Joan drove Luther forward but stopped halfway through the checkpoint.

"Hope you're calling in some help." He'd need it if that bloodling reappeared.

"Believe me, I will." His expression turned uncertain and grave. "For what it's worth, I'm sorry about your loss. Trevon was a good man."

So. He knew who she was. The urge to turn around and drive back the way she'd come was so strong, she almost gave in.

"I appreciate that." What else could be said? She hadn't spoken to her father since she'd left.

She stuck her hand out the window, ignoring the chill. "Joan."

10

He tugged off a glove and his grip was cool and dry. "Dayton."

"First name or last?"

"Just Dayton." He smiled, and his whole demeanor changed from stoic brick wall to lumberjack teddy bear. "Welcome home."

She nodded as she drove past but didn't correct him. Calvert wasn't home anymore.

The sign marking the town's limits wasn't the only way Calvert greeted witches.

A tingling warmth passed through Joan's body as she crossed the border's plane, so different from other places she'd been with a similar boundary. The metaphysical ward was common, often found surrounding an area protected by a binding witch or a coven magically bound to its land.

The boundaries were designed to sicken vampires with a debilitating nausea making it easier to overpower them. In Joan's experience elsewhere, the wards were icy cold.

She hadn't felt the warmth of Calvert's boundary in eight years.

Nervousness roiled her insides, but Joan wasn't the same kid who'd left her binder witch roots behind to become a war witch instead. What did she have to be nervous about? The only person who could truly judge her wouldn't be waiting.

She blinked away tears. For so long, her father had been a constant, though they hadn't spoken in years. How many times had she argued in her own mind with her father as a foil?

The thick woods on both sides of the highway were soon broken by a few small homesteads. These houses used to look more inviting but now they were boarded up, their fences fortified against invasion. The kind of homey touches that had given Calvert its personality—flower-lined driveways and front lawn vegetable gardens—were all gone.

Most of the businesses in town had locked down for the night though the sun hadn't yet set. A few more doors closed as Joan drove the streets in silence. She noted how many storefronts had shut down for good in her absence, the buildings now covered in graffiti. A wide banner above the door to the bakery proclaimed regular hours, but plywood blocked the windows. The florist had been closed a long while if the burnt-out entryway was any indication.

On one side of the town square, the fire station sat next to the small sheriff's office. The rest of the square was framed by City Hall, the library with an adjoining coffeeshop, and the largest church in Calvert with a plot of land taking up an entire block.

Joan parked in front of the station, killed the engine and opened the door. A spike of pain through her head made her gasp as she stood. The hit on the asphalt had been a hard one, but hopefully not bad enough to cause a concussion.

She had only taken a few steps towards the station's office door when it opened in front of her.

"You are a sight, Joan Matthews." Gretchen Wilson, her voice warm in welcome, was a little heavier than the blade-slender form Joan remembered, and her straight chin-length hair was more white than gray, but she was otherwise unmistakable.

The Wilsons had lived across the road from the Matthews family for decades. Gretchen, head of the Calvert coven, had taught her almost as much about witchcraft as Joan's father had.

Freckles stood out against her suntanned skin, and her blue eyes were as piercing as ever. "Could hear you a block away in that thing."

Joan felt like a teenager again, coming in late for dinner. Gretchen was only as tall as Joan's shoulder, and Joan had to bend a bit to hug her properly. It was awkward but not unwelcome.

"I didn't think you'd come," Gretchen said.

Joan bit her lip and swallowed down the sobs wanting to

break free when Gretchen embraced her. These arms had held Joan when her mother died, when her father had closed himself off, heartbroken at his own loss and forgetful of Joan's.

Those times were past, and the man who'd committed those sins, gone.

Gretchen clung to Joan's shoulders with surprising strength as she pulled away. "Look at you. Still so beautiful. Probably out there breaking hearts."

Since a broken heart had driven Joan from Calvert, she hadn't been inclined to do the same to anyone else.

Joan cleared her throat. No need to mention that. "I'd better get inside."

"I've already checked you in here. How about a ride to the house in this monstrosity of yours?"

Joan nodded in agreement, then caught herself. Following Gretchen's directions without question might have been her habit when she was younger, but she wasn't a damned kid anymore. Hadn't experience taught her to think for herself?

Gretchen secured her seatbelt as Joan guided Luther onto Main Street. The clash of familiar memory and unfamiliar present quieted Joan. The woman beside her had shaped her training for years, but they hadn't spoken since Joan had left Calvert behind.

Then again, she wasn't here to talk about the past. The plan was to find out what had happened to her father, attend his pyre, and get out of a town that held nothing for her anymore.

At one of the few stoplights, Joan turned toward Gretchen and asked the only question that mattered, though she feared the answer. "What happened to him?"

If it had been a vampire, she'd hunt the culprit down, stake him to the ground in broad daylight and kill him slowly.

Gretchen's widening eyes made Joan realize she'd lowered her voice and leaned forward, a tactic she'd used many times to intimidate someone into revealing their secrets. Guilt drove

Joan to ease back in her seat.

Gretchen folded her hands in her lap as if she hadn't noticed.

"It really was a heart attack. The doctor found no hint of spellcraft or poison. Trevon's heart just gave out." Gretchen sighed. "He'd been working too hard these last few months. The outer farms were attacked, and when he couldn't convince those folks to move into town, he insisted on helping them vitalize their land."

Gretchen pushed a few tendrils of gray hair behind one ear. "Why anyone would want to take their chances out there vulnerable to the monsters is beyond me."

In Joan's experience, the open roads were safer than most places as long as you got to safety before the sun went down, but Gretchen wouldn't believe her.

Silence fell between them.

As she drove, every familiar landmark sparked memories of her life here. The person most prominent in those memories wasn't her father. She shoved away those thoughts and focused on the landscape.

Joan had forgotten how it felt to be in a place as big as Calvert, though it was still a small town by most standards. When she'd left, the population had been in the thousands. She hadn't traveled anywhere with a population larger than a few hundred people in months, and had spent all that time defending those tiny places from vampires eager to establish new territory.

Less than a mile from the town square, evenly spaced town streets gave way to country lanes, and the sidewalks ceded territory to large front lawns. The houses sat farther back from the road.

Her heart raced as the old neighborhoods closed in around her. The thumping in her chest echoed in her ears and pulsed in her aching head.

"I suppose you'll contest the house ownership clause," Gretchen said.

Joan had left her father's house behind long ago, and in spite of the many memories it held, ownership of the family plot sounded like responsibility—one she'd avoid like any other. War witches didn't stay in one place for long.

"I'm just here for the pyre, then I'll get back on the road. Besides, I'd imagine Pierce has been living there for a while." Joan hadn't spoken Pierce's name since she'd left and it was still bitter on her tongue. "I'm not kicking him out."

As her father's apprentice, Pierce would have taken up residence with Trevon while training under him. She had no love for the binder witch who had occupied the position Trevon wanted her to fill, but she wouldn't oust a man from his home, even if he wasn't family.

Even if he'd been the cause of so much of her pain.

Gretchen stared out the window, her jaw set and her lips pursed. "Pierce was . . . taken."

A local euphemism for a grisly death. A kinder way of saying someone had been snatched by vampires and drained of blood. No human deserved that. Not even the man who'd replaced her in more ways than one.

Joan braked at a four-way stop. A crow landed on the front grille, squawking and flapping its wings before it settled down, turning its beak toward the windshield. If Joan didn't know any better, she'd swear it looked right at her through the tinted glass before flying away.

With Pierce dead, who would take her father's place?

"How long ago?" she asked.

"About two years," Gretchen said, and Joan swallowed her shock. "Trevon didn't take on another apprentice." She didn't sound like she approved, but Joan cared more about other details. Ones she couldn't bring herself to ask about.

Joan's heart rate surged when the house came into view. Home—or what used to be. She still dreamt about it far more than she liked.

On this block, with four houses on one side of the street and three on the other, the Matthews house was the oldest. The spacious two-story Craftsman farmhouse had a wrap-around porch and a carved oak front door. A few fall blossoms remained in the low hedges surrounding the porch, and the slanted sunlight showed where the white paint had chipped away.

Much of its splendor and magic—both real and imagined—had faded over time.

Joan pulled into the long gravel driveway where a handful of people waited to greet them. To see them lying in wait only reinforced her plan to leave as soon as possible.

"So, who owns the house? You?" Joan asked. Maybe the coven had plans for it.

Gretchen climbed from the front seat as she spoke. "Trevon updated his will two weeks ago. He left the house to Leigh Phan."

Joan jerked back at the mention of the one person she had been trying not to think about—the woman who had turned her back on Joan and chosen Pierce instead.

CHAPTER 2

On her knees in the Matthews backyard, Leigh Phan wished she could disappear into the dirt as easily as her fingers did. Hiding herself was second nature now, even in a place as beautiful and safe as it was here.

Row after row of everything a binding witch like Trevon might have needed—sage, lavender, mint and rosemary—filled an extensive garden long enough for two full tennis courts to fit inside its edges. He'd tended them every afternoon, a solitary, meditative ritual of pulling weeds and removing bugs, trimming stray branches that tried to encroach on another plant's territory—especially the mint.

Leigh wasn't a farmer, but everyone in Calvert knew something about the land. Now that Trevon was dead, she did the tending. For the third time today, she swallowed her panic at his absence.

She forced herself to calm. Each breath was rich with the scent of the herbs, cleansing and settling at once. The sun through the trees shouldn't have been warm enough to cut the late October cold, but she closed her eyes for a moment and let it seep into her skin along with the new and surprising warmth from the earth itself. For the moment, she was safe and whole.

Since her arrival three weeks ago, she'd worked beside Trevon, and it had soothed her. Seeing someone as powerful as Trevon doing something so mundane had been a welcome change. In her experience, the powerful ones ordered others to do the dirty work.

Leigh shook her head to dislodge bad memories. *Enough. Focus on the task at hand.* She pulled her fingers from the dirt and brushed her hands together.

With delicate care, she trimmed a young branch of jasmine from its base, shaping its form as she passed, then did the same with the passionflowers planted at the end of each row. When the tending was finished, she collected several herbs as Trevon had taught her. He had emphasized the importance of each and its quantity. The price of a mistake was too high to contemplate.

Leigh pushed that thought from her mind. One day—one moment—at a time. She couldn't imagine a future now that Trevon was gone, and wasn't sure how much longer she could continue on her own.

Suddenly in shade, Leigh looked to the sky—pale yellow earlier but pink and gold now, refracted light on the sparse high clouds. Less than an hour until dusk. As if summoned by the change in light, the low roar of an engine grew louder, peaked at the front of the house and then cut off.

She froze in fear as surprise spiked through her. Someone was here. This late in the day meant trouble. The urge to run almost drove her to escape, but that wasn't what Trevon would have wanted.

The sound of doors opening and closing drew Leigh to the garden's side path. She walked on the grass instead of the noisy gravel lining the path to the garden gate. Her fear shifted to something unrecognizable when a long-unheard, yet familiar voice mingled with several others.

Joan.

Leigh didn't know if she should run away or rush closer. The need to avoid attention battled with the need to see for herself what had happened to Joan. Had Joan ever thought about her during the long years since they'd last seen one another? Had she forgiven Leigh?

"She just got back into town herself not too long ago," Mrs. Wilson was saying.

Evidently, Leigh was already the subject of conversation, but that wasn't what made her stomach flip. Mrs. Wilson led the town coven and Leigh had avoided them since her arrival.

"What? Where's she been?" Joan didn't even bother to lower her voice. Did she know Leigh was listening?

"You'll have to ask her," Mrs. Wilson said, "but first let me introduce you to the Calvert coven."

The fear in Leigh's stomach now froze her whole body. The coven was in the front yard, and with Joan here now, there'd be no escaping them. When had they arrived? Had she been so oblivious in her melancholy that she'd missed it?

"We wanted to welcome you home," a man said.

Home. It wouldn't mean the same thing to Joan that it did to these other people. They wouldn't understand that. Trevon certainly hadn't, but Leigh had known Joan better than anyone.

Leigh peeked around the corner of the house, the gap in the cedar-plank gate wide enough to reveal a section of driveway. She gasped, one hand against her chest, over her racing heart.

Joan was dressed for war—all black and foreboding—with a knife in her boot, another strapped to her thigh, and a sword's hilt poking past her jacket at her waist. Her long hair was neatly braided in wide, thick rows, and Leigh was stricken by the visceral memory of twisting those braids between her fingers.

Lean and hard, Joan had been tempered by the outside world into someone stronger and more formidable over the last eight years.

Leigh wanted to rush forward and throw herself into Joan's arms, but that beautiful frown on Joan's face was not welcoming.

"We're so sorry about Trevon, Joan," one woman said. In her mid-forties, her mahogany brown, almost-familiar face was

19

drawn from stress or fatigue. Maybe the librarian at the high school? The woman pulled her cardigan tight across her chest and crossed her arms. Her over-bright smile looked forced. "He was such a wonderful man. So thoughtful and generous. Once, he offered to cast a protection spell for my daughter when she decided to join one of the hunting parties."

Reed Hill, another person Leigh had always managed to avoid, stepped forward. A tall, thin man with a shockingly thick head of hair and a robust beard, he seemed more deferential than the man in Leigh's memories. "Trevon was kind that way. He helped me keep the general store stocked after we lost the supply lines from the city."

One by one, each of the group told a story of how Trevon had helped their farms to prosper, or their businesses to stay open, or saved their loved ones.

The old discomfort played on Joan's face as these people kept talking about things that clearly bothered her; she shifted her weight more than once. This was one of the reasons Joan had always said she wanted to escape—the constant press of duty and obligation on her family.

"We're so glad you're here, dear." Mrs. Wilson had a way of drawing the force of everyone present to her leadership. The others quieted when she leaned forward, her hands clasped before her. "It will be good for the town to see you here when we reconsecrate the ground."

Every full moon, a powerful binding spell was cast to keep the boundary strong and protect the town. Trevon had performed the rite for decades, but now the duty would fall to someone else, or the boundary would fade and leave Calvert vulnerable.

Another woman leapt at the chance to speak. A generation younger than Mrs. Wilson, she seemed eager to add something to the conversation. "But now that you're here, you could do it."

Joan blinked with a start, though Leigh noticed Mrs. Wilson's quickly hidden frown.

"I'm sure a full coven can handle Calvert just fine," Joan said.

Leigh shivered at the thought of being anywhere near so many witches.

A wan man, dressed like he'd come in from the fields, cleared his throat. "Trevon was the most powerful of us, to be sure, but the six of us are more than enough to strengthen the boundary." He spoke with a Spanish accent.

"Six." Joan looked at each of them in turn. "That can't be—I mean, how—what happened to the rest?"

The silence said a lot, but eventually, Mrs. Wilson filled the void.

"Calvert isn't quite the same as when you left."

"Trevon always said you were so strong." The librarian smiled again, but there was a wildness to her eyes.

Joan shifted a hand to the hilt at her waist, a sign she was unnerved. Leigh remembered what Joan was like when she felt attacked.

"Maybe even stronger than he was," Reed Hill said.

"Reed." Mrs. Wilson's harsh interruption silenced him, and she turned to Joan in apology. "We all know how skilled your father was, and I'm sure you've inherited some of his prowess. Though of course, I do remember the first time you called the directions."

Mrs. Wilson sounded proud. It seemed hollow to Leigh, but Joan had always been treated like a prize pupil.

"Trevon told me that story." This time it was a man's dry baritone, someone outside Leigh's field of view. He sounded full of awe even though she couldn't see his face. "He said the winds sent a token from all four points."

"I heard an eagle flew over the ceremony that day," the man with the accent said.

Other voices joined in, showering Joan with accolades, but Joan didn't acknowledge them. They all seemed to care more about what Joan might do for them, completely oblivious to

21

Joan's lack of response.

To see Joan uncomfortable twisted something in Leigh's chest, no matter how much stood between them, or how much Leigh feared the coven's attention.

A creak in the gate turned their eyes toward her. Shocked, Leigh realized she'd opened the gate without thought, and it was too late to hide from their scrutiny.

Everyone looked at her in surprise, except for Joan. All the breath in Leigh's body escaped at Joan's first glance. Eyes dark as a moonless night made Leigh want to freeze in place, but she walked toward the group—toward Joan.

Joan's clothes were disheveled and her knees muddy. Was that blood on her cheek? A tightness around her eyes made her look tired. Had she traveled far? And what did it mean that she'd avoided Calvert and her father for years, but returned when he died?

"Good evening," Leigh said, grateful her voice didn't shake. She summoned her courage and caught Mrs. Wilson's eyes. "It's getting close to sunset. Perhaps all this should wait until after the pyre."

The meaning was clear. Joan had come to town for her father's funeral, and they were talking coven business as if Trevon's death meant nothing.

To Leigh's surprise, Mrs. Wilson blushed.

"Of course." Mrs. Wilson collected herself and in an obvious attempt—to Leigh at least—to control the conversation again, she drew everyone in with her gaze. "The town hall is set for the pyre tomorrow, and most everyone will be there to honor Trevon."

She stretched a hand out to touch Joan's arm. Joan flinched, but Mrs. Wilson pretended not to notice.

"We've already prepared him for the pyre, unless there's something you'd like to do privately, dear."

Alarmed, Joan glanced at Leigh, who recognized the look

for what it was—a grounding moment with the least threatening person in an otherwise hostile space.

"No." Joan spoke, her voice faint. She cleared her throat and spoke again as she looked back at Mrs. Wilson. "I'll pay my respects at the pyre."

"Wonderful." Mrs. Wilson stepped back. "There'll be plenty of time for us to talk about the rest afterwards." She gathered the rest of the townspeople with her as she walked down the path. At one point, she looked back over her shoulder with an assessing glance at Leigh and Joan before she crossed the street to her own house.

Leigh wished she'd avoided the attention, but it was too late now and there were more pressing things to address.

Like Joan.

Joan had been a young idealist when she'd left years ago, but now, she was battle-ready and deadly. Her stance was menacing, but it wasn't fear that made Leigh's heart race as Joan looked her over, slowly. Joan's power and presence drew her forward, but the tension stole any words Leigh might have mustered to start the conversation.

Joan turned toward the street where the coven climbed into their cars—all except Mrs. Wilson who disappeared into her own house.

"Six." Joan's tone implied she wasn't expecting a response. "How can the coven be down to six people? Calvert's had at least a full coven for decades."

And then she turned her attention at last to Leigh.

"So you live here now?" Joan asked, her voice lower and snide with anger.

Leigh tucked her hands in her back pockets. She wasn't trembling. She *wasn't*.

"Your father let me stay here when I got back to town." It might have been Trevon's pity more than his generosity, but the result had been the same.

23

Joan's eyebrows lifted, though the anger was still apparent. "What's wrong with your place?"

Another thing Leigh didn't want to talk about. "It's not . . . mine anymore."

Joan scoffed. "So you moved in with my father? I thought you two didn't get along."

With a shrug, Leigh tried to convey the oddness of the situation. "We made our peace."

It was an understatement, but what had passed between her and Trevon was private and loaded with information not easily explained. There were enough reasons for Joan to hate her. Leigh didn't want to add any more, and some secrets kept her alive.

"So you could stand one of the Matthews family. Amazing." Joan made a sound like a laugh, but it felt like a punch to the gut. "And what did Miss Perfect do that was so bad your grandmother threw you out?"

Joan's words could still cut Leigh until they drew blood. Some things hadn't changed.

"Ba noi died before winter solstice three years ago." Leigh swallowed the old pain. "Some folks from out of town bought the place."

Regret and sadness washed over Joan's face as it fell. For as much time as Leigh had spent at the Matthews house when they were teens, Joan had spent the same with the Phans. Years of shared meals and family holidays, all broken when Joan had left.

Perhaps their common grief would help them put some of their other history aside for a little while.

"I know this isn't easy for you," Leigh said.

Joan took a step closer, and Leigh was overcome by the scent of her. Joan stood a full head taller than Leigh, and the visceral memory of every time Joan had staked a claim washed over Leigh's body in a hot wave. She swallowed as her diaphragm dropped.

24

In an instant, Joan's grief was gone and the anger returned. "You don't know a thing about me anymore."

That much hadn't changed either. Leigh remembered now how quickly Joan's moods shifted, how anger was replaced by remorse and compassion—or vice versa.

Leigh winced and clenched her fists until the nails dug into her palms. There would be no forgiveness. No mending the rift between them.

She would not cry in front of this woman. Leigh stiffened her back. *One day, one moment at a time. No past, no future. Only now.*

She met Joan's glare with as much strength as she could muster, praying that she looked more certain than she felt, but Leigh wasn't a mouse anymore, no matter how much she'd been batted around.

"You're right. I don't."

It was too late to go anywhere. Sundown meant barricading doors—not wandering around looking for shelter.

Leigh cleared her throat. "If you can bear me staying in the guest room until the day after the pyre, I'll find another place to stay."

Where she might go was impossible to guess. She'd never had a lot of friends in Calvert and all of them were dead or gone. Trevon had most likely only meant for Leigh to hold the place for Joan's arrival, and though Leigh had never believed Joan would return, Trevon had been right.

Joan's frown deepened as she considered Leigh's request, and for a moment, Leigh feared she'd have to run full speed to the church half a mile away. It was the nearest shelter that might take her in.

"Fine," Joan said, her jaw tight.

Leigh held back a sigh of relief. "Thank you."

Something swirled in Joan's eyes and Leigh steeled herself for whatever knife-sharpened words might come next. Joan was never one to hold back.

"From what I hear, it's your house now anyway. Guess you've earned it."

Leigh turned away so Joan wouldn't see her tears. How long could she keep it inside, though? They'd be in the house together and Leigh had never been good at hiding her feelings from Joan. Sooner or later, Joan would see through her.

Then again, Joan wouldn't be here long enough for it to matter. She'd made it clear all those years ago there was no room for her here, that there was more for her out in the world, outside Calvert's boundary.

Leigh wrapped her arms around her body as she walked back towards the gate. The old familiar pain returned, of feeling most at home in the one place Joan didn't want to be.

CHAPTER 3

Joan's relief at Leigh's retreat was short-lived.

Alone in the empty living room, Joan stood unmoving as mourning ripped through her guts. The spirit she imagined in the air, the unseen ghost around her, would never again have form.

What would happen to this place filled with mementos of lives lost and people gone? Her mother had died a week before Joan's twelfth birthday after years of battling leukemia. Joan's older brother, Marcus, had been taken by the vampires when she was in high school. His death had driven her to become a war witch instead of a binder.

The list of the dead had grown longer since she'd left. Leigh's grandmother. And now, Joan's father.

Too many changes—and the space around her contained more. What should have been familiar was instead unsettling.

The leather couch she'd often sprawled across as a teen had been replaced with some mission-style sofa, though the old throw her father had knit at her mother's bedside was tossed over its back. The ancient burgundy leather wingback chair, where no one but Trevon ever sat, still filled the corner in the living room near the fireplace. Her mother's porcelain dinner service remained proudly displayed in the glass-doored cabinet in the dining room. Trevon could never bear to get rid of any of it, though they never used it again after her mother died. Everywhere, dust thickened the corners and bevels in the wood.

All the same, but different—smaller, more worn, dingier. Overwhelmed, she rushed upstairs, past the wall of pictures of all those dead people and so many more, down the unlit hall to her old room.

What she found there knocked the grief into overdrive.

The linens on the queen-sized bed had been changed and the room had been dusted, but everything else looked the same—a snapshot of who she used to be. Half a dozen books she'd read more than once were stacked on the nightstand. The closet door stood half open and her old, threadbare clothes hung inside. A hobby model she'd never finished sat on the shelf above a desk still covered with notes from studies she'd abandoned. The same posters and art hung on the walls—some of the paintings and sketches crafted by Leigh's talented hands.

Like her father's absence somehow filled the downstairs, the specter of her long-ago-broken relationship with Leigh crowded this room. Weeks had passed since Joan last slept in a bed, but she wasn't going to get any rest in here.

Another night in Luther's back seat, though, sounded terrible. Back in the hall, she stopped at the linen closet for the familiar store of spare blankets and opted for the living room couch.

Downstairs, a wide hearth framed by bookshelves and windows occupied one whole wall. Above the mantel, a vibrant mosaic inlay depicted the seasons and circle of life, a symbol of the family's standing and history.

Enough wood rested in the cradle next to the fireplace for a roaring blaze. From one corner of the sofa, Joan stared into the dancing plasma of flames and tried to slow her racing mind, but all she could think about was Leigh.

The same perfect golden skin, the same thick black hair that fell past Leigh's shoulders and down her back. Her runner's build still had subtle curves that had compelled Joan more than once to mold her hands to those hips, to lean in to kiss her warm, pliant lips. Leigh's voice had once been a calm, collected contralto of reason, of positivity and light.

Until Leigh had said she didn't want Joan. That Joan was selfish and arrogant, and never gave a damn about anyone but herself.

Maybe that had been true once. And arrogant Joan might still be, but she had done nothing but sacrifice herself to the greater good for years, just like every other war witch she'd ever met.

Leigh's guarded eyes in the front yard had suggested much had changed for her, too.

Joan leaned back on the couch as the old heartache seized in her chest. The fire crackled and spit, its hissing a whispering lull.

The next thing she knew, insistent tapping pulled her from an uneasy sleep. Sunlight slanted through the high windows on either side of the fireplace. The fire she'd made last night had long since died, and the room had a slight chill.

A crow sat on the ledge outside the window, tapping its beak rhythmically, shifting its head rapidly back and forth.

Joan blinked at the bird from where she lay on the long couch. The crow croaked and flew away.

She stretched beneath the pile of blankets and rolled onto her back to stare at the ceiling. Her first thought matched the last one from the night before.

Seeing Leigh had hurt, and pain always made Joan lash out. So many times, she'd tried to change that one thing about herself, the need to wound someone back, harder than ever. She didn't even remember what she'd said to Leigh last night, but Joan absolutely recalled the way Leigh's shoulders had shrunk as she pulled in on herself.

When they were younger, that was how Leigh had tried to protect her own heart from attack, from the disbelief and betrayal that someone she trusted could hurt her in such a way. The carefully constructed blank look that followed would wipe away all trace of Leigh's pain, and that, too, was its own spike to Joan's heart.

Leigh didn't have any right to look so damned hurt. She'd been the one to break things off. She'd been the one to say that all they had shared between them didn't matter anymore.

Anger made the blankets too tight, too close, too warm. Joan pushed them to her waist.

Dust motes danced in the sunlight across the room. She hadn't slept this late in months. She patted her braids out of habit and blinked the grit from her eyes as she stood, details from the previous day on her mind.

Calvert had a limited coven and its binding witch had died with no apprentice. Add that to her own unsettled and unwelcome grief, the news about Leigh's grandmother, and Leigh's presence itself . . .

The house was silent.

Where was Leigh? Had she left without saying goodbye?

Joan didn't know what she might have said to Leigh, but she didn't want it to be nothing at all.

A low bell sounded, followed by another. The grandfather clock in her father's study.

Not much time left. Soon, the town would assemble for her father's sending.

Joan didn't want her grief on display for the whole damned town, but this was why she'd come to Calvert. To make sure the monsters hadn't taken him. Now that she was here, she couldn't leave it unfinished.

A shower washed away some of the aches from her body, but not the restlessness. At the end of the upstairs hall, she stared at the reflection of her usual fighting attire, but with the addition of her ceremonial tunic and the cowl of her father's spare robe.

Her hands twitched with the need for a fight, but there was

30

none to be had, and she wasn't likely to be challenged by anyone at the pyre. Not that she wanted her father's job. She didn't need anything from anyone here.

When Leigh's face passed across her mind, she ignored it.

Joan took another breath but tried not to breathe too deeply for fear of tearing a seam. Her ceremonial tunic was years old, and while it was looser in the waist than it had been when she was younger, it was also tighter in the chest and the shoulders.

Yet another reminder of how much things had changed.

Though she wanted to carry her usual weapons, she limited herself to one gun and two knives. It shouldn't be that dangerous in broad daylight in the center of town.

A stiff wind greeted her when she stepped onto the porch, and she paused to taste it on her tongue. Bittersweet, like overripe fruit and the acrid tang of smoke. Calvert had always tasted fecund to her, like possibility and hope. Now peril and strife soured her tongue. Was it because Trevon had died?

In the front yard, she closed her eyes as she knelt to touch the dirt. She broke a few clumps between her fingers, felt the familiar warmth of the boundary—but its energy, the essence of the earth itself, was tainted with a faint oily residue.

Another puzzle, but no time to unravel it.

Joan opened her eyes and stood to assess the neighborhood. Pale sunlight washed out most of the color, leaving a lot of gray as a backdrop to the trees. Dry leaves rushed across the grass, the only sound on the entire street. Maybe everyone here had already gone into town.

The hall was less than a mile away, and a walk in preparation sounded better than a short drive. Luther was overkill on calm streets, and she preferred to get a sense of the land by walking it.

She strode down the middle of the street, updating her memories as she went. Familiar trees along the way stretched tall, but the flower boxes and beds were long dead or graveled over. One of the houses was completely boarded up, and almost all of them were barricaded.

This part of town used to be one of the safest places in Calvert. When had it become so guarded?

With each step, she centered herself, shifting her weight as if stepping into battle, muttering the incantations for strength, for spirit, for peace, but her concentration was broken by a distracting hum, like a vibration at the base of her skull. How hard had she hit the ground in the fight on the road?

A cacophony of cries wove its way into the wind as scores of crows rested on power lines and in the trees, bringing back the headache that had eased somewhat with sleep. The number of scavengers increased every year, but it was rare for so many crows to be in one place, and the oddity was like an itch she couldn't scratch. The swarm swirled as she walked toward the hall, with nothing but the sound of her boot heels on the asphalt and the wind for company.

After a few blocks, the asphalt gave way to dirt when she reached the clearing where the hall stood. The hall was the spiritual center of Calvert, even though the town had a few churches. The huge circular building stood in the midst of a space big enough for two side-by-side football fields.

She was one of the last to arrive.

Outside the hall, Joan stood in the shade of the awning, watching a few townspeople file inside one of the four entrances. No one came near her, and she was glad for the space to collect her thoughts before she stepped through the large double doors.

Made of oak, reinforced with silver and iron, the walls rose from a stone base. The silver was a superstitious precaution, but the iron burned vampire skin, and if somehow infused in their blood, it made them sluggish. The walls curved upward, with fist-sized diamond-shaped holes every six feet to allow the light in, until they reached a ring of iron and silver mesh open to the sky so the smoke within rose to the heavens.

Even a protected boundary like Calvert's wouldn't stop

bloodlings or human thralls, so this had been constructed to provide a safe place to send spirits onward.

Inside, a couple of older boys—high schoolers she'd guess—helped Dayton stack more wood. The pyre would burn all through the night and into the next day. Dayton himself was dressed much like she was, in a long gray and black tunic that fell to his knees with wide gaps on the sides. A small axe was tucked into a strap on his pants. Dayton's dog sat on his haunches nearby, and for some reason, Joan was glad they were here.

The hall was built like an amphitheater, with row after row of hewn wood benches arced in a great circle around the center space. Every row was filled, and Joan guessed that most of the town was here.

In the stone floor, a pentagram several strides wide had been carved within a circle marked with the cardinal directions. In its heart stood the pyre platform of pine and walnut where her father's body lay shrouded in linen and wrapped with hemp rope. Joan stared until her eyes hurt from not blinking.

Leigh stepped through the entrance across the building. She wore an ankle-length black dress and a strand of knotted hemp as a belt. With a start, Joan recognized it as one of the last gifts she'd given Leigh—a blessed length of braided rope for protection and meditation.

Joan couldn't look away. Leigh wore no jewelry or makeup. Her long hair fell unbound, and sunlight streaming through the crevices in the stone and wood walls kissed her golden skin. Her dark eyes met Joan's and Leigh's lips parted as she crossed her arms, then looked away. She looked the same as she had years ago, as if she hadn't aged a day since she'd torn Joan's heart from her chest.

Yet, as much as it pained Joan to see Leigh at all, Joan was still soothed somewhat by her presence. Faces she remembered were few here, and many of these people likely knew her father far better than she ever had. Joan chose to watch Leigh, who

33

stood staring at Trevon's unlit pyre.

Gretchen and the other members of the coven waited on the outer edge of the altar, a curved, waist-high table set at the northernmost point of the pentagram. Gretchen nodded at Joan and tipped her head in the direction of the center position.

Of course. As Trevon's daughter, Joan was expected to perform the ceremony. How could she have forgotten? She didn't want to do it, but . . .

She evaluated the implied disrespect to her father against her own need to avoid the demands of this place—all of it weighed too damned much. She shouldn't have come back here, but how else would she have found out the circumstances of his death?

Gretchen's face shifted into concern, and Joan realized she was taking too damned long to decide. She chose to rely on her own rules: when all else was in doubt, do what needed doing, no matter the cost.

Joan took her place at the inner point and faced the sacred space. The top of the table had been cut from an enormous oak, and its grain stained dark. Five short, fat candles were spaced along the table's length, and interspersed between them was a small bowl of water and another of salt, a small hand bell, and a ritual hammer.

Centered on the table was a square blue cloth no longer than Joan's arm. Upon it, outlined by a silver cord, a small ceramic bowl sat empty as the symbolic representation of Trevon's spirit. A simple unadorned athame lay beside the cloth.

As far as Joan knew, a war witch hadn't led a ritual in this room in her lifetime. Other towns welcomed war witches, mostly because one was usually standing between them and vampire invasion. Calvert had tolerated visiting war witches, but never called on their services. Trevon had always said fighting only led to more unnecessary death, that binding to the earth was enough.

Yet here she stood to commend him to the spirits. She didn't let herself think of what he might have felt about it.

Joan drew a dagger sheathed along one thigh. For her, it served the same purpose as the athame on the altar. She touched its tip inside the bowl of water in ritual cleansing, then again in the bowl of salt to purge impurities, and then lay the blade across the bottom length of the cloth.

She turned her back to the altar, faced the center of the room and took a deep breath before she spread her hands out from her waist, palms to the sky. The low hum from earlier now vibrated through her shoulders and feet.

"Welcome, children of the earth and the wood, as we join our hands, hearts and spirits to send our beloved forever to the Summerlands."

"Blessed be." The low response to Joan's call filled the room.

The headache intensified, but Joan took another cleansing breath, returned to the northernmost point of the circle, and spread her arms again.

"Guardians and Watchtowers of the earth, I call on you to protect this circle."

The words to invoke the spirits of the cardinal directions came to her lips without thought. So many times, her father had led her through these rituals, and she said them now by rote. Pain spiked through the base of her skull again as she spoke.

"Guardians and Watchtowers of the air, I call on you to protect this circle." Even now, she felt guided by the man who lay dead before her—his hands leading her hands, his voice speaking her words.

"Guardians and Watchtowers of fire, I call on you to protect this circle."

Above her, beyond the mesh of the dome, the cries of circling crows intensified.

"Guardians and Watchtowers of water, I call on you to protect this circle."

She finished her call at the northernmost point, where she

lifted the bell and struck it. The low tone echoed in the vast space. "We honor this soul and send our love with him on his passage from this place. So mote it be."

The silence stretched long, and Joan realized everyone was waiting for her to say something about Trevon. Before pyres were lit, it was customary for loved ones to speak of the people lost.

Now that the invocations and ritual invitations were complete, Joan had no more words. Her chest tightened and her eyes ached with a dryness that blinking did nothing to dispel. Why had Gretchen or any of them thought she could come in here after all this time, stand before an entire town of people who didn't know a thing about her anymore, and talk about what her father had meant to her?

Their last words to each other had been nothing but awful. She couldn't reveal those private thoughts here. They were caught in her chest, in her throat.

Joan grieved not only for her father, but also for her inability to share her loss with anyone.

CHAPTER 4

With the hall seats full, Leigh stood at the end of one row where she'd attract the least attention. A few others stood nearby, enough so she didn't stand out, but she did her best to blend in without standing too close to anyone.

Leigh had attended countless pyres over the years, but she'd never seen the elements themselves answer the calls to the guardians.

When Joan called the earth, a slight vibration reverberated through the stone. As Joan stepped past the eastern ward point calling the air, a breeze blew through the hall, rustling the linens of the platform, swirling hair, and blowing away dust. Every single torch lit in the wall sconces sputtered and flared as one when she summoned the spirit of fire.

At the final call for water, a small cloud formed over the platform, swirled towards the ceiling, and evaporated. Outside, a crowd of birds blocked the light from above as Joan completed the circle, their cries almost deafening in a space designed to carry sound.

Joan had always had an affinity for earth and air, but her skills must have developed during her absence. Leigh herself had never shown much aptitude for magic, but she'd spent enough time around the Matthews family to know this was impressive.

Leigh wasn't the only one to notice. Mrs. Wilson looked

unhappy until her face went carefully blank.

When the time came for people to take turns speaking of the dead, no one wanted to speak before Joan. Trevon had been loved by many and respected by all, and he had saved the lives of many of the townsfolk several times over, but Joan was his only living relative.

Joan's jaw tightened now that she wasn't speaking, and her fists clenched. Perhaps someone who didn't know Joan might think she was hard and uncaring, or angry, but Leigh knew Joan was seconds away from falling apart.

Leigh stepped to the edge of the circle, not far from where Joan stood, before she lost her nerve.

"Trevon was a father to me when I had none," Leigh said. The words were unplanned, but every one of them was true.

Her voice wasn't loud, but it filled the hall. "He taught me that I wasn't defined by my mistakes, and . . ."

She faltered and looked at her own feet. "He taught me forgiveness. He wasn't perfect, which reminds me that no one is. He was also the best of us, and that means we all can be something more than who we think we are." Her eyes blurred with her tears. "I will try to follow his example for the rest of my life, and I will never forget him."

When her eyes met Joan's, her own thunderous heartbeat filled her ears. No matter what had happened between them all those years ago, they had both lost a father.

One by one, members of the coven and the town stood to speak tribute to Trevon Matthews. When the lamentations fell silent, Joan sighed deeply enough for Leigh to feel it in her bones.

Back at the altar, Joan moved her athame to the side and pulled the cloth into one hand. She wrapped the bowl in the cloth, then tied the silver cord around it, her movements slowing the closer she got to the end of the ritual.

Leigh wondered if Joan might be prolonging the inevitable,

but then Joan raised the hammer and let it fall once. The crack was muffled, but the bowl was broken. Joan's hand trembled as she set the hammer aside, picked up her athame, and sheathed it once more.

For a long moment, no one moved. The threat of sobs quivered in Leigh's chest, but she fought it down. Later—she could cry later when she was alone.

Joan turned without looking up and walked toward the platform. With fluid grace and deceptive ease, Joan conjured flame at her fingertips and lit the kindling points.

Leigh remembered that spell. Joan had taught her once, but that skill had fallen away from Leigh, like so many other things.

Once the fires were lit, many of the town's residents stood quietly and left, but a larger group of people stayed. A handful of stewards would remain with the pyre until the flames died. Besides the crackle of the fire, the room was mostly silent, any conversations held in whispers and low murmurs.

The flames licked the shrouded dead as Joan stood unmoving.

The heaviness of Trevon's absence pressed on Leigh. He hadn't been a big man, but he'd been such a strong presence. Perhaps it had been his power, but—like Joan—he'd been a commanding person even without it.

She wasn't sure how she would manage without his gentle refusal to judge, something no one else had offered her since her grandmother.

At least she had another day before she needed to find somewhere else to live. Calvert didn't have any official shelters for people like her—people without families to take them in or homes of their own—but perhaps after a night or two at the church, she'd figure something else out.

Leigh wondered what would happen to the house she'd called home for the last few weeks, once Joan left. Maybe the coven would take over, since Joan would no doubt be gone in the morning. Leigh couldn't stay there without Joan's permission, and Trevon had only meant for Leigh to keep it in case Joan returned.

At least, that's why Leigh thought he'd left her the house.

Joan coughed at the smoke, and Leigh looked at her again. Joan's boots made her seem taller, and the tunic revealed the muscles Joan had developed over the years. Leigh fought the blush she could feel warming her cheeks when Joan caught her looking.

She cleared her throat as she walked to stand beside Joan. "Will you stay with the stewards tonight and close the circle?"

Some people did—stayed overnight until the pyres burned to ash and the four directions were released and closed. The doors were locked and guarded at night against intruders.

Joan shook her head slowly. "No, I . . . no." She frowned but didn't say anything else.

Leigh wondered what she was thinking.

Joan wiped eyes red from smoke and sighed. Her shoulders sank, and Leigh realized how tired she must be.

Leigh glanced out one of the doors. Almost sunset. "I'm going back to the house," she said. She'd been out in the open long enough.

"I will, too," Joan looked around as if she'd forgotten something, but then looked at the pyre again and sagged even lower.

Leigh reached out to wrap a hand around Joan's arm, and Joan flinched. Leigh squeezed once before she pulled away. Perhaps she'd gone too far, but she hadn't been able to help it. Joan was obviously in pain, and so close . . .

No. All that was done and forever in the past. She must be careful to not reach out again.

"Come on," Leigh said. "Before the sun goes down."

Joan nodded without looking at her and turned towards the door.

One more night, Leigh thought to herself as she followed.

For tonight, she would spend a little more time with Joan and try to ease the grief for both of them, trying not to think about tomorrow when Joan would most likely leave again, taking Leigh's heart with her a second time.

The flow of pedestrian traffic thinned the closer they got to the house. Leigh said nothing as they walked, and Joan seemed to be looking everywhere but at her.

"Jesus, what happened here?" Joan asked.

Leigh tried to see Calvert through new eyes, but the sad state of the town was well known to her, the boarded-up houses common and the extra fortifications normal. The question might have been rhetorical, but she answered anyway.

"Dwindling supply chains, more people lost or taken, fewer resources."

"Why didn't the coven or the watch do more to protect the supply lines? I've never heard of a single call for a war witch to come to Calvert."

Leigh wondered if Joan would have come if she had.

"The coven never let word get out, and no one wanted to face the truth," Leigh said. "You know what it was like around here. Nobody ever wants to admit there's a problem until it's far too late."

Together in their teens, they'd convinced each other of their own sanity when many in the town wouldn't face the growing threats in the world. How many conversations had they had like this one, pointing out the lunacy of the choices made by their elders?

Awkward silence returned, this time weighted by all the things between them, but Leigh had no idea what to say. Joan had always been the one to cave first when things had been tense.

Finally, on the gravel path to the house, the dam broke.

"We can't keep dancing around this," Joan said. "Why were you staying with my father?"

Leigh was growing weary of the subterfuge herself, but

there were some things she couldn't bring herself to say.

Once again, she relied on half-truths.

"I don't want to recount every single fuck-up of my life. Let's just say I made a lot of bad choices. I went to Trevon to see if he could recommend somewhere for me to go to get back on my feet but he insisted I stay here."

Joan stared as if trying to find holes in her story, but everything Leigh had said was true. When the air between them became too thick, Joan looked away.

A squawk from circling crows interrupted the standoff.

"Have you ever seen anything like it?" Leigh asked before the question finished forming in her head. "The way the crows acted at the pyre?"

Joan's confusion contorted her face. "What?"

"There must have been dozens of them. They showed up when you called the corners."

Joan leaned away from her. "What are you talking about?"

"You didn't hear them? They were so loud I could barely hear you."

"No idea."

Maybe Joan had gotten better at lying, but Leigh didn't see or sense any of her tells. In fact, Joan looked suspicious of Leigh, which was troublesome on its own.

Perhaps it had been a simple coincidence.

The house had grown cold in their absence. Joan rubbed her arms and went straight for the fireplace to rebuild the fire. There were more efficient ways to warm the house, but natural gas and oil were expensive and hard to get. For all the effort it took to obtain wood and keep it dry through the Oregon seasons, it was still easier to come by.

Out of habit, Leigh lowered the metal guards on the windows. She was halfway through securing the dining room when she realized that Joan might want to do all this herself.

"What are you going to do with the house?" Joan asked.

Leigh whirled in surprise but recovered, though she wondered if Joan could read her mind. "It's all yours now, Joan. I think he only left it with me so the coven didn't take over before you got here."

"I figured you and Pierce—"

"No," Leigh said, though there was so much more to it than that.

Joan frowned, and Leigh steeled herself. That look meant Joan was going to ask about something either provocative or painful.

"What really happened with the coven?" Joan's voice sounded distant, almost absent-minded as she stared into the flickering low flames. The larger logs hadn't yet caught.

Leigh sat down on the arm of the sofa, hiding her relief at receiving a question about something other than herself.

"A couple years back, things started getting worse. The feed store took over the ammo runs to Portland along with some of the farmhands. It was dangerous, of course, but they knew the risks. People said that last run was cursed from the outset—problems with the goods for trade, and the truck kept breaking down. One of the hands showed up high before they were supposed to leave, and got his ass kicked in front of half the town."

Joan nudged the fire with a long iron poker. The curve of her jaw, the regal line of her profile brought a long-forgotten itch to Leigh's fingers for a pencil. She used to draw Joan's likeness every day.

Leigh remembered the day she'd stopped.

"Are drugs as bad here as everywhere else?" Joan asked.

"I don't know what you've seen elsewhere, but it's been horrible here. Where anyone can find heroin these days is beyond me, but meth labs keep popping up no matter how quickly they get shut down." Leigh shrugged though Joan didn't see. "Anyway, on that last big run, they made the deal in Portland and were on their way back with the trade goods when the truck broke down. They were picked off one at a time on their way back, including a couple coven members."

Joan stashed the poker and stood.

Leigh fought the urge to squirm under Joan's direct gaze. "I heard one of the other elders took part in a duel that was . . . questionable. Trevon—" She stumbled over his name but rallied and kept speaking. "Trevon thought that he'd been baited since the challenger wasn't from Calvert. Some laborer working his way from farm to farm up the valley picked Elder Winslow out of a crowd and backed him into a corner. Said a duel was the only way he'd accept satisfaction. The guy turned out to be a crack shot, and he was gone before anyone could track him down the next day."

"That sounds fishy as hell." Joan crossed her arms over her chest. Outside, the sun set, and the light in the room shifted.

"Yeah," Leigh said. "The others—they happened far enough apart that it would be a stretch to think they were in any way connected, but it was weird how only members of the coven were targeted. Totally explainable each time, and yet somehow . . ."

Joan made a noncommittal sound. "Who do you think is targeting the coven?"

Leigh was surprised Joan took her words at face value. Joan certainly didn't have any reason to trust her or her judgment.

She navigated her way around dangerous topics. "Some folks thought maybe vampires in Portland."

"Doesn't make sense. If that were true, they wouldn't have bothered with sending goods back to Calvert. They'd have kept the entire shipment."

Leigh didn't disagree, but hearing Joan say those words gave her goose bumps.

Joan scratched her head and sat just outside the reach of Leigh's arms. "Whole covens don't get targeted like that, though I suppose someone would eventually try it. Still, if the coven doesn't replenish their numbers, they're going to be easy pickings, and Calvert is a pretty attractive target."

She sighed. "Or, I guess, it used to be."

Leigh bit her tongue, trying not to state the obvious solution. Joan would never take her father's place.

Joan turned her powerful gaze on Leigh. "You gonna tell me your story or do I have to pry it out of you?"

How much to tell her? How much to admit without giving the deeper truths away?

She owed Joan nothing, but the thought of adding to the wall already between them . . . it hurt. She would tell as much as she could, and hope Joan didn't suspect the rest.

"After—after you left," Leigh said, speaking quickly to keep Joan from interrupting with questions she didn't want to answer, "I fell in with some bad people."

What an understatement.

For weeks after Joan had left, Leigh had holed up in her room and cried. Ba noi had finally chased her out of the house, insisting she get a job in town if only to keep her from moping during business hours.

Fortunately, Leigh had found a job as a checker at the grocery market. Unfortunately, she met some of the other workers a few years older than she was. They weren't into anything crazy, but they weren't the most responsible people either. It started with lazing about on their off days, smoking weed and doing a whole lot of nothing. But as months passed and stories about bloodsuckers grew closer to Calvert, a few of her crowd— including the woman she had briefly dated—started doing harder drugs. To protect themselves, they'd said.

Eventually, Leigh had joined them.

The people she'd thought to be the in-crowd had turned out to be drug-addled, shiftless losers with no plans and no real future. Leigh had fit in shamefully well.

"Turns out a couple of them were dealers, and I was too clueless to catch on. By the time I did, I was high and dry in

Boise with no way back."

Joan looked shocked. "You left Calvert?"

Leigh looked at her hands, acutely aware of the irony.

Strung out, addicted to opioids and meth, she'd eventually come home and earned her way back into Ba noi's good graces. "When I came back, I found a job on one of the local farms, got clean and sober." She could see the past clearly in her mind's eye: dinner every night with her grandmother who never said a word about her time away or her mistakes.

And then her grandmother had died.

"Ba noi died of natural causes. No witchcraft, no weird circumstances. Went to bed one night, mad at me because I hadn't cleaned one of her pots well enough, then died in her sleep."

But dead nevertheless, and then Leigh had been alone. There was no one to help her pay the mortgage—who would she ask? Trevon barely acknowledged her after Joan left. Her sketchy friends lived paycheck to paycheck just like she did. And while people came to mourn her grandmother, they didn't exactly reach out to comfort Leigh. She'd always been the odd one alone in the corner. Only Joan had ever gotten to know her, had ever learned who Leigh really was.

Joan was long, long gone by then.

Now, Joan rested one hand on Leigh's knee. She gave a little squeeze before pulling away. "I'm so sorry. She was an amazing woman."

Leigh took the small win of Joan's touch to heart but didn't press for anything further. The welcome ghost of Joan's warmth spread up her thigh.

"She was. No surprise that I didn't take her death well."

Alone and broke, Leigh had haunted the home she'd once treasured until she finally relented and gave in to the only companionship she could get. She went back to her drug-using friends, and then everything she thought she knew or understood changed, and she learned what true terror was.

"I left town again and . . . relapsed." Leigh stared into the fire so Joan wouldn't see the lies in her eyes. "I ran around for a while with horrible people. When I came back, the house had been foreclosed on by the bank, and someone else had moved in. I don't know what happened to Ba noi's stuff."

That was all of the tale Leigh wanted to tell, and she hoped Joan was satisfied.

"Gretchen might know," Joan said. "I could ask her."

That was unexpected. Leigh hadn't thought Joan would show her any kindness. Not after what she'd done.

"I can tell there's more, Leigh." Joan leaned forward, her elbows on her knees as she stared at the fire. "You don't want to talk about it, and I can let it be, as long as it doesn't have anything to do with my father."

Leigh swallowed. It technically didn't have anything to do with Trevon, but . . .

Joan continued as if measuring every word. "I can't forgive you for what you did, but I can put it behind us. Don't get me started on how ironic it is that you left town not once, but twice, considering you didn't want to leave with me at all."

"That's not true—"

"Save it. We don't have to open every scarred-over wound. Not tonight." Joan's eyes were guarded but direct. "Just know that you're not getting away with anything."

Leigh stared back, defenseless. What if she did tell Joan? What were the chances that Joan wouldn't kick her out if she knew?

A sharp rapping on the door interrupted their stare-down. Leigh flinched, but Joan leapt to her feet, a six-inch blade suddenly in hand. They hadn't yet put the barricade board across the door, every home's last-ditch effort against invasion.

The knocking persisted. Joan stepped closer to the door and took a deep breath to yell something but before she could, a muffled voice shouted through the door.

"Joan? It's Dayton. I'm sorry but I need to talk to you."

Joan made sure Leigh was behind her, and then opened the small viewing cage set in the door below the peephole.

"Not such a bright idea paying a visit after sunset," Joan said.

Leigh couldn't move. The watch was on the doorstep. What if there were more but they were lying in wait?

"Sorry I didn't call first," Dayton said. "But I didn't have your number."

"Whatever it is," Joan said, "it's gonna have to wait until morning. Today's been long enough."

"I know my timing sucks, and I'm sorry about that, too, but we've got a situation and I need your help."

"What kind of situation?"

"Bloodsuckers hit the Clark farm and the watch is down a few guys because of the pyre."

Leigh's heart pounded so hard, she felt lightheaded. *Vampires inside the boundary?* That wasn't supposed to be possible. She stood in alarm as Joan opened the door.

Dayton stood taller than the doorframe and was still dressed in his clothes from the pyre. To Leigh's relief, he didn't make a move to come into the house.

"Two other guys are fucking high and therefore useless," he said. "I'll kick their asses later. Right now, I need to make sure the Clarks are okay, and I could use some real muscle."

Joan laughed, but with little humor. "You sayin' I'm tougher than your boys?"

Dayton didn't skip a beat. "Honestly? Yes. You might be tougher than anyone else in this town, including me. I'd be an idiot not to ask for your help."

Joan reached for the hem of her ceremonial tunic and lifted it over her head. "Give me a sec. We'll take my rig."

"Roger." He turned and stomped off the stairs.

"Can you lift the barricade?" Joan asked, and without

thinking, Leigh nodded. Setting the board was usually a two-person job.

"Good." Joan grabbed her jacket and a bag that lay on the floor beneath the coatrack. "Don't let anyone in while I'm gone, no matter who it is or what they say. Got it?"

Leigh found her voice. "Be careful."

Joan nodded and walked into the descending night.

CHAPTER 5

Thick, heavy clouds blocked the moonlight. Joan took the lead on the twenty-minute drive to the Clark farm, with Dayton and two guys from the town watch piled into Luther. Another pickup full of armed townspeople and Dayton's dog, Willy, trailed behind her on the otherwise empty back roads.

Against a single vampire, there was safety in numbers. Superhuman strength and speed would overwhelm one person, and perhaps a few more, but a crowd of well-armed and well-trained humans with the forethought to deal with one bloodsucker would prevail.

Unless more than one awaited them.

"What's the word?" Joan asked Dayton.

"Bina Clark said they heard the livestock screaming. Her father and brother went out to check and never came back. Her mother won't let her leave the house. They're barricaded on the homestead."

Joan scraped her memory for details. "Wait. Aren't they inside the boundary?"

"Yeah, and not on the edge, either."

"We don't need her, man." Someone in the back seat spoke up.

Joan had no patience for naysayers. "Dayton, tell this bitch if he wants to walk to say some more shit while I'm right here."

These guys might not know her, but they were in her ride.

The upstart tried to backpedal. "I'm just saying that we can take care of this ourselves. I mean, you just lost your father, so I'd imagine you'd want to stay home and mourn or whatever."

Here it was. The welcome she'd expected from Calvert— the overall perception that the town didn't need war witches. Leaving in the morning sounded better all the time.

Joan was ready to kick this guy out, but Dayton shifted to face the back seat. "Shut the fuck up, Halsey. Even if she wasn't Trevon's daughter, believe the hype. Joan took down three bloodsuckers—three—all on her lonesome, and after sundown to boot. Show some respect."

Joan decided right then she liked Dayton just fine, though she didn't want to think about the experience he'd mentioned. Yet another memory of a close call that had left her bloody and unsure if she'd survive.

The rest of the ride was quiet.

She drove Luther into the wide gravel space by the farmhouse's back door. Like many in the area, the house and barn had been built decades ago and renovated over time with added rooms and modern windows on older frames. A young woman burst from the house, waving her arms, eyes wild in Joan's headlights.

Dayton and his boys jumped out, but Joan lagged behind to loosen all her weapons for draw. This time, she brought her gun when she climbed from Luther.

"They took radios with them," the woman was saying, "but they're not responding to our calls."

Dayton reached out a hand to calm her. His voice was even and authoritative. "Which way did they go?"

Bina Clark's directions sent them to the southern field. Dayton urged her inside and assured her they'd check in once they found her father and brother.

Joan figured Evan Clark and his eldest son James were dead,

drained, or worse, but she kept that to herself.

The watch fanned out to either side of her, and Dayton stalked in her wake armed with an axe in one hand, a pistol in the other, and his dog at his heels. Willy's training had to have been extensive since he didn't race off on his own.

Her battle senses yielded little beyond a silent pasture. Nothing stirred in the night, and they navigated the exsanguinated carcasses of cattle until they found the bloodless husks of Evan and James Clark, lying lifeless on the wet grass of their pasture. James's neck had been broken, his jaw dislocated above the torn flesh on his neck.

Halsey, or someone like him, vomited while Dayton cursed.

"I don't understand," one of the other roughnecks said. "This is inside the boundary. How did they even make it this far?"

Dayton stopped beside Joan, and they shared a worried glance.

Joan licked the ends of two fingers and a thumb, then rubbed them together. "*De tenebris lucem producat.*" *Of darkness bring light.*

Her fingers were only a focal point, a gesture to center herself. Her body was the conduit for the spell as it pulled any available light to brighten the dark places, but if there was nothing nearby but shadow, it drew its energy from Joan herself. The muscles in her arms, legs and abdomen tightened with the effort as the shadows backed away and the area around Joan became more visible. A slowly growing circle expanded from where she stood until the meadow grass of the Clark farm's pasture was lit as if by moonlight. Her chest heaved with her breathing. Sweat rose on her skin, and she fought a shiver against the night's chill.

She could still put up a fight if required, but they needed to see what might be lurking in the dark. Tomorrow she was definitely sleeping in.

"Thanks." Dayton spoke low enough that she was probably the only one who heard him. He called to the others. "Spread out. Stay in groups of three, and if anything moves, shoot first then sound off."

She had to give the watch credit. They all moved to do as they were told without any back talk or reluctance. It said a lot about them, since bloodsuckers were something to fear.

She watched Halsey in particular. He stood in the area she had brightened and stared at her. She stared back.

Halsey looked away. She guessed he'd figured out their respective positions in the food chain.

Joan looked at the bodies again, something about the scene irritating her hindbrain.

"No blood," she said, trying not to gasp at the effort of holding the spell.

Dayton frowned in confusion, and she realized she'd stated the obvious. Of course the bodies were drained of blood.

"No, I mean around the bodies. There's no blood. They were drained elsewhere and dumped here." Were they killed outside the boundary, and then dumped here by thralls as a threat?

His confusion morphed to something more cautious—fearful. "Why would they leave their farm at night?"

Good question. Nobody went outside after dark if they could help it, and no one traveled outside the boundary without a damned good reason and armed support.

Twenty minutes later, the pasture was cleared.

Whoever—whatever—had done all this damage was gone. Joan released the spell and tried to catch her breath without heaving like an oaf. At least she hadn't needed to fight at the same time. She'd done that once before, and it hadn't been a good night though she'd lived to tell the tale.

Dayton had laid out a white tarp next to Evan Clark and motioned for Joan to help lift the body into its center. Evan had been a bear of a man who wasn't any lighter dead. Joan almost dropped his feet but managed to set him down, though she lacked any grace.

"How many people on the watch these days?" Calvert had always been well protected with a robust group of over a hundred people.

"Nineteen," Dayton said.

She stood, fighting the urge to stretch her lower back. "You gotta be kidding me. How did that happen?"

Dayton pulled another white tarp from his backpack and shook it out on the ground. Joan followed him over to James Clark and they repeated the grisly procedure.

"Some folks left for bigger towns south of here. At least one group went to Portland thinking they'd be safer in an established vampire territory, as crazy as that sounds."

It was crazy, but it wasn't unheard of. The northern section of Portland, called Black Rose City, was self-contained vampire territory, one with an old hierarchy of vampires who only drank from human volunteers. Every month, names were drawn from a collective record and the lucky winners had mandatory blood draws. No one was hunted, the donors lived to see another day, albeit down a pint or two, and balance was achieved.

Joan hated the idea. Humans weren't meant to live like that—tithing their blood to the monsters.

Dayton finished securing the tarp around James with some rope. "A few were taken. Mostly, though, a lot of people just weren't fit for watch anymore because they were taking vampire bane."

As a general rule, the bloodsuckers didn't want contaminated blood of any kind. A few drinks or marijuana only mildly affected the quality, but serious drugs made the blood taste unpleasant.

Heroin and methamphetamine use spiked as a result. Most never considered the fact that the drugs were only a deterrent of taste. A hungry vampire wouldn't give a damn about their altered condition and would drain them nonetheless.

But humans were a superstitious bunch. If they believed that inverted crosses and garlic and meth would keep the monsters at bay, then that's how they'd arm themselves.

"How long do you think you can operate with only nineteen people?" Most people had jobs and families to feed. Working the boundary, checking the roads, fighting off any invasions—it was 'round the clock work, and securing a town Calvert's size meant that people were pulling double and triple shifts just to stay alive.

It wasn't sustainable.

"I just need to last until the full moon," Dayton said as he stretched his lower back, their gruesome task complete. "Once the boundary has been secured, I'll talk to the village elders about a long-term strategy. Gotta say I wouldn't mind your help."

Before she could tell him her plan to leave in the morning, a crow squawked in the night. Joan squinted in the direction of the sound—south, near the farm's fence line. The edge of the forest lay beyond the pasture.

Crows made little noise at night, but this one wasn't far from where they stood. It set off alarms her subconscious recognized even if she wasn't sure what it meant. Without really understanding why, Joan wanted to get closer to that sound.

Her back to the heart of the farm, Joan walked away from Dayton and the bodies of the two hardworking men who'd died trying to protect their family's land. Dayton called after her, but she waved him away.

She walked about twenty yards through the ankle-high grass toward the fence and the wall of trees beyond it. A warm shiver passed through her body, and she stopped in surprise. It was a sign she knew well, and she stepped back once to feel it again. Her heart pounded, and the sweat of fear slid down her back.

It was the invisible line of the boundary. The protected space that should have extended a few more miles towards the mountains now ended here.

The boundary wasn't just fading. It was failing altogether.

In towns like Calvert, protected places with established boundaries, the magic had to be periodically replenished or it faded. Every full moon, a binding witch or a coven had to perform the ritual to reinforce the boundary. If not, the border weakened, but never in her experience had a boundary receded.

What the hell was happening here?

Joan stepped forward without thinking and the stench of death hit her like a wall. When she looked down, she didn't need light to see the dark stains on the ground, the trampled sections of grass from a one-sided fight.

The Clarks had been killed on their own land. Human thralls must have moved them closer to the house, but why?

Joan retreated, unanswered questions more terrifying than the dark as she rejoined the watch. She pulled Dayton aside where the others couldn't hear.

"We've got a problem. I think the boundary's fading."

He frowned at her as if she was mentally deficient. "Yeah."

"No, I mean . . ." None of the others stood anywhere close to them but Joan lowered her voice anyway. "The boundary is well inside that fence." She tipped her head in the direction of the place she'd walked to, not wanting to point and call attention to it.

"Joan, the boundary that way is the county highway."

She leaned closer and Dayton stepped back, moving his hand towards his axe. He probably didn't realize he'd done it, but if she'd scared him, good.

"Listen to me," she said, and to her own ears her voice was little more than a growl. "I know where the fucking boundary is supposed to be, but something is wrong. It's not just losing power. It's receding."

Voices across the pasture signaled the return of the others.

"Do you think it's because . . ." He tried to dance around mentioning her father's death, but Joan was tougher than that.

"No. It shouldn't be collapsing in on itself, if that's what's happening. Maybe something's working against it somehow, but I don't think—"

"Victor." Anger clouded Dayton's face.

"What?"

"Who." He glanced at the others as he spoke only to her. "We've got a lot to talk about, but not here. If word gets out, I'll lose what few people I have left, and then we're all fucked. You don't know me, but, please, trust me on this."

Joan stared at him as the others joined them, and something in his eyes led her to give him the benefit of the doubt.

Dayton and four members of the watch made sure Evan and James Clark were delivered to Bina and her mother. Joan kept to the shadows as the shrouded bodies were carried into the barn.

The mystery of the boundary ate at her guts like ulcers.

Dayton emerged, calling out assignments. This time, he and Willy were the only ones who climbed into Luther.

He waited until they were off the farm and back on the road.

"Victor is the nearest vampire lord."

Joan cursed. Rural vampire lords were the worst of the two kinds of bloodsuckers in the world.

Most belonged to the guilds, led by Firsts, who were older vampires with the experience of centuries to guide their decisions. They saw human civilization as a necessary nuisance and planted themselves into existing city structures. They fed from the populace but didn't kill rampantly. For the most part, they solicited volunteers. There were always idiotic humans who were willing to trade pints of their life substance for their continued mostly comfortable existence.

And then there were the vampire lords. Usually younger vampires, the lords were unaffiliated and often thought their power was enough to bend the world to their will. The smart ones stayed hidden or at least didn't attract the attention of the Firsts. The dumb ones were either killed by the Firsts or knocked down a few pegs until they assimilated into the older guilds. Either way, humans paid the price.

Dayton stared out his window into the black.

"He set up in a vineyard between here and the coast."

At least they knew where the vampire kept shop.

"This guy moves in on the towns and farms he thinks are in his territory. If they send him tribute, by which I mean humans to drain, he takes 'em off his shitlist. He doesn't even keep a low profile, which means he doesn't care who he pisses off."

Joan absorbed this new information as she drove. Sooner or later, this Victor was bound to attract the attention of the vampire guild in Black Rose City a few hours' drive to the north, but who knew how long that might take? Calvert might not survive in the meantime.

Dayton clenched his hands into fists and relaxed them twice, his frustration evident. "Rumor has it he reached out to the coven after your father died."

Why would the coven consider something they'd found abhorrent for decades? Had Calvert changed that much? "Did they take him up on it?"

"Not that I've heard, but honestly? It wouldn't surprise me to learn they were considering it. They all bow to Gretchen Wilson, and she's a dangerous woman."

That pulled Joan up short.

"No way." Joan never would have considered Gretchen to be this kind of threat.

Dayton laughed without humor. "She'd strike a deal if it meant saving something she cared about. These days, all she cares about is having the coven perform the binding."

Most places with boundaries were protected by covens. Very few towns had a history like Calvert, which had always been protected by a binding witch from Joan's family. As far as Joan knew, Calvert had always been a triumvirate of sorts, with a Matthews binding witch, the coven and the watch working together to protect the town. Most of the time, the binding

58

witch had been a member of the coven as well, like her father had. He'd always been the spiritual and magical leader in the town.

This was the first time Joan had heard of any schism in the town structure.

Dayton's weariness bled into his voice. "She's said more than once Calvert should work like other places, with the coven as its guiding light. I think Calvert worked just fine with your father in the lead. He was still on the lookout for an apprentice when last we spoke.

"Although truth be told," he said as he turned his head in Joan's direction, "Calvert needs a war witch more than a binder."

Joan decided she'd let that hint lie until tomorrow, after she got some sleep. The other questions pistoning through her aching skull would have to wait until then as well.

The only thing she knew for certain was that she wasn't leaving Calvert in the morning.

CHAPTER 6

Leigh paced the stretch of floor behind the living room couch. No good could come from a late-night visit from the town watch. Who had died this time? Death was common enough in Calvert—tonight's pyre was the third in the last month.

With each breath, she tried to let go of her fear of discovery, her worry for Joan, and a greater urge to run outside into the night. She shivered though she wasn't cold. The fire Joan had made blazed in the fireplace, barely contained by the grate, but none of its warmth could defrost the dread inside her.

She tried not to envision the corpses of people she knew in town, not that she'd spoken to any of them recently. Then she tried not to picture Joan as one of those corpses. Trevon's death, the coven dwindling, the watch on high alert. The delicate balance of a mad world in stasis could soon tip toward the worst possible outcome. She knew that better than anyone.

Once she might have soothed herself by pouring her disquiet into a sketchbook, channeling her fear into her art, but those days were so long ago they seemed like another life. She couldn't remember the last time she so much as sketched on a piece of scrap paper. Now the only peace she found was in the dirt, in the rows of herbs in the garden, though she didn't want to do that after dark. The Matthews homestead might be the safest place in Calvert, but human thralls had been known to raid houses when ordered to by their vampire masters. Best to stay inside.

Now, every single day was the same. She rose before the sun. She did whatever it took to survive to the end of the day. Hoped for a dreamless sleep. Rose to begin the cycle again.

The only difference now was Joan's return, though she wouldn't stay long and when she left, things would go back to what passed as normal. Leigh would be on her own, though she would have to find somewhere else to stay. Joan would probably sell the house to Mrs. Wilson or someone else in the coven.

Leigh would find another way to survive, one that didn't attract too much attention. Maybe get a brainless day-labor job on one of the farms, one that would keep food on the table, no matter where that table was. A cot to sleep on and one meal a day were enough to keep her going, though she wasn't likely to live long.

When Joan's monster of a vehicle pulled into the driveway at seventeen past three in the morning, Leigh rushed to the door.

She lifted the thick four-by-four oak board from the bars of the barricade and set it to one side before opening the door.

Joan lumbered across the threshold, fatigue in every motion. "You should have checked me first, babe."

Warmth washed over Leigh at the sound of that forgotten affection.

Joan covered her misstep with a cough. "I could have been anyone." She tossed her gear bag full of who knew what near the coatrack and removed her jacket. No one opened a door at night without checking to make sure an attack wasn't waiting. Too many tales of old friends returning as thralls of the undead filled local lore.

"I knew you weren't . . . I knew it was you." Leigh reseated the board in the door brackets.

"Let me catch my breath and I'll help. That thing is heavy."

It was too late to feign weakness. "What happened?" Leigh asked. She didn't think herself ready for the answer, but she wanted to talk about the door even less.

Joan sighed as she headed for the kitchen. "Vampires got to the Clark farm. Evan and James didn't make it."

Leigh gasped, fingertips against her lips. She'd gone to high school with James Clark though she hadn't known him well.

"Their farm is so far within the boundary. How is that possible?" Had Victor and Nathaniel found a way inside? Cold terror ate at her insides.

Joan sagged against the frame of the kitchen's entryway. "I can't right now, Leigh. Honestly, my head is screaming like a motherfucker, and I need to eat something."

Action staved off Leigh's horror. If she had something immediate to do, she could pretend nothing had changed. At least until she was alone.

She slipped past Joan but pulled her by the sleeve of her shirt. "Come on. I found some lasagna in the freezer."

Joan laughed, though it was fainter than usual thanks to her weariness. "And you didn't eat it all? Wasn't that your favorite food, even though Ba noi didn't make it?"

Leigh pulled up short and swallowed against the rising bile in her throat. "Yeah. I'm, um, well, I don't eat much meat these days."

"Glad you left me some, then. I'm starved."

Leigh tried not to breathe as she plated a healthy serving and delivered it to Joan.

At the small kitchen table, Leigh cupped her hands around a mug of tea while Joan ate. The metallic clink of the fork hitting the plate was the only sound for a while until Joan paused.

"I haven't had a chance to . . ." Joan stared at her half-empty plate as she toyed with the frayed ends of a napkin. "I'm sorry about Pierce."

A full minute passed before Leigh understood what Joan was talking about. The middle of the night was not the time for this conversation, but here they were. Leigh gave in to the inevitable.

"I wasn't here. I left Calvert months before he was taken." Leigh shifted in her chair though the tremble in her knees didn't settle.

"Oh." Joan's attempt at a normal tone was somehow worse. "I didn't realize . . . I mean, I didn't know when you . . . broke up or—"

"We were never together." Leigh hadn't spoken to Pierce since the week after Joan left town.

Memories Leigh had cast aside returned in technicolor. A small band of war witches had come to the summer carnivals that year and joined some of the farm competitions. All summer long, Joan talked of nothing but their skill and purpose.

When the witches came back through that fall, Leigh knew Joan wanted to join them.

"But I . . . I saw you . . ." Joan's hands trembled slightly, too.

Leigh and Pierce had been standing in the corner of the barn at the harvest party. Pierce had said he'd always liked her, offered her a hit of the joint he'd been holding, and when Leigh saw Joan with one of the war witches on the other side of the bonfire, she'd done the unthinkable.

Old shame dug new wounds. The aged linoleum on the kitchen floor was easier to look at than Joan's face.

"Pierce and I only kissed that one time." Days later, Pierce had been angry because he'd been used. Trevon had been angry that Joan had been driven away. "I was high at the party, but that's no excuse because I knew exactly what I was doing."

For weeks after, Leigh had hidden in her grandmother's house, mourning the loss of the sanctuary next door and agonizing over Joan's absence.

"It was stupid and reckless and mean, and I did it anyway." Leigh's voice was little more than a whisper. "I led him on, and I made you believe it was real."

Leigh's eyes filled with tears as she stared at her own hands. "After everything we'd done together and been to one another, you wanted to leave and I didn't. You were going to break up with me."

"That's not true."

And there it was in Joan's eyes. All the old hurts and something else Leigh couldn't decipher.

"To get what you wanted, Joan, you would have broken my heart. So, like an idiot, I kissed a boy I didn't want to make it look like I'd dumped you first. It was childish and unforgivable." How many times had she beaten herself up over one stupid mistake? She'd been convinced that she deserved Pierce's ire and Trevon's rejection.

It might have been smarter to let the conversation end there, to put some distance between them, but this hadn't been the only revelation of the night.

"D-did you see . . . any of the, um, vampires, at the Clarks?" To ask such a thing was to get too close to truths Leigh didn't want revealed, but she had to know. How had they gotten past the boundary?

"No." Joan pushed her plate away with restrained disgust. "No, they were gone by the time we got there. We just found the dead livestock and . . . and the bodies."

Oblivious to Leigh's panic, Joan stood and stretched, then flinched and raised her hands to her head. She paused as if she might say something about Leigh's earlier admission, but then left the kitchen without another word.

Leigh wanted to call after her, but fear kept her silent. The vampires were getting closer, and she was running out of places to hide.

CHAPTER 7

After not nearly enough sleep, Joan forced aside her grief for her father, her confusion about Leigh, and her fatigue from the night's spellcraft. Urgency drove her to survey the boundary.

Walking wasn't fast enough. She drove Luther along the wide town streets and narrow rural roads and re-familiarized herself with Calvert's edges. With her father's pyre behind her, she looked at the town's decay with more critical eyes. Calvert was a dying mess, many of its larger buildings in the industrial sector empty, graffiti-covered and burned out. Whole swaths of the town were deserted, blocks where the houses were gutted, entire rooms open to the elements. A watch of only nineteen people couldn't possibly protect this place against a siege if this upstart vampire lord decided to attack in force.

And that wasn't the only thing that gave her pause. A longing ache—a loneliness she hadn't noticed before—accompanied each rediscovered space, places she'd forced herself to forget. The diner where she and Leigh had spent almost every summer afternoon drinking soda and eating fries. The now-deserted drive-in where they'd gone to see every movie whether they liked it or not. Neither of them had owned a car so they'd watched from folding chairs.

Calvert used to be home. Joan hadn't had one since.

She slowed as she pulled into a cul-de-sac by the baseball

field where Marcus had played his senior year. She and Leigh had shared their first kiss behind the aluminum bleachers. The field was overgrown now, rarely if ever used, but Joan stared into the past until she forced herself back to task.

The cawing of swarming crows every time she stopped only made her headache more pronounced, but she soldiered on, eager for answers. To her ever-growing consternation, the hum in her head persisted and she began to wonder if it had nothing to do with the hit to the head.

Three hours later, Joan finished her circumspect circuit. With growing confusion, she drove into the heart of town. Not every person stopped to watch her drive past, but most did.

Dayton owned a construction company—no surprise, considering his build—where he'd said he'd be working today between shifts with the watch. Joan parked across the street from his warehouse and pulled the hood of her jacket over her head against the light rain.

Near one of the burnt-out graffiti-covered buildings, a few people stood beside worn tents and propped tarps. Why on earth would anyone live on the streets and risk getting snatched by thralls after dark?

Determining their age or gender was tough—all of them dressed in baggy oversized clothing, their heads and hands covered by cheap gloves and skullcaps.

A tall, lanky man with splotchy pale skin and a scraggly beard spoke louder than the others, his gestures sudden and jerky like a meth addict. Another fool who thought drugs made them impervious to vampires. His flighty eyes assessed Joan like a target as she crossed the street. One look from her and he waved his arms like he meant no harm and turned back to his group.

Dayton's Contracting and Lumber was the busiest establishment on the block, though only a few pickups sat in the parking lot. Joan stepped through one of the bay doors into unnatural fluorescent light.

The indoor lumber yard was larger on the inside than it had looked from the street. Racks for lumber, piping and insulation were stacked from the floor to the rafters, but long overdue for restocking.

One man operated a forklift and loaded a pallet of four-by-fours onto the back of a flatbed truck. Nearby, a woman with a clipboard made some notes on its attached papers. A handful of others walked with purpose around the warehouse, moving supplies from the poorly stocked shelves.

Joan walked the periphery of the warehouse looking for Dayton until she found the door to the front office. Inside, he stood behind the counter having a tense conversation with two men in the customer area.

Dayton somehow looked bigger without the heavy-duty jacket he'd worn the night before. Broad shoulders and thick arms pushed at the seams of the long-sleeved flannel he had buttoned like a dress shirt and tucked into his work pants. His large hands made a clasped pencil look like a toothpick. Today his long hair was tied back into a neat ponytail. A pair of reading glasses poked from one chest pocket.

Joan caught his eye. He nodded as he wrapped up his conversation and guided the men to the door. Once he locked it behind them, he flipped the "open" sign over to "closed."

"Let's talk in my office." He pointed toward a door at the other end of the room.

She followed him into the spacious but sparsely decorated office: just a few filing cabinets and one bookshelf full of binders. Willy raised his head from a huge dog bed in one corner, then huffed at the interruption and went back to sleep.

Walnut-stained wainscoting wrapped around the room from the floor to waist height, and the walls were a functional gray. A barred set of windows looked over the street. Behind a dented metal desk, another bank of windows showed the warehouse floor.

"I did a circuit around town this morning," Joan said after he closed the door.

"We did, too," he interrupted, though not unkindly, as he sat in a rolling office chair that squeaked in protest. "But now we've got bigger problems. I just got word the roads around Calvert have all been blocked."

Shock rendered Joan speechless. They'd moved in quickly. She'd checked the ingress points not two hours ago and seen only the watch.

Dayton lowered his voice. "Tree fall on all the smaller roads, and the highway's blocked north and south by bloodlings and thralls. We can't get out without a fight, and nobody from outside can come through."

"Guess the hits keep on coming," she said without humor, and took the seat across from him. "The southwest section of the boundary has receded by about two miles."

Dayton stared at her, frowning in disbelief. "You sure?"

"I wouldn't be here if I wasn't." She restrained the urge to yell at him.

He held up his hands in placation and sighed. "Of course you are, and no one would know better than you. I just don't want to believe it's possible."

Trevon had never warned her of any magic that could accomplish such a thing, and she didn't recall anything in the training texts or reference journals.

She pulled a rough sketch from her inside pocket. Unbidden, she thought of how Leigh might have drawn something better than her own kindergartner scrawl.

"Here's my estimation of the new boundary. There were a couple of places I couldn't get to, so I erred on the side of a further recessed edge."

He took the map and frowned at it. "I'll make sure the watch is there before sundown."

Joan shifted in her chair. "I haven't told anyone yet, but we should inform the coven."

"You're right, but . . ." He stared out his warehouse window, collecting words before he spoke again. "This might be bigger than I thought."

Dayton turned his measuring gaze back to Joan. "A few months back, we heard a rumor that other covens might have been targeted the same way ours has been. That maybe Victor hadn't just drained them."

Joan did the math and didn't like the sum she came up with. She scoffed. "You think he's put together a dark coven? Man, those are just legend. No one is stupid enough to go against the high covens *and* the Firsts."

Vampires who could wield magic were a rare occurrence, but it was possible. The idea that several of them would band together to form a dark coven, however, was improbable.

Back before the first settlers had come to the area, most of the country's territory had been under contention. After decades of conflict and countless deaths, an uneasy peace between the vampire guilds and the witch covens was achieved with what were now generations-old treaties. They'd pledged to leave each other's territory alone as long as the guilds only fed on volunteers.

The witches insisted on another stipulation: no vampire covens.

Joan's temples throbbed with the headache that was only getting worse, just like this whole situation.

Dayton shrugged. "Well, it may be bullshit, but ask yourself: if you've never heard of anything like a receding boundary, but had to imagine a power capable of executing that type of magic, wouldn't the old legend fit the bill?"

She hated the idea, but it was sound logic. If Victor was building a dark coven, he had to know the guilds would come for him eventually. What kind of long game was he playing?

"I don't like this fucker at all," she said, muttering to herself.

"Agreed."

They stared at each other while Joan pondered those and other terrible possibilities—like what would happen if the vampire crews at the blockades decided to attack the town all at once.

Dayton leaned forward and folded his hands on his desk. "Gretchen is going to lead the coven in claiming the land at the full moon, and I don't know if anyone else in this town is gonna ask, but I sure will. Will you stay until then?"

And that was the rub, wasn't it? She didn't want to stay, not when there were so many bad memories here. Even if she did, Calvert had never wanted a war witch. Dayton might welcome her, but she doubted anyone else would. Though the roads were closed, she could maneuver Luther overland. It would suck, but she'd tried it before in other places and succeeded.

Leaving felt like a cop-out.

The people here might not know her as well as they used to—and she might not know any of them at all anymore—but she couldn't do less for Calvert than any other town she'd helped protect.

Which meant sticking around a little while longer. The full moon was only a few days away.

Dayton must have sensed her decision. "I hate to beg, Joan, but my watch is running thin and you're a goddamned legend."

She had to laugh though she didn't think of herself that way. She did the jobs that needed doing, and let her actions speak for themselves. "You sucking up to me now? Playing to my ego?"

"Will it help?"

She laughed harder, even though there was nothing funny about it. Whether he'd asked or not, Joan couldn't turn her back on the people of Calvert.

There were still too many questions, though. "What's your beef with the coven?"

He looked uncomfortable, as if he had something to say

but wasn't sure about her response. "Truthfully, I don't trust Gretchen. She and Trevon butted heads about almost everything and she didn't seem all that torn up at his passing. Not only that, but she hasn't done a thing to replace any of the lost coven members. She may want the coven to lead Calvert, but if I had my way, I'd want someone else for the job—someone a little more transparent in their motives."

"Who else in this town is an option?" If there was another powerful binding witch in town, Joan hadn't heard of them.

His long stare suggested she might do it, and she started to protest but the sound of approaching running feet drew their attention.

Willy growled just before a wan woman in her mid-twenties poked her head through the door to the warehouse. "Thralls are inside the boundary."

Several hours later, the ring of Joan's phone woke her, thanks to its loudest setting. She surged upright in Luther's driver's seat and turned the key in the ignition before she answered.

"It's Joan," she said, glad to hear some power in her own voice. The catnap had restored a little energy. She glanced to both sides, checking for threats, then faced front. Parked next to the city square, she was the only thing moving in this part of town this late at night.

It wasn't yet midnight. Dayton and the watch had been slammed with attack after attack all over town. Unlike vampires, human thralls passed through the boundary without any effect, allowing them to terrorize Calvert whenever it suited their masters.

In the hours since her meeting in Dayton's office, livestock had been stolen, several townspeople taken, the fortifications around the youth center destroyed, and at least two homes set on fire.

Every time the town got hit, her phone rang.

"Cramer Field," Dayton said. Someone screamed in the background on his end.

The old baseball diamond was less than two miles from her current position.

"Eight minutes." Joan hung up before he responded. She shifted into drive and peeled into the street without checking for traffic. There wasn't any.

For the fourth time that night, she mentally checked herself for preparedness. Deep breaths did nothing to ease the headaches, but they helped the tension in her shoulders. Her ankle ached from an earlier twisting, but not enough to keep her from driving or walking. She'd have to pull any kicks so she didn't make it worse.

She'd seen this in other towns. Packs of thralls attacking around the clock, picking at the vulnerable spots until a whole area was completely under vampire control.

Rain suddenly splattered against the windshield. She cursed and set the wipers to maximum. An open fight in the elements would make a complicated situation worse.

She pressed harder on the gas. Most of the houses were dark, barricaded against the kind of attacks she and the watch had fielded all night. Main Street ran the length of town, then ended in a T-shaped junction. Right led to the highway currently blocked by vampires and thralls. Left was a road that dead-ended at the forest by Cramer Field.

The edge of the forest was technically within Calvert limits. Until recently, the boundary had stretched over a mile past this road. When she reached the parking lot, she jumped the curb, ignored the single lane of slots along the first base line, and slammed Luther into park right behind the backstop.

Dayton and four members of his watch brawled against the same number of human thralls. It was an odd place for a fight—

72

they were in the heart of the unpainted baseball diamond, near the overgrown pitcher's mound.

One glance yielded a working theory. The house across the street from the parking lot, like the field, pressed against the woods. Its freestanding garage still smoked from where someone—or the rain—had put out a fire.

If the boundary were full strength at its usual perimeter, the house might have been fine, but with the receding edge yielding territory to the vampires . . .

Thralls must have set the fire to drive the inhabitants outside. Instead, they themselves had been driven to the field by the watch.

Two more thralls appeared from the woods on the other side of the third-base foul line, and now Dayton and his watch were outnumbered.

Lightning flashed, thunder rolled, and the rain turned into a deluge.

What a fucking mess. She couldn't use her gun in this kind of melee—chances were high she'd shoot through a thrall and into a friendly. She tucked her gun into the back of her waistband, and then drew her short sword.

Joan ran into the fray, heading for the closest fight. Two thralls doubled up on one of the watch. She picked the one as tall as she was, a white, corn-fed American male who held an eight-inch Bowie knife with some familiarity.

He looked like he'd been eating well. Maybe he was a new thrall, one who hadn't been denied any meals yet.

"*Aqua* pool." Water wasn't her strong suit, but she had a lot to work with. She centered her weight, anticipating the coming change.

The water beneath his feet swelled to an ankle-deep pool wider than his stance. He swung his knife at her but slipped in the mud. The blade sliced through her jacket and her shirt, confirmed when icy rain spattered against her hot skin. He overcorrected, shifting his weight to keep himself upright.

His broad chest was undefended.

No time for mercy. Joan stabbed him below one pronounced lower pectoral, blade horizontal as it slid between his ribs. Surprised, his jaw flapped though no sound escaped. He collapsed, dead.

Maybe after the fight, she'd have time to wish his spirit safe passage.

The wind picked up, which meant spells fighting against the air's natural flow would have an extra layer of difficulty. The rain pummeled her, soaking through her clothes and pissing her off more than the headaches.

She breathed out the anger with her next exhale. Being tired was already making things difficult. Being pissed on top of that would only cause mistakes that would turn a bad situation worse.

The watch had killed two more thralls. She sagged, trying to catch her breath. They might win this one.

Lightning flashed again, and a new form stalked into view.

Fuck.

A bloodling—the same one she'd seen on her first day outside of Calvert—and he was headed directly for her.

"Joan!"

Dayton obviously wanted to help, but he was too far away to do any good anyhow. If this piece of shit wanted to come for her, so be it.

She swallowed the fear, adjusted her grip of the short sword's hilt, and shook the rain from her face.

"*Terra* shifted."

The ground rumbled and shook between them. The bloodling swayed but kept coming. One thrall tripped into his path. He reached out to grab the man by his head and twisted it so quickly, Joan gasped.

He stared at Joan as he tossed the thrall's corpse aside. So much for solidarity on their team.

He was bigger than she was, and he'd be fast. He'd be strong—they always were—but she had more than speed and strength on her side.

He wore a shirt this time, and was barehanded, the cocky motherfucker. Whatever. She was no easy meat.

The bloodling spread his arms, a transparent attempt to menace her and grab her in a bear hug. Bullshit move. She stepped diagonally past him, twisting out of range as she passed. He grabbed nothing but empty air.

He turned toward her, growling in irritation or frustration. She sliced her blade across his chest from one shoulder to the opposite leg. He grunted and reached for her again.

She blocked him with a cross of her blade on her upswing, against the inside of one thigh. Another slice.

He grabbed her other arm, right above the elbow, and squeezed as she twisted away.

It still fucking hurt.

She stabbed him in the stomach, sinking half her blade into him before he pulled away. She'd perforated something—the stench of his entrails cut through the wind and rain.

He wiped one hand through his own blood and whatever else might be leaking out of him, then licked it from his palm and grinned.

Ugh. *Gross.* Bloodlings acted like they were invincible.

It might have rattled someone else, but she'd seen worse. Someone nearby screamed, but she couldn't spare a glance. Wings flapped in the rain, hinting at the presence of more damned crows, but she couldn't be distracted by that either. Nothing mattered but the fight.

Mr. Cocky came at her again. Desperate, she lowered herself to one knee and plunged her free hand into the mud.

"*Terra* liquified."

His next step sank into mud halfway to the knee, throwing him off balance. As he fell forward, Joan shouted as she slid her blade through his torso, this time deep enough to carve a gouging gash through his flesh.

He collapsed with a resounding splat, his face in the mud. He tried to push himself up, but she must have cut into his heart—his movements slowed, futile, until he stilled, his head half-buried in the ground.

Her chest was tight, ravaged from heavy breathing. The cold night air tasted of woodsmoke, fresh blood and sour mud. Her breath fogged in front of her every time she exhaled, a cloud large enough to block her vision. She forced herself to breathe through her nose. Visibility was the most important thing until this battle was done.

Wearily, she pushed herself to her feet.

Tonight wasn't a night for loose ends. She planted a boot on the back of his head to hold him in place, and stabbed her sword into the hollow at the base of his skull. One violent twist of her wrist severed his spinal cord.

She'd never seen a bloodling rise from the dead, but this one definitely wasn't coming back.

The rain pounded the ground, the standing water making it sound like a shower stall. All the remaining thralls were dead or dying. Dayton and two watch men stood next to a woman who knelt beside another body. Judging by her expression, it was a compatriot who wouldn't rise again.

Dayton helped the woman stand—the same woman who'd come into the office earlier that day. Her shoulder looked dislocated, and she cried out with every step as Dayton guided her back towards the parking lot. The two men lifted and dragged her friend's dead body between them.

Joan tilted her head back. The rain washed some of the sweat from her skin. When she opened her eyes, Dayton had stopped walking. He reached into his pocket and pulled out his phone.

A moment later, he looked at her, the meaning of his gaze clear. Joan muttered a simple incantation for strength and endurance—one she'd inevitably pay for later with a hard crash.

She marched herself back to Luther, picking up speed as she got closer.

The night wasn't over.

In the midst of another incursion, the smell of dawn hinted at a possible reprieve though it was still fully dark.

Joan hoped a break was coming. Raising her arms took effort now, and she wasn't sure how much longer she could keep the fatigue at bay.

The rain had eased to a drizzle but the frenzy had not. This fight's front was the receding southern boundary line, now stretching across the parking lot of a long-empty warehouse. Amber streetlights glowed over four double lanes of parking spaces as Joan, Dayton and the others stood between the thralls and a multifamily apartment building on the other side of the lot.

If the watch fell here, those families would be exposed to the enemy.

This killing field was more brutal than the others had been— the thralls came in waves, a handful at a time, surging from the side streets. Several bodies lay still and would never move again.

Another watch team had joined the handful of people working with Dayton. A dozen in total struggled against too many thralls to count. Joan fought on the edge closest to the boundary line, overpowering the thralls while keeping an eye out for greater threats.

Two of the enemy closed in on Halsey. He backed up too quickly and slipped, but caught himself before he collapsed completely.

The thralls were close enough to each other that she could aim her battle spells at both. *"Ignis lampyridae."*

A dozen floating fireballs the size of fireflies materialized before their faces. One of the thralls walked face-first into the flurry and screamed when the fire burned his skin.

Halsey scrambled to his feet and stabbed that one in the chest. By the time the fireflies faded, he was steady enough to fight the remaining thrall.

The boundary kept shifting, and no one but Joan could tell where it was. A scream drew her attention to the far side of the lot by the warehouse. A bloodling, its irises glowing gold, grabbed one of the watch twenty yards away beneath the tattered awning over the boarded-up entrance.

Joan lunged ahead of the others and closed half the distance, but she couldn't move fast enough.

The bloodling buried his teeth in his victim's neck and bit hard enough to tear the flesh at her jugular. The woman fell to the ground.

"Clear left!" Dayton yelled, coming up behind Joan. Fighting in tandem for hours had yielded some battle synchrony, and Joan lunged to the right.

Dayton's axe flew past her, whipping through the air. Its bit plummeted into the bloodling's chest. The wannabe-monster fell backwards into the plywood of the barricade, then sank to the concrete.

Joan ran to the woman, hoping to cast a patching spell to slow the bleeding, but it was too late. The woman bled out in seconds.

No time to even curse. An itch pulled Joan's attention elsewhere.

Two male vampires—one tall and Black, the other shorter and white—lurked at the edge of the lot.

With her gun in one hand and her short sword in the other, Joan rushed to plant herself between the vampires and the rest of the watch, splitting her attention between the greater threat and the possibility of a thrall sneaking up her backside.

Peals of thunder mixed with the growls of the fight.

The pale vampire ran towards her. Then abruptly, he fell to his knees and vomited a stream of viscous blood. He tried to turn around, but succeeded in crawling only a few feet back the way he'd come as he vomited again.

He'd crossed the boundary.

Joan fought the urge to puke with him, but it didn't stop her from stashing her gun and grabbing the hilt of her sword with two hands, eager to claim the advantage.

His terror and fear greeted her—uncommon expressions on a vampire—and he didn't have fangs. A young vampire, then. Less than a decade undead.

She yelled with the effort as she swung the blade at his neck. It wasn't a clean blow. Her blade slid free when the vampire's head fell to the side, connected by decayed tissue.

Mostly decapitated was good enough.

The other vampire roared but stayed put.

None of the thralls or bloodlings had snatched any of the watch. The enemy had hit hard at precise points and never let up, not even when they were losing. Joan had killed over a dozen thralls tonight in addition to the bloodling at the baseball field. Victor served his minions up like fodder, but she couldn't find reason in sacrificing so many of his thralls.

Unless the only point to all this was to tire out and decimate the watch.

A wave both iron hot and ice cold passed through her from front to back as the boundary shifted again. The remaining vampire moved forward as if he'd expected the shift.

"Fall back!" Joan stood her ground and redrew her pistol, trying to give the watch some cover.

One glance to make sure everyone was behind her was a mistake.

"Look out!"

The shout was all the warning she had before the vampire

closed in on her, growling in malignant humor. Fangs poked across his lips, and the sclera of his eyes were red, almost black in the amber lamplight. His skin was a charcoal ash color, and his long, hugely muscular arms, naked to the elements, were slick with mist. His fingernails were long, like talons. Only the long undead—fifty years or more—could grow those.

It had been years since Joan had fought one of the older ones. She hadn't taken that one down and barely escaped with her life.

Focus. Memories didn't help a fight.

The stench of his half-dead flesh made her gag. He was too close for distance spells. If she tried anything now, it might blow back on her.

"Oh, I bet you're delicious," he said by way of greeting, his voice a raspy baritone.

"Fuck you, bloodsucker."

"Not my type, blood bag. But I'll drain you dry once I rip that pig-sticker out of your hands."

"Come at me, then." Exhaustion or no, she wasn't giving ground.

The battle raged behind her, but she couldn't divide her attention. Either the rest of them handled themselves or they didn't, but she had to direct her effort and skill on this waste of existence in front of her. The old terror of falling to a vampire surfaced, but she poured it into the fight.

She would not die here tonight.

He was bigger and would be faster. She had to kill this fucker quickly—before she tired out. The rain was back, heavy enough to spatter her skin, but not enough to block her vision.

In close quarters, a clean shot to the head was impossible. He kicked a leg beside her and swept his leg back to try to sweep her off her feet, but she jumped clear. The jump gave her enough space to shoot him in the side of his knee, blowing out his knee-cap. He yelled in pain and anger. Thick, reeking congealed blood spattered from the wound, droplets landing on her lips. She spit in disgust.

Had he been human, the shot would have crippled him. No such luck. He'd push until the leg failed altogether. She couldn't wait that long.

He swung his arms in an attempt to grab her in a bear hug. A cold whiff of rot choked her as she ducked, stumbling out of range of his improbably long reach. His frustrated growl juddered against her teeth. Fuck the gods and all their mothers, but she hated vampires.

"*Ignis lampyridae,*" she said, but as the fireballs appeared, the rain doused them.

The vampire snickered and reached for her sword hand. He caught only her tattered sleeve, but she couldn't shake him loose. Her fingers slipped down the hilt but she managed not to drop the short sword altogether.

Too close. No room. They fought on asphalt, so no earth. The rain eliminated fire as an option. Water wasn't her strong suit and she couldn't catch her damned breath for any air spells.

No time. She was fucked.

Joan shifted one shoulder back to throw a wild, sloppy punch with her gun hand. *Stupid, stupid, stupid.* The pistol barely grazed his jaw, and her wrist cracked with the pressure. It wasn't broken, but the twinge *hurt*. She cried out.

The vampire threw his head back and laughed, a dry cough of a sound despite the rain.

His grip on her sword arm loosened.

It gave her a half-second last chance. Joan shifted her weight, pulled her knee to her chest and channeled all her strength into a side thrust kick to his mid-section to give herself more room. He grunted from the impact as she kicked herself free, but he grabbed her boot when she tried to pull it back.

The ankle popped and she screamed. He shoved her hard, sent her flying backwards a few yards away and she slammed into the ground. Her short sword clattered away and splashed into a shallow puddle.

Joan lay nearly flat on the asphalt of the lot, pain blooming in her lower back and one arm from landing hard. She was going to have bone bruises after this shitstorm. At least she'd kept her head up.

His smile was gruesome, fangs jutting across his thin lips, so certain was he that he'd secured an advantage, but Joan felt better about her chances. Plenty of room now.

Relief helped her correct her grip. She raised her gun and shot him right between his blood-tinted iridescent eyes, wincing at her bruised knuckles. Her other palm ground into the asphalt, gravel digging into her skin.

He fell backward with an awkward plop.

It took her a moment to catch her breath and get back to her feet. Gingerly, she tested the weight on her ankle. It ached like hell, but she could walk. She retrieved her short sword from the ice-cold water of a puddle.

A few yards away, Dayton slit the throat of another bloodling, then pushed it away to clear enough room for him to decapitate it in one blow. He grimaced in distaste as he shook the blood off his blade, a three-foot monstrosity of questionable origin.

None of the thralls remained alive. Two more of the watch were dead. The rest sagged where they sat or stood, exhaustion evident in their hanging heads.

When Joan moved to join Dayton, she walked through the boundary again.

"Here," she said loud enough for the remaining watch. With surprising speed, considering how tired they all were, the watch moved beyond the line of her position. Three more thralls appeared from behind the warehouse, but one of the other women in the watch raised a rifle and shot them down in rapid succession.

Joan checked her gun, made sure it was clear and ready for

another engagement, though she prayed they were done. She needed to sleep, to eat, probably in that order though she was starving. And a gallon of water sounded better than sex.

Standing not far from her, Dayton cursed, and she didn't blame him. They'd won the battle, but lost more ground in the fight as the boundary receded.

With a few seconds to breathe—to fucking think—she calculated the distances and locations where they'd battled tonight. Calvert's boundary had lost half a mile of territory so far, which shouldn't be possible. How was Victor doing it?

Dayton's suggestion of a dark coven might not be as much bullshit as she'd thought.

"Bloody hell," Dayton muttered. She thought he was responding to her own macabre thoughts, but he stood still, tense.

Joan turned to look and tried not to groan.

Two vampires, their hands clawed to demonstrate their long talons, stalked closer in a slow confident gait.

The watch lined up where they stood, beside the vehicles they'd lined up sideways for cover if they had to fall back. Many of them held guns, and now that they had open field between them and the vampires, they had a small advantage.

"Wait 'til the boundary weakens them," Dayton said. "And then mow the fuckers down."

The vampires stepped past the last known line of the boundary.

"Joan."

He was asking if the boundary had shifted again, but Joan hadn't felt a change.

"I don't—I don't know. I don't think it did." These vampires had walked *through* the boundary.

It should have been impossible, and for a moment, Joan wondered if this whole war had just been lost to Victor.

Gunshots sparked and echoed across the lot. The vampires

took hit after hit in their arms, legs, torsos, but they kept coming.

She couldn't go hand to hand again. She'd lose.

The watch deferred to her first action: she knelt to touch the dirt in a parking divider. It was like sinking her hand in muck—it wasn't only the mud. Whatever Victor was doing to the land *felt* wrong, even inside the boundary. Cold and slimy, yet not just physically. She'd never experienced anything like this. She tasted the air while she was at it. Bitterness coated her tongue like it was laced with anise and not in a good way.

Too much input.

She wrestled back her fatigue, and summoned a swirling tornado of earth to surround her opponents' legs. It would wall them in, halt their movement, leave them vulnerable to distance weapons.

"*Terra* mob boots." One of her first incantations. Stupidly worded, but effective. The asphalt cracked and the earth bubbled up as if pushed from below, but sifted away from their legs as they pushed forward. She'd have to use air to hold it—a cluster spell of two elements. Dangerous in the best of times, but mid-battle . . .

"*Aeris* silo."

It was risky, though, because as tired as she was, she ran the risk of . . .

The rebound pounded into her, the dirt scratching her face and hands, the air knocking her back a few steps. She tasted bile and swallowed it down, desperate to keep her stomach in check. She shook her head to clear it, regretted it instantly when the headache pounded in her temples, and looked at the vampires again. Something shimmered around them, something familiar —

Before Joan could shout that something was off, they were close enough to shoot in the head. They collapsed dead, one with his leg bent unnaturally backward beneath him, the other with legs splayed wide and obscene. A final insult to their long-abandoned humanity.

Nobody moved. The watch all stood, Joan sat on the ground, and they watched the shadows, waiting for the next monster to reveal itself. Across the lot, one of the thralls lay dying, crying out for mercy, but Joan couldn't spare it. Not until she was sure no reinforcements were lurking in the shadows. Experience had taught her caution.

Dayton kept checking his phone, but . . . nothing.

Twenty minutes later, the eastern sky lightened. The dying man's cries stopped.

She tried to force herself not to relax, not to assume it was over, but some small part of her nearly wept.

When the incongruent and somehow obscene trills of predawn birdsong began, when the entire lot was silent and nothing else stirred, the watch began to collect the bodies for final burning at the landfill. So many of them. She'd lost count of the people she'd seen fall over the years.

Joan pushed herself to her feet, staggered, and stopped to catch her balance. The headache she'd ignored for hours was back with a vengeance, and her equilibrium was shot. Queasy with fatigue, she marshaled herself to join the watch.

"We've got this," someone next to her said.

It was Halsey, the smart-mouth punk from her first night with the watch. Jesus, she was losing it if this asshole could appear out of nowhere without her noticing.

"You've done enough for tonight, I'd say," he said, looking her dead in the eyes as he spoke. One of his eyes had swollen up from what had probably been a punch to the face. His gaze and tone held nothing but deference and respect.

"Thanks," Joan said.

He nodded and joined the others.

It was a simple thing, this exchange, but it meant a lot. Maybe these weren't her people anymore, but they were people, and she didn't want to let them down.

War witch or not, Joan was now an unofficial member of the

Calvert watch.

This time, they didn't bother with tarps or rope, and decapitated the corpses on the spot, separated the heads from the torsos, and loaded them into the back of the nearest pickup.

"Oh, fuck." One of the less talkative members of the watch stood over one of the final two vampires. His eyes were wide with fear. "This one's human."

They all moved closer. No fangs, no elongated discolored talons, no red-tinted eyes.

"It's Javier, from the feed store," someone said.

Joan looked at Dayton in question.

He sighed. "Taken on the last supply run."

They checked the other vampire, but it, too, turned out to be human—another former Calvert resident who'd been taken months before.

No one spoke.

Joan wanted to scream. Up close and dead, their appearances were disturbingly obvious and human, but someone had cast a glamour spell over them to appear otherwise.

"This is not your fault." Joan pulled herself to her full height, no matter how tired she was. She stared at each member of the watch in turn.

"He's doing this to test your resolve. He thinks if he makes you stop to consider whether the person across from you is a human, that you'll hesitate. That you'll back down in fear."

She hadn't planned the words, but they were true. Her voice lowered in anger. Not at these people—at a pretender vampire who thought he could take what he wanted, no matter what the cost, and she wasn't having it. She ignored the stench of fresh death and spoke once more.

"Don't give in to him." They weren't going to like it, but it had to be said. "These people were already dead. If Victor hadn't pushed them through the boundary, intent on having us kill them, he would have done it himself. These people were never going to survive."

Her voice rose. "This isn't on you. It's on him. Maybe these people were just like you, just trying to get by, until he took them and twisted them to serve his purpose."

She sheathed her weapons and walked among them, drawing their attention to her channeled fury, her belief that they would prevail because she never backed down and she certainly wasn't starting now.

Joan had enough conviction for all of them.

"Don't waver. Don't falter. Keep up the hunt. But know that when you finally see that bastard, when you kill him and burn his corpse and leave his head for the crows, that you'll be avenging each of these people as well."

There were no more decapitations. They collected the rest of the bodies and covered the truck beds. No one wanted to look too closely anymore.

Dayton amended his plan, dejection weighing on his shoulders as he sagged against Luther's tailgate. There'd be a pyre at the landfill instead of a mass heap into the crematorium.

"There's no way we could have taken them to the hall," he said by way of explanation an hour later as Joan drove him home. "We'd only have to explain what happened and it'd lead to panic. People are already hounding us for answers, and I've got jack shit to tell them."

Joan didn't have any words of wisdom either. She dug her nails into her palms as she gripped the steering wheel.

Dayton rubbed at his eyes. "Know what's worse? We only got hit tonight in our blind spots, Joan."

It took a minute for the implication to sink through her fatigue. "Someone's talking."

He probably thought it was Gretchen, but Joan couldn't believe it. Still, the mysteries were stacking up and she was too damned tired to unravel them.

When she pulled up in front of Dayton's house, a single-story white ranch with fortified windows, motion detectors sensed their arrival and two spotlights on the front yard blinked to life.

She shifted into park out of fear that her exhaustion would make her foot slip from the brake.

He climbed slowly out of his seat, every motion indicating he was just as exhausted as she was. Once on his feet again, he turned around to lean his head back in, just clearing the door with his tall frame. "Jesus, what a clusterfuck this is." He shook his head, his long hair matted by sweat and blood and morning mist.

She didn't disagree. "Rest up."

"Night, Joan. Morning. Whatever."

Though the whole situation was dire, she couldn't help but laugh a little. "Right."

Calvert was waking up as she drove back to the house—a farmer in his garden, a few more trucks on the roads. First light meant safety to some, but she wondered how many of their routines had been wrecked by all this madness. Her own regimen—which wasn't very formal to begin with—was nowhere near as centered as she'd hoped. She hadn't meditated in two days because her head hurt too much to focus. If she kept this up, she'd lose her mind for real.

Smoke rose from the living room chimney as Joan drove Luther into the driveway and a yearning seized in her chest. Leigh was awake, then, and had built a fire. Joan tried to remember when she'd eaten last and decided it was too hard to think.

The moment she set foot on the porch stairs, the door opened. Leigh, fully dressed but barefoot, welcomed her inside. As always, her hair was down and free, and her gaze held nothing but Joan. When things between them had been good, Leigh had always made her feel like she was the center of the universe, ten feet tall and bulletproof. Joan didn't feel like any of that right now, but Leigh's presence made the awful just a little bit better.

"Hey," Leigh said, locking the door behind her.

Joan prayed she didn't ask how the night had gone. She had no strength to talk about any of it.

Leigh stepped close enough to touch, though she didn't. "I put some vegetable stew in the microwave. Figured you'd be hungry. I can find some meat to add if you want." Her face twisted in displeasure.

So different from who she used to be, yet so much the same.

"Sounds fine just the way it is. I could eat my fucking hand right now." She hung her jacket on the rack by the front door.

Leigh looked her up and down and crooked an eyebrow. "You sure you don't want to clean up first?"

Joan wondered if that was commentary on her current state of uncleanliness, but Leigh continued.

"It'll help ease some muscles before they get too stiff."

Hot water sounded like heaven. Joan bit back a moan.

"I'll take that as a yes," Leigh said with a smile.

She guessed she *had* moaned out loud. She'd be embarrassed but she was stunned speechless by Leigh's smile—something she hadn't seen since she'd been back in town. It made something long forgotten—a kind of longing welcome—twist inside her.

Not long after the bath in the downstairs tub and a bowl of stew at the kitchen table, Joan stumbled down the upstairs hall dressed in a ratty old bathrobe she didn't recognize. She'd wondered where it came from, then decided she didn't care. It was clean and helped her cover the distance to her room.

Halfway to her bedroom door, she remembered she didn't want to sleep here, but a bed sounded too comfortable to deny.

Leigh appeared with a thick blanket in her arms. "Thought you might need an extra."

Her golden skin was lit by the first rays of sunlight through the hall window. The sun had risen while Joan had been in the tub. Everything about Leigh appeared angelic right now, except for the tense set to her jaw.

Joan leaned over and planted a kiss on Leigh's head as she passed. "Thanks for everything." She closed the door behind her as she went inside her room and collapsed into the bed.

A few minutes later, curled under the blankets and almost asleep, she realized what she'd done.

At first, Joan didn't realize she was dreaming.

How had she gotten outside? She sat in a tree, staring at her bedroom window. The image shifted between contrasting angles, as if from different branches of the same tree.

Next, she was looking at the front porch, then her rig in the driveway, but the vantage point was off. She floated above everything.

She must still be asleep. Weird, though, to be so cognizant in a dream. So aware of each moment passing.

The street. The parked cars unmoving in the weak sunlight. Houses on both sides of the road. The front of Gretchen's house, then her porch, then the tiny window in her door. Gretchen sat in an armchair in her living room, talking to a tall man dressed in black who sat on her couch. Only the back of his head was visible from the window, but he leaned back in repose, his arm resting along its back like he had all the time in the world. Gretchen leaned forward, tension in every muscle.

Gretchen glanced out the window at her, then squinted. Joan tilted her avian head to the side, and Gretchen's face went wide with alarm. She rushed to the door and threw it open.

The image went blurry, like looking out a car window trying to focus on one point while the car sped forward.

Joan sank back into nothingness, deep, dark sleep covering her once more.

CHAPTER 8

Leigh sat alone on the bed in the guest room. It was only her imagination, but she still felt the press of Joan's lips to her head and thought of little else. It reminded her of the times when Joan would study so hard, she said her brain felt heavy. She'd kiss Leigh good night, embrace her so tightly Leigh's bones would crack, then offer one last kiss to the top of Leigh's head.

Old habits, or perhaps accidental muscle memory, but it had been so warm and wondrous to have Joan forget the distance between them.

Even if Joan didn't know the truth.

Morning sunlight splashed over the hand-stitched quilt on the bed. In the last six months of her life, Joan's mother had been too weak to climb the stairs. She'd insisted on being moved to this room on the main floor to be closer to her family's daily lives. Trevon had painted the walls a warm yellow, brightening it year-round.

The walls were still decorated with Leigh's framed charcoal portraits of Trevon and Joan, of Joan's brother and mother. Leigh had been surprised Trevon had kept them considering all that happened later.

Leigh looked away from the reminders of her younger self, back when she'd been a visionary, an optimist, madly in love with Joan and hopeful of a life they could share together. Back before Leigh understood that Joan was too big for a small town like Calvert.

Before Leigh's choices made everything so much worse.

Leigh wiped a hand over her face to clear her mind and looked out the window. She'd wasted another hour staring into nothing but the past, with no change whatsoever to the outcome, and work needed to be done. The house was old, but she'd kept it immaculate since her return—a way of showing Trevon her gratitude.

In the garden, Leigh reveled in the sun on her skin. Since her return, working amidst the plants was the only thing that felt . . . good. She clipped a few branches of sage and lay them beside the rose petals and a clump of moss in the small basket at her side.

One row of herbs had nearly died off before her arrival, but they'd recovered surprisingly quickly over the last few weeks. Many of the raised beds were empty, tilled over in preparation for the coming winter. On the far side of the yard sat a memorial garden for Matthews family members who had passed away. Narrow stone pillars, each knee-high and etched with a name, commemorated a person who had lived on this land.

Would anyone build one for Trevon? Or would this all be lost?

Yet another thing outside of her control. She busied herself with digging out the new weeds near the stones until noon, an arbitrary pause in an otherwise formless day.

Back in the kitchen, Leigh put another pancake on the stack warming in the oven, then poured more batter into the cast iron pan on the stove. Joan wouldn't be up again for hours after such a late night, and she'd be starving when she did.

On another burner, Leigh placed a small saucepan of water over a medium flame. Making the rosewater was the last step of preparation.

She forced herself to cook bacon. Her stomach roiled at the

odor—like spoiled meat though it was recently slaughtered—but Joan would expect it and a few minutes of discomfort was worth the chance of avoiding dangerous questions. Besides, the bacon would cover the scent of the roses.

She transferred the rosewater to a tiny ceramic pitcher and tucked it behind a flowerpot on the kitchen sill. It would lose its potency if left too long, but should be fine for now, as long as—

Boot heels warned her of Joan's approach, but there wasn't time to hide anything. More time had passed than Leigh had thought.

Joan appeared in the space between the dining room and the kitchen. As usual, the sight of her made Leigh's heart rate increase.

"Morning," Joan said. She stood dressed in black jeans and a loose black tunic, and tucked one hand into a front pocket.

Leigh smiled, but she knew her nerves were showing. "Afternoon."

Joan wiped sleep from her eyes and took a step closer to Leigh. "Do I smell bacon?"

Leigh lifted a spatula and nudged it in the direction of the table, hoping to distract Joan from the extra pans on the stove. Best to pretend everything was normal. "Nice try. You know you do. Have a seat."

Joan frowned at the four-person kitchen table where Leigh had set a place. "You're not eating?"

"Already did." Leigh carried the tray of pancakes and bacon towards the table. She hadn't eaten at all, but admitting it would only prompt more questions. She offered a tight-lipped smile as she served a healthy portion onto a ceramic plate.

Joan sat and draped a napkin across her lap. "You know, you don't have to . . . take care of me like this."

"It's just breakfast."

"Join me anyway?" Joan's earlier animosity, the cold shoulder she'd given Leigh, was gone.

Leigh thought of the kiss on her head and pushed her reservations aside. She refreshed her tea and sat at the table. Joan ate without speaking—another typical trait of hers—then joined Leigh quietly at the kitchen sink to clean up.

Joan cleared her throat. "So, listen, um, I—"

Here it was. She was going to say the kiss was a mistake or an accident. Something that would erase the magic of what had happened. Leigh liked that Joan had forgotten herself.

Joan wiped her hands on a dish towel. "I want to apologize for getting in your personal space."

Her eyes held no judgment or regret, only nervousness and hesitation.

"Don't take it back, please." Leigh looked away, not wanting to give away too much. "I . . . I liked that you didn't think about it, okay?"

"Okay." Joan finished wiping down her plate and put it back in the cabinet. "Look, I . . ." She turned around to lean against the kitchen counter, still within arm's reach as she looked everywhere but at Leigh.

Leigh steeled herself against the impending inquiry. She couldn't lie to Joan if asked a direct question. It'd be impossible. For all that had changed between them, Joan still knew her too well.

"I appreciate what you've been doing around here. Everything is so nuts right now, and you're . . . you're helping me get through it, so . . . thanks."

Leigh stared. This was a more mature Joan than the young, impetuous woman she'd loved long ago. The lines of fatigue around Joan's eyes made her look older but couldn't detract from the grace of her jaw and cheekbones. Her braids were a little fuzzy now, probably from her tossing and turning, but it softened the hard edges that made Joan who she was.

Joan had been beautiful when they were younger, but now she was breathtaking. They were close enough that Leigh could see the black pupils in the dark, dark brown of Joan's eyes, eyes that had always made Leigh feel like she mattered. Right now, whatever was behind those eyes was anyone's guess, but Leigh couldn't turn away.

Her knees trembled. They were getting dangerously close to the truths left to speak between them.

Joan's phone rang. With a start, Joan stepped away from the counter and reached into her pocket.

"Yeah?" she answered as Leigh returned to her task. "Where and when?"

Leigh looked up, and Joan was staring right at her, her business face on.

"I'll be there."

Leigh tucked a kitchen cloth into the rack on the outside of the oven. "Another attack?"

The frequency of attacks over the last few days was terrifying. She didn't think that they would come any closer to the house, but sooner or later, she was going to have to deal with the fact that perhaps even this house wasn't safe enough to protect her.

A house couldn't change what had happened to her, or the ticking clock that she counted every day.

Joan tucked the phone back into her jeans, her brow wrinkled in thought. "I'm taking the watch to meet with the coven."

Leigh's heart leapt into her throat at the mention of the two groups she was trying most to avoid.

Joan frowned at the items on the counter and Leigh froze in fear of discovery.

"Do you have to do this now?" Joan asked. "Or can it wait until we get back?"

Leigh tried not to reveal her relief, but she was surprised that Joan wanted her company. Now still wasn't a good time— she didn't have long to do what needed doing.

"Do you really need me to come with you?" Leigh couldn't hide forever, but things had been going so well. "I don't think I'd be any help with any of . . . that. Why don't I stay here and . . . um, get dinner started?" It was a weak excuse, but it was all she could think of.

"It's not about help, but it is important. And you want to stay here?"

"I . . ." What could she say to explain herself without revealing the truth? "I don't want to be outside . . . so close to sundown, I mean . . . I . . ." Joan would never buy that—sundown was still hours away.

One piece of truth then. She looked up at Joan and couldn't fake the fear in her voice as she whispered. "I'm scared, Joan. I don't think I can leave the house right now. Please?"

It was a deliberate pull on Joan's heartstrings. Joan stared at her as if she were an overwhelmingly challenging puzzle she was trying to solve, but just when Leigh thought Joan might push the issue, she relented with a nod.

Leigh tried not to sag with relief.

Joan turned towards the dining room. "Call me if anything happens."

"Wait, what's the meeting about?" Her mind filled with several options that were potentially dangerous for her in particular.

Joan shrugged into her jacket and checked the position of all her weapons. "The boundary is receding and we don't know why, and Victor has blocked all the roads."

The countdown in Leigh's head sped up. As Leigh grappled with this horrifying information, Joan offered an almost tender look as she walked out the door.

"I'll be back as soon as I can."

After she left, as Leigh barricaded the door, she wondered if even Joan could protect her from the horror Leigh faced if the boundary fell. The trembling started. It would overpower her if she didn't find something to do, something to pour the fear into.

One glimpse of her reflection in the living room mirror

reminded her that her schedule was already decided, and that it wasn't only fear that made her feel unsteady.

In the mudroom by the back door, Leigh placed a pint-sized mortar and pestle in front of her on the workbench. She ground the collected herbs to a fine powder, then added a few grains of sea salt to the mix and ground them in.

Mounted on the wall below the window was a narrow shelf, perhaps three inches deep and covered in bottles and boxes of other ingredients Trevon had found useful.

Leigh picked up a small brown bottle. Very carefully, she removed the stopper, and sifted a tiny clump of iron filings into the mortar, then restored it and put the bottle back on the shelf.

More grinding. When she was certain she'd broken everything down as finely as she could, she poured in two tablespoons of the concentrated rosewater she'd made earlier.

She transferred the potion to a small bowl. Then she removed all traces of her work and carried the bowl in her hand back to the guest room. She locked the door and drew the curtains, sealing herself off completely from the world outside.

Alone, secure in the knowledge that Joan was out of the house and couldn't interrupt, Leigh removed her clothes. A short cold bath in the small adjoining bathroom cleansed her body for her ritual. She avoided looking at herself in the mirror and returned to sit in a chair next to the closet.

With a deep breath, she settled herself for what came next.

The tiny bowl sat on the table next to her, as did a small black bundle, no more than four inches long and an inch in diameter. Inside lay a simple sewing kit, complete with a selection of needles.

Leigh removed the largest needle, pricked the end of a finger before she lost her nerve, and let three drops of blood fall into the bowl.

She dipped the middle finger of one hand into the mixture and ignored the slight burn when it touched her skin. With focused attention, she rubbed the ointment into the pulse points of her wrists, behind her knees, at the junction of her thighs, and both sides of her neck. She repeated the routine until every bit of the mixture was gone.

Leigh closed her eyes, and as she did every day, fought the urge to cry. It wasn't the burning sensation all over her body that brought her to tears, but the fact she had to perform the ritual at all.

CHAPTER 9

The parking lot at the library was full. Joan parked on the street. She glanced at another cluster of crows, the only noise in an otherwise quiet main square, as they clashed and surged from tree to tree. The block-sized park was empty despite the daylight.

Back in her teens, there'd always been some event here—a farmers' market, a herd of preschoolers on a park outing, a meeting or convocation of some kind. Now the fountain in its center was dry, the surrounding benches covered in mold and moss, the hedges lining the paths overgrown and untended.

Had the heart of Calvert died long before her father?

Inside the library, Dayton paced in the narrow hall near the conference room where the coven held its meetings. Through the floor-to-ceiling window next to the door, Gretchen and the others sat in mismatched chairs before a blank whiteboard.

"What are you doing out here?" Joan asked.

"The watch isn't invited to coven sessions." Dayton's displeasure deepened the frown on his face.

Joan rolled her eyes. This kind of local political bullshit was what she'd wanted to avoid. "Well, we don't have time to spare feelings."

She knocked twice before opening the door, but that was about as much courtesy as she could muster.

Gretchen stopped speaking mid-sentence and the others

present looked at Joan in surprise. Reed Hill, who sat closest to the door, half jumped from his chair before he sat back down in embarrassment.

"What brings you to the coven meeting, Joan?" Gretchen's greeting sounded forcibly casual.

Joan kept her back against the open door. Dayton stood just inside the room on the other side of the entrance. Smart—the room was only large enough for the conference table and chairs, and didn't have another exit.

Five people joined Gretchen around the conference room table in the beige, boring room, the same people Joan had met outside her house the day she'd arrived. On the far side of the conference table, Pablo Cortez didn't move, though his disapproving eyes assessed Joan and Dayton in turn. Reed Hill now smiled wide enough to show all his teeth, but the sentiment didn't reach his eyes. Ashley Gaines, the youngest person in the room, couldn't sit still in her seat. Ella Williams leaned back with her arms crossed over her chest, her library badge clipped to the large front pocket of her cardigan. A burly bear of a man whose name Joan couldn't recall, with a crewcut and a pentagram tattoo on his neck, nodded at Joan in confusion.

Every one of them looked weary, not that Joan could blame them.

Though all eyes were on Joan, she focused her attention on Gretchen. "Got some news for the coven that can't wait."

"Are you leaving town already?" Gretchen glanced at the others as if in confidence. "I'm sure you've all heard she's the most famous war witch west of the Cascade Range from British Columbia to Baja California. Joan has single-handedly defeated over two dozen vampires in the last three years."

That introduction left Joan unsteady. Since when did Gretchen cater to her ego, or follow her career?

"Not just yet," Joan said.

Suspicion washed over Gretchen's face before it disappeared.

Had Joan imagined it? A fissure of warning spiked through Joan's head. The dream she'd had that morning, the weird one with all the blurry, jarred images, came to mind, and she remembered the one where Gretchen had stared at her.

Gretchen had been dressed much as she was now. Was it some kind of portent? Joan's natural suspicion led her to hold on to this new piece of information.

"What's so important?" Pablo said as if he had somewhere else he wanted to be and Joan's presence was dragging things out.

Joan had little tact or skill for mincing words. "The boundary is failing."

A long silence greeted this, which surprised her. Did they already know? A few of the coven members exchanged looks, and then stared at Gretchen as if expecting her to deliver some news of her own.

"We know, Joan." Her tone was meant to sound kind but came off as condescending instead. Had she always been like this? "The power of the boundary weakens until replenished on the full moon, but the ebbing is . . . more evident since your father's passing."

Joan stepped forward. "No, I mean its locational border is receding."

Someone gasped.

"That's impossible." It was the young witch again, the one who couldn't seem to contain her enthusiasm. "That's not how it works."

These people tested Joan's nerves. "I know goddamned well how it works. I grew up watching my father prepare for and conduct that ritual. What I'm telling you is that the area the boundary covers is shrinking."

"Preposterous," Gretchen said.

"It's true," Dayton said, and while Joan was annoyed that her word wasn't taken at face value, she didn't blame him for trying

101

to help. "Since the Clark farm was hit, the watch has repelled six more attacks. I just found out about two more that happened on the southern edge of town, but those folks didn't call the watch until this morning."

Low murmurs around the table took the focus away from Joan. She shifted her weight to one side, though she didn't feel relaxed. "It sounds like this local vampire of yours has a bead on Calvert."

Gretchen folded her hands together on the table, taking the reins once again. "The boundary is the coven's concern. Seems to me the watch should focus more on protecting the town than meddling in coven affairs. Perhaps we can send a message to this Victor and find out what he wants."

Joan scoffed. Vampires only wanted two things. Blood and control, not necessarily in that order. "You think you can negotiate with a vampire? Broker some kind of deal? He'll break it and Calvert will suffer. Don't be stupid. I'll work with the watch until this Victor is out of the picture."

"I'm not sure that's necessary," Gretchen said. "I don't doubt your skill, but I'm certain other matters require your attention. Just yesterday I heard there's a vampire horde attacking the towns along the California border. Surely someone with your prowess is needed there."

She glanced at the other members of the coven and then back at Joan. "Rest assured this coven will protect Calvert."

How much more could this dwindling coven handle? They were supposed to tend to the town's rituals, to the high holy days fortifying the community so the binding witch could focus on keeping the boundary strong. With Trevon dead, how would these six people meet all those needs?

"Look," Joan said. "We need to stop this vampire lord and find out what the hell is happening to the boundary."

"No offense, Joan," Pablo said, while clearly meaning the exact opposite. "But you have no say. You haven't been here, and you don't know what we've gone through."

Dayton laughed without humor. "Are you fucking kidding right now? She's had nothing but trouble since she got here and has fought more than once to protect people in this town."

"And a lot of us are grateful." This from Reed, the tall scarecrow of a man with the easy smile. He seemed hopeful as he asked, "Are you planning to stay?"

"No," Joan said, without apology. "I'm only here until I find out what's going on with the boundary."

Ashley piped up again. "But why not? You're the most—"

"Joan," Gretchen interrupted, with a side glare at Ashley. "It's best that we do our own research into that."

Joan squinted at Gretchen. *Seriously?* Despite Joan's training and experience, despite what Gretchen knew she had taught Joan herself, this was the tack these folks wanted to take?

What the hell was going on?

"And the blockade?" Dayton asked.

Gretchen shook her head. "I'm sure that's a coincidence. Once the boundary is restored, those opportunists will no doubt give up."

She couldn't be this uninterested. Something else was at play.

Joan crossed her arms and fought against huffing in disbelief. Dayton might not want to ask, but she sure as hell would. "Can you at least put out the word for more folks to aid the watch? That southern part of town is under constant attack, and they're stretched thin."

Dayton glared at her, but didn't deny the validity of the request.

Gretchen offered a tight smile, and though her tone was conciliatory, the impact was not. "I think Dayton should focus on sobering up the people he already has, don't you?"

The way Dayton puffed up meant this was about to get even uglier, but before Joan could say anything, Gretchen stood.

"Why don't we take a short recess?"

Dayton looked like he wanted to push the issue, but his phone interrupted him. He side-eyed Joan, incredulous, and stepped into the hall.

Ashley and the others stood to stretch, while Reed and Pablo had a side conversation in low voices. Gretchen approached Joan and with a glance, drew her just past the door.

Joan followed.

"You should be careful of that Dayton, dear." Gretchen's tone was kind, but her eyes were hard.

Had Gretchen always been so suspect, so duplicitous?

"Why?"

Gretchen tucked her hands under her arms and gave the impression of pulling Joan into her confidence, but Joan wasn't going for it.

"He's new here, and I don't think he understands all of us yet. I can't help but wonder if these attacks would be happening if he had accepted the coven's guidance. I'm not happy with the idea, but perhaps we need to let some of those outer farms go and move those people into town. We can't protect everyone. And why isn't he doing something about the number of drug addicts on our streets? Half of those people aren't even from Calvert. We don't have to let them stay."

Shock stole Joan's response. The Gretchen she remembered hadn't been this lacking in compassion. Had she?

Gretchen shook her head in disapproval. "We've got limited resources as it is, and these attacks on the livestock aren't helping. We should set up a system of distribution for the people who belong here."

And then Joan knew just what to say. "So, these outsiders, the people who haven't lived here and don't belong here, they should fend for themselves. People like me." Perhaps she wasn't considered a local anymore.

Gretchen paused her puritanical tirade and plastered a wide, loving smile on her face. "I know you've been away, but you're more like the prodigal daughter, aren't you? You're one of us."

"And Calvert takes care of its own, right?"

"Well, of course, we do! There's nothing we won't do for a resident of Calvert. That's why we're here. In fact, I wanted to let you know that we'd be happy to take care of the house for you when you leave. It's too much for Leigh to handle alone and I'm sure she'd appreciate our taking the responsibility off her hands."

Subtle as a thunderstorm.

Joan shifted her jacket and took a step forward into Gretchen's personal space. "If all you care about is protecting the citizens of Calvert, if even a delinquent like me is welcomed back with open arms, how come my father was the only one willing to take in Leigh when she came back?"

Gretchen shook her head in contrived pity. "You've always had a weakness for that girl. Regardless of how you may have felt about her in the past, she's not the same person you knew. After you left, she spent years running with drug dealers and abandoned her poor grandmother."

Her tone was consoling. "It's sweet that Trevon took her in, but the truth is, she's never really been part of this community."

Too far. Leigh had been born and raised in Calvert, just like Joan.

Gretchen took a half step closer, grating on Joan's nerves. "I know you have places to be, so let us keep an eye on things for you until you decide what to do. Leigh will find somewhere else to stay, I'm sure."

If Trevon had wanted the coven to have the house, he'd have never left it to Leigh. Leigh, who'd had no other place to go because . . .

Anger tightened Joan's shoulders. "She was grieving, bereft, and on the street but you couldn't take her in? You couldn't work with the coven to see if there was some way to save her grandmother's house?"

"It's not that simple—"

"Either we care about everyone, or we pick and choose and someone gets left out in the cold. Common decency should have made it easy for you to help her. The help you say you're giving to me now, but the truth is, you want something."

Joan leaned forward, and she saw the surprise in Gretchen's wide eyes, her hand on her chest in mock—or perhaps serious—distress as she tilted away.

Joan tasted her fear. "I mean it. Because I don't buy this 'I'm just looking out for you' crap, so what is it?"

The silence stretched between them as Gretchen turned thoughtful. She lifted her chin.

"Well, I should get back." She smiled and rested a hand on Joan's arm, persistent even when Joan bristled. "My offer stands if you change your mind. Safe travels, Joan."

Without another word, but with a parting glance that made Joan want to scream, Gretchen returned to the conference room and closed the door.

Fights with vampires were a lot easier to navigate than small-town machinations.

The mysteries of her weird dreams, of Gretchen's behavior, of the damned boundary made the irritating hum in her brain more of a headache.

Then she thought of the kiss she'd planted on Leigh's head, the way Leigh had seemed to like it, Leigh's considerable fear. Trying to make sense of it all made Joan's head too tight.

Dayton's tone of voice caught her attention. He ended the call and shoved the phone back into a pocket of his jacket as she approached.

"You're not gonna believe this. An emissary of Victor's wants to meet with the watch at the western checkpoint at sundown."

The familiar surge of pre-battle adrenaline coursed through her limbs. "Not without me."

Dayton glanced behind her. "What about them?"

Joan arched an eyebrow and nudged her head in the direction of the exit.

"Right," he said, and didn't argue.

She guessed he got the point.

The last rays of the sun brushed the treetops as Joan once again drove Dayton along the meandering back roads. The western checkpoint was the most remote, a stretch of two-lane road past the industrial section of town. The buildings were all abandoned and burnt out, or locked and dark. Joan slowed to a stop before the railroad tracks.

A dozen human thralls and three bloodlings by Joan's count blocked the road. It was a blatant show of muscle. Only a handful of the watch were present—the others were delegated to defending Calvert. Parley with an emissary was supposed to mean there would be no concurrent attacks, but Joan trusted no vampire contingent to follow the rules.

"You get any sleep this morning?" Dayton's low rumble was loud and abrupt in the silence of the vehicle as they sat waiting for sunset's conclusion.

"Hmm? Oh, yeah." Joan thought about kissing Leigh's head before she pulled herself back into the game. "You?"

"Some, but now I feel like any relaxation I managed to muster is shot."

"How many people know about this meet?"

"You, me and the watch guys I trust the most."

On the other side of the old railroad ties, a large charcoal SUV arrived followed by a black limousine, its gray exhaust steaming in the cool twilight air. It looked so out of place that she scoffed and Dayton laughed, but they both turned serious when doors opened across the road.

The dog growled from the back seat. As if he sensed the

upcoming threat, Willy seemed more wolf than dog, hackles high and blue eyes focused on the road ahead.

"Willy, stay here," Dayton said as he turned to Joan. "Ready?"

"Not even close." Joan pushed open Luther's door with a sigh.

The clouds roiled red and purple as she stepped to the tracks and confirmed the warm presence of the boundary, then returned to stand in front of her rig. While Dayton joined her, two decade-old pickups parked on either side of Luther, blocking access from the road perpendicular to the one they'd used to travel here. Of course, no one else was likely to be out here after sundown. Not unless they had a death wish.

The watch joined Dayton and Joan, forming a line to face the enemy.

Across the tracks, the monsters climbed from their cars like mobsters, threatening and in sync. Two vampires, their blood-tinted eyes giving them away, and two bloodlings. None of them looked familiar.

Dayton spoke low enough that his voice didn't carry. "When did the fog roll in?"

Joan reluctantly pulled her gaze away from the limo. The woods beyond the vampire convoy were hazy with fog, a thick cloud slowly enveloping their vehicles and crawling toward the warehouses and the watch's three trucks on this side of the railroad tracks.

Fog didn't move like that, which meant someone in the vampire party had the skill to conjure it.

"Magic," she said, stating the obvious.

If the fog enveloped them, the thralls and bloodlings could pick them off one by one. It was against the rules of parley, but it said a lot about what to expect from these bastards. They were only willing to honor a truce if it served their purpose.

No matter. She muttered an incantation as she crossed and uncrossed her fingers. The fog dissipated in the area between the warehouses and the woods.

"Neat trick," Dayton said, his admiration evident in his dry tone.

She wondered who it was in the emissary's party who possessed such skill. Casting countermeasures wouldn't deplete her—not unless she had to do it all night—but it would be distracting.

"How about we just kill these sonsobitches now and go home?" A beefy guy everyone called Huck spat a brown gob near his boots, then used his tongue to secure his tobacco wad in his cheek.

"Other than the fact they outnumber us three to one?" Dayton glared at his team. "Because then Victor will send someone worse. For once, we don't have to fight first. Let's find out what they want."

He looked at Joan in question, as if she might have something else to say about it.

Joan opted to follow Dayton's lead, for now.

One of the vampires moved like a snake—a cold predator focused on nothing but his prey. As tall as Dayton and lean like a runner, he had black wavy hair that fell past his ears. He could have been Middle Eastern or Latino—it was tough to tell at this distance—and he walked forward in unhurried measured steps until he stood on the far side of the tracks.

He looked at each of them in turn, as if sizing them up for slaughter, and held her eyes just a beat longer than the rest before moving on.

She itched with the need to take a weapon in hand and wipe this gruesome, offensive stain from the earth.

"I am Nathaniel, Legate to Victor." His voice was low and sinister, his words crisp as though English wasn't his first tongue, but he spoke with no discernible accent. Legate meant that he'd been the first vampire sired by Victor, also evidenced by his lack of talons.

His quiet menace suggested indescribable violence if provoked. "Which of you speaks for this little burg?"

Always so goddamned condescending. Every time she'd dealt with one of these young vampires, though they weren't even middle-aged by human standards, it was always the same. The antiquated posturing. The gothic dress, or worse, the ones who dressed like monks. At least this one had normal clothes. He wore a well-tailored black business suit over a white dress shirt without a tie, like he was on his way to an after-hours business negotiation with a bunch of real estate developers.

Come to think of it, he was dressed for the occasion—not that it mattered what kind of clothes the monster wore.

Dayton shifted his weight. Joan hoped no one else could sense his unease. "What do you want?" he asked.

The vampire's smile wasn't kind. "I'll be brief, since you're not in the mood to talk. Victor offers his protection, and I am here to collect payment."

"Calvert doesn't need his protection," Dayton said. "And we won't pay him anything—or anyone."

Nathaniel crooked an eyebrow. "No? Ask around. You might be surprised to learn some in your town don't agree with you and have no faith in your pathetic watch."

She and Dayton shared a glance and did the math. The vampire could only mean he had sources in town.

Nathaniel laughed, a cold, dry sound, as he watched their silent exchange. "More than one resident has offered themselves to Victor in exchange for . . . security."

"Is that what slow death is called?" Joan couldn't help speaking up. Nathaniel looked at her, sizing her up. Having drawn attention to herself, she regretted having spoken. She was supposed to be the ace in the hole, not the distracting bait.

He arched an eyebrow. "Perhaps you should speak to someone in your paltry excuse for a coven."

Joan froze. He knew something—but what, and from whom?

Nathaniel didn't raise his voice, but his words were clearly enunciated. "Accept Victor's protection and consent to a donor rotation, and we'll lift the blockade."

Joan couldn't help herself. "It'll be a cold day in hell before your master strolls in like it's an all-hours diner."

The other vampire and both bloodlings spread out on the far ends of the line, moving into attack positions.

Nathaniel focused on her now. "From what I hear, you won't be staying in Calvert long, so it's not your concern."

Their spy was good. That gave Joan pause, but she would never sacrifice the people of Calvert just to make sure some vampire Johnny-come-lately got his fix.

"You keep killing people every night, you're not gonna have a well to drink from anyway. Whether you kill us now or drain us later, there's no incentive to stand down. I don't mind taking a few of you with me."

She widened her stance, took a deep breath and arced her fingers in a counter-clockwise circle at her waist. She turned towards the flanking vampire and clapped her hands in front of her.

A thunderous, swirling ball of air the size of a large tumbleweed swerved towards the vampire and slammed into his chest. He flew back ten feet into a towering oak and fell to the ground, too dazed to move.

So much for her low profile.

Dayton took a step forward, hands still empty and his voice little more than a growl. "There is no way we're setting up donors for Victor. Stop dicking us around and give us something we can use."

Nathaniel squinted at Joan. "Perhaps Victor could be convinced to move on to other pastures if we come to a different agreement."

Something in the vampire's tone drove a chill through her.

"There is one in your little village who owes me."

"The attacks on the border, the people you've taken," Dayton said. "All of this over one person?"

Puzzle pieces shifted and Joan didn't like the way they settled.

"We're not giving you anyone," she said.

Nathaniel looked at her for a long moment before speaking. "My mistake for suggesting it was a choice." He tilted his head and raised a hand from his side. The bloodlings stopped moving.

Joan looked back and forth between them and Nathaniel in confusion and then she felt it.

A whooshing sound of wild wind preceded the popping of her ears as the air pressure changed. An invisible force boxed her in, holding her limbs fast, and the sounds of the evening— the wind in the trees, the idling engines—were silenced by the pressing air. She reflexively muttered the counterspell, freeing herself, and the sound resumed.

Dayton stared ahead but didn't move. Joan glanced at the other members of the watch. They were all in a similar stance— as if time had stopped and they were frozen, though still breathing. This changed the game entirely, because she was the only defense the watch had against someone this powerful.

Nathaniel smirked with arrogance. She wondered whether he'd been a witch as a human or if his attunement had changed after he'd turned. She'd heard that was even more rare than a witch keeping his powers, but there was no way now to know. It made her hate this undead thing all the more.

Alarmed, Joan drew her Bowie knife from her thigh. It was only useful in close quarters, but it felt good to have something in her hand. Nathaniel was evidently some kind of necromage, an undead practitioner of spellcraft.

She stepped forward. "So, this is how Victor parleys? Release them."

He looked at her as if he hadn't expected her to speak. It wasn't surprise or annoyance. More unanticipated—as if a dog had suddenly meowed like a cat.

He offered an unnatural shrug. "Merely taking advantage of an opportunity."

The thoughts flew furiously across her mind as she did the fast calculus of searching for an edge in this confrontation.

Without guild sanction, a young vampire lord like Victor had no right to expand his territory. Joan had never heard of him before coming to Calvert, and she'd been all over this region. Maybe these guys were actually smart, with the plan to secure larger territory before they petitioned a guild for membership—a rare possibility but not without precedent.

It would mean higher standing for them overall if they brought their own house to the guild table—otherwise they'd be relegated to lower roles with less influence. And vampires did love having influence, even over other vampires.

"Does the Black Rose City guild know Victor's staking a claim on Calvert?"

Nathaniel stared as if retaking her measure. "What does a human know of the guilds?"

"Enough to know this is against the rules."

He stepped forward, and an odd sound tunnel weaved between them—pushing the ambient noise aside but allowing them to speak in private.

He tilted his head in a way that should have been nonchalant, but it was too precise, too crisp of a motion to be truly casual. "Since you seem to care so much about saving the sheep, you will do what I ask."

Joan wasn't going to like this at all. "I'm not doing shit—"

"You will bring me the one I seek," he said, and his expression turned hostile. "A donor—young, Asian, long black hair— who took something that did not belong to her."

If Joan didn't know any better, she'd swear her heart stopped beating. It was possible that he was describing someone else, but she added it all up—the timing of Leigh's return, the way she'd hidden herself from everyone but Trevon, the lack of friends in town.

Now she understood why Leigh was so terrified to leave the house, why every time Joan mentioned anything about the attacks, Leigh seemed frozen solid with fear.

Leigh had been held captive by a vampire, used as a donor, and somehow escaped.

Nathaniel offered a gracious smile. It turned Joan's stomach.

"You'll want to consider every option, of course, before you realize it's futile, and I wouldn't want to distract you. We ourselves could use a respite from our hard work protecting your town, so we'll rest tonight. You have until tomorrow night to recognize the benevolence of my request. Bring her to me and I will persuade Victor to . . . focus his attentions elsewhere."

He lowered his head and shed all pretense of congeniality. "If she hasn't surrendered herself to me here by moonrise tomorrow, Calvert will fall."

Without waiting for Joan's response, Nathaniel spun on his heel and returned to his limousine. Sound rushed into the vacuum of the dispelled air pressure. One of his associates opened the back door to let him climb inside, then joined the driver in the front.

Dayton twitched, finally drawing his gun.

"What the hell was that? I could see his lips moving, but I couldn't hear anything and I couldn't move."

Oddly, the other vampire rolled his shoulders as if he'd just been released as well, and looked pissed as he returned to the limousine. Had the conversation with Nathaniel been unheard by anyone but her?

Dayton turned his head to look at Joan, though his weapon was primed to shoot at the vampires if necessary. "What did he say to you? Who are they looking for?"

She couldn't find any words. Why hadn't Leigh told her the truth?

In less than a minute, the vampire convoy turned back the way they'd come. Half the thralls and one of the bloodlings followed on foot. As a final insult, unnatural fog closed around them as they faded into the night and disappeared.

The remaining members of the blockade made no move towards the tracks, but Dayton left two more men with the watch at the checkpoint before he climbed back into Luther where the dog barked in welcome.

Joan wasted no time leaving the meet. She drove the empty streets faster than was wise, gripping the steering wheel so hard it creaked. The other watch members drove to their respective residences, or to fortify some of the key protection points for the night. Now Luther was the only thing moving on the streets.

Dayton had stopped asking her what had happened while he'd been incapacitated. She pulled up in front of his house. He opened the door, then paused, ignoring Willy's whines for release.

"Look." The wind had picked up since they'd left the meet, and it blew strands of his hair into his mouth. He used his other hand to pull them loose. "I get that you've got way more experience than I do, but whatever this is, don't tackle it alone. Half the watch may be dead weight, but the rest are folks I've trained myself, and I didn't go easy on them. They'll back you one hundred percent because I will."

She didn't trust herself to speak yet. What he offered was a precious gift and she reined herself in enough to at least nod in thanks.

"Good talk," he said, and climbed out. He opened the back door and Willy jumped free.

"Dayton." Nathaniel had known everything. "Now we know for sure someone is talking."

His eyes bored into hers, but he said nothing more.

"We need to find the mole," she said.

Dayton nodded and closed the door. She waited until he was inside before she drove away.

Her brain boiled with everything she'd learned tonight. Nathaniel, a necromage vampire who'd turned out to be more calculating diplomatic envoy than bloodthirsty feral monster.

Nathaniel wanted Leigh. Leigh had been a donor, captured and tamed. How could Leigh keep something like that to herself?

Was it some twisted work of the vampires shrinking the boundary? Joan couldn't imagine anyone she knew having that kind of power—not a vampire, not the coven. Not even her father might have been powerful enough to do something that immense. Bindings strengthened over time, and borders became almost permanent. They might weaken, allowing stronger vampires to overcome their magically imposed sickness, but they didn't recede.

She hated herself for it, but a thought came to her that she wished she could burn from her mind, one that terrified her with its possibility.

What if Leigh had something to do with Trevon's death? She wanted to toss it out immediately, to believe Trevon had died of a heart attack as she'd been told. Leigh would never do something to hurt him, she wasn't capable of it, but if Leigh had been holding back information this serious, wasn't anything possible?

Joan thought her heart would stop beating if that were true. But the only way she was going to ease those thoughts and purge them from her mind would be to finally have a conversation with Leigh putting all the cards on the table.

The harsh wind stirred the leaves on the roads into a storm of debris that forced her to turn on the wiper blades. She turned down her street and slowed, hoping the diesel engine wouldn't wake anyone on the block. Every house was dark except for theirs.

With some chagrin, she realized that she'd stopped thinking of it as her father's place and started thinking of it as hers. Hers and Leigh's.

By the time she parked in front of the house and climbed from the rig, the wind was cold enough to bite her skin, hinting at the hard winter to come.

She stomped up the porch stairs as Leigh threw the door open.

"Are you all right?" Leigh asked, her face wide with worry.

Joan stalked through the door and slammed it. After the face-off against Nathaniel, Joan trembled with exhaustion and anger, the soreness and fatigue battling with the waning adrenaline and the ever-present headache. It was almost arousing in intensity, in its need for some sort of physical outlet. For a split second, Joan wondered if she could actually hurt Leigh.

"I want the truth, Leigh, right fucking now."

Leigh stepped back, away from Joan's ire. "What are you talking about?"

The tone was all wrong, too fearful to come off as confusion. She was hiding something.

"Why didn't you tell me Nathaniel is looking for you?"

CHAPTER 10

It was a chilling dichotomy to hear the name Leigh dreaded most from the only voice and lips she had ever craved.

The terror crept like ice water through her body. Leigh closed her eyes, focusing instead on how she might eke out what Joan knew. It couldn't be everything. Otherwise, Joan would have done a lot more than ask a question. She would have tossed Leigh out the door, or worse.

Then again, maybe that's what was about to happen.

If this was it, if this was what Leigh had feared and tonight was to be her last on this earth, she would be damned if she went out like some sort of sniveling weakling. Not anymore. She'd hidden her own strength long enough.

And what good had hiding done for her?

Leigh took a deep breath and opened her eyes. "Why would I tell you about the most traumatic, horrible experience of my entire life? Why would I talk about that with anyone, much less someone who—"

She bit off her next words. "You show up after eight years without a single word to anyone here. Why would I tell you anything?"

Joan's mouth fell open, though she recovered quickly. "Are you fucking kidding right now? A vampire is looking for you. *You.*"

They would kill Leigh if they found her. Or worse. "I didn't think I mattered. I was just a donor."

Joan's face fell. "Blessed Gaia, why didn't you *tell me*, Leigh?"

"Because I didn't want to talk about it!" Leigh paced between the living room couch and the dining room table, desperate to run. "I don't even want to think about it! It was hell, the worst thing that's ever happened to me." *Besides you leaving town*, but she couldn't say that. Even now, she wouldn't speak hurtful things to Joan—not if there was a likelihood she wouldn't live long enough to take them back.

Tears she couldn't fight fell from her eyes, but she wiped them away.

"He—they, his—his thralls . . ." She squeezed one hand closed, let the nails dig into her palm to remind her she wasn't weak. "They picked me off the streets. I was strung out, and the people I trusted to watch my back left me alone. I was tied up in their fucking dungeon for weeks, kicking the drugs I thought would save my life. You know how people say that they don't care if you're an addict? Oh, no. They chain you up until you dry out, feeding you paste and water until you stop puking it all back up."

Joan's face was frozen, perhaps in disbelief, or maybe it was horror. Leigh couldn't look at her long enough to decide.

"I thought I'd die so many times. I *prayed* that I would, so I didn't have to go through what came next, because I heard the other junkies who'd kicked already. Then came round after round of dry heaves, muscle and joint pain that felt like my body was on fire, the incessant itching, the sores that wouldn't heal."

Her own shame bled out as anger, and she fired every word at Joan as if it had been her fault.

"Lying in my own puke and . . ." She couldn't bring herself to say the rest. "Screaming for help that never came. And when it was over, then the fun really started."

She crossed her arms over her chest. "I didn't see the sun for weeks. They kept us in a dark room and all they did was take our blood. Nathaniel uses the drug addicts to feed the lower-ranking vampires, or the ones that have pissed him off. He wouldn't let them drink from us directly, because then he couldn't control them."

Leigh clenched her fists as she uncrossed her arms, holding herself back from shrieking in anger. She wanted to pound on Joan's chest, to make her understand, to not hate Leigh as much as Leigh hated herself.

That was probably a losing proposition. What did restoring Joan's opinion of her matter if Nathaniel was so close to finding her?

She couldn't contain the sobs. "You don't know what it took for me to get out of there. What kind of person I had to become."

She turned her back on Joan, though part of her wondered if that was such a good idea. Why not, though? Why not let Joan end it all for her right here and now? There were far worse deaths waiting for her in the darkness outside, things that would kill her faster than the loneliness and shame eating her alive.

"I did what it took to get better, because it meant that I could get out of the pit. I became someone I didn't want to be, *ever*, someone Ba noi would have despised. Someone I—I despise, just to survive."

She whirled on Joan, though she could barely see through her tears. "And now you want to know why I didn't want to fucking tell you?"

Leigh threw herself down in one of the dining room chairs, her head in her hands and her elbows resting on the table. She had to pull herself together or else she wouldn't live through the night.

"How did you get away?"

Joan sounded cold and distant, and Leigh didn't want to look. If Joan looked down her nose at Leigh, looked at her like some kind of vermin, like most people looked at fools like herself

120

who'd been donors, she thought she might die of heartbreak.

But she couldn't answer the question, either.

Leigh leaped to her feet and whirled on Joan, fists clenched at her sides. "I said I *don't want to talk about it.*"

Joan took a long, slow deep breath, her face not giving any clues to her thoughts. "You don't have a choice. You have to tell me everything, because . . . Nathaniel stopped the attacks on Calvert for the next day. If you don't surrender to him by tomorrow night, he says he'll come for you himself. I don't think he can cross the boundary, but the thralls will cut through this town like a blade."

Leigh sagged. She'd thought she'd lost all hope, but the loss she felt meant there was an inkling left.

She wasn't worth a whole town of people.

"Well, I'm sure you'll only be glad to see me go." She hadn't meant to say that, to be cruel.

Joan grunted. "You think maybe you've got that backwards?"

It was too much.

When Leigh spoke again, her voice was lower than she'd ever heard herself speak, each syllable enunciated. "I know you didn't see it back then, but now you must be blind. I have never wanted you to leave, but you didn't want to stay, Joan. You told me—*me*, and to my face, Joan—that there was nothing for you in Calvert."

Shock played across Joan's face. "That's not true. I would have asked you to come with me—"

"It is true!" Her face now inches from Joan's, Leigh spoke the words she'd always held back. "You knew damned well that I didn't want to go, but you were going to leave anyway. Asking me to come would have been a token offer at best, a crumb tossed in my direction, so you didn't feel bad when you left me behind. Well, I wanted none of it. All that bullshit with Pierce was just enough of a push to kick you out a door you were ready to run through."

Joan still looked incredulous. "I thought you didn't want me anymore."

Leigh laughed, and her own bitterness made her cringe. "I never stopped wanting you, but it wasn't enough."

The dam broke for good, an endless stream down her cheeks. "I loved you, and you left me here."

It was pathetic now, how she couldn't stop crying. It changed nothing, and she needed to get her shit together because she had to think. She'd always known her time was finite, that this had been inevitable, but she had to find the courage, make a plan. Maybe a poison that wouldn't take effect until after they'd gotten back to—

It took a few deep breaths before she was able to speak again. "I'll be ready by sundown tomorrow."

"You're not going anywhere."

The words didn't penetrate at first.

"What?" Leigh wiped more of the annoying tears from her face.

Joan relaxed enough to take off her jacket. Beads of sweat had formed on her forehead from the over-warm room, thanks to the blazing fire.

"Even if it wasn't you," she said as she hung her jacket on the rack by the door. "There's no way that I would let a human—any human—turn themselves over to those bloodsucking cockroaches. Never gonna happen. And something else is going on. This isn't just about you. Nathaniel is hiding something. Plus, there's a mole somewhere in this town. Could be in the watch, might be in the coven, I don't know yet, but some things aren't adding up, and until I find out what's going on, I'm not giving an inch."

Since when did Joan represent Calvert?

"You—you're not leaving?" Leigh wouldn't let herself hope. Hope was foolish . . . and dangerous.

"No," Joan said, her face unreadable. "Not yet."

CHAPTER 11

Maybe the difficult conversation had taken its toll, or maybe it was only the lateness of the hour, but Leigh had curled into the arm of the couch and fallen asleep. How she had survived and escaped was unfathomable. She'd never been a fighter, though Joan had never thought her weak, but to have been through all that madness and remained the gentle soul she was—Joan couldn't help admiring Leigh for her resilience.

Leigh was tougher than she'd ever thought.

Joan herself was still antsy, still processing all Leigh had shared as well as her earlier confrontation with the vampire. Nathaniel had claimed a cease-fire, but that didn't mean she believed him.

The kitchen was dark, but she didn't bother turning on the light. Though it was half past midnight, Joan called Dayton to apologize for being a dick earlier. He answered on the first ring.

Guess he couldn't relax either.

"Did you tell anyone outside the watch about the meeting?" Joan asked once the apology was out of the way.

Dayton scoffed. "No, but I'm not sure how long it'll stay quiet."

She kept her voice low, hoping not to wake Leigh. "If we don't say anything, the mole will still know something happened and they'll ask about it." She tumbled the puzzle pieces in her

123

mind, trying to get any kind of picture about what was happening. Nathaniel wanted Leigh, but that seemed separate from Victor's aims—and Victor was the one who'd blocked the roads.

Wait.

The blockade against Calvert wasn't about supplies or forcing a donor arrangement. They could just attack the town until Calvert gave in. Victor wanted to limit the flow of information.

"What about the person he said he was looking for?" Dayton asked.

She didn't want to lie, but she didn't want to tell him, either. "I think it's a distraction. We need to focus on keeping the boundary line protected, and then get someone through."

"Huh."

His disbelieving grunt and the headache that had expanded to the base of her skull fed her irritation.

"Look, Dayton, I'm not trying to tell you how to do your job, but if they're successful at blocking us in, secure in the knowledge that we can't notify the High Coven in Portland or the Black Rose City guild that they're coloring outside the lines, we're fucked."

"Understood," Dayton said after a long pause, though he sounded wary. Joan signed off.

Back in the living room, Leigh wasn't relaxed even in sleep, her tense shoulders hunched in. Joan tried to reconcile all she thought she'd understood about Leigh with everything she now knew. Leigh, the kindest person she'd ever known, a strung-out donor in a vampire dungeon.

The woman would get a crick in her neck trying to sleep hunched over like that. Joan decided to wake Leigh before turning in herself.

When Joan sat on the couch and touched Leigh's arm, though, Leigh bolted upright, eyes wide with fear.

Joan pulled her hand away, held up to show she meant no harm.

"Sorry," Leigh said with a barely covered-up yawn, and looked away in embarrassment. "I didn't mean to fall asleep on you."

"S'okay," Joan said, but didn't touch her again. "We should go to bed."

Leigh gazed at her in mute silence.

Joan bit her lip, wondering when she'd lost command of the English language. "I'll walk you to your room." Which was the most ridiculous thing she could have said, but it did dispel the idea they were going to the same bed.

Jesus, the headaches were making her stupid.

Leigh hadn't moved. "How do you think you can stop them, Joan? There are so many of them."

Right. Leigh had been on the inside. "How many?"

Leigh shrugged. "I don't know for sure. Five others were in the detox pit when I was there. Then seven or eight in the room besides me when they imprisoned us after I got clean, but there were other rooms, too. I don't know how many thralls." Her words were measured, hesitant. "I heard he had a dozen vampires in what he called his court."

His court. Pretentious murdering asshole. And how many of them were necromages?

"I'd like to relieve this motherfucker of his delusions of grandeur." Joan's fatigue made her voice sound like a growl.

"You're so different now."

Surprised and wary, Joan peered at Leigh. "Different bad?"

"No." Leigh laid a hand on Joan's knee, then pulled back before Joan could respond. "Not at all. You seem more . . . powerful."

"Hmmm." Joan shifted her gaze to the fire. "I suppose everybody changes over time. I guess I picked up a few things after I left."

"I'll say. You look like you can take on the watch all by yourself."

Joan shrugged. "Probably could."

"Even Dayton?"

"Definitely Dayton."

Leigh's lips perked—not quite a grin, but close.

Joan was taken aback. "What? It's the truth."

Leigh laughed. It changed her whole face, softened her posture. Joan might have smiled in surprise, if she hadn't been so damned offended.

"Did I drool on myself or something?" Joan asked, affronted.

Leigh tapered her laughter. "Where on earth did you find that machine you drive around in?"

"Luther?"

"Oh, my god, you gave it a name?"

Leigh covered her mouth against another laugh until she pulled herself together. She'd smiled more in the last half minute than the entire time Joan had been back. Was it from the freedom of the night's earlier revelations? Or borderline hysteria?

Joan gave Leigh's shoulder a gentle shove with her own. "Luther has saved my life more than once," she said, a bit of levity in her tone. "Show some respect."

Slowly, Leigh's humor leeched away as she turned thoughtful, and Joan wondered if the brief magic between them, the temporary ease of how they'd once been with each other, had passed.

"How different is it, Joan? Being a war witch, I mean."

Joan hadn't anticipated Leigh would want to hear about her life after leaving Calvert. Not the way they'd left things. "Baby, I could tell you stuff that would blow your mind."

Why had she called Leigh that? So many old habits . . . "Every summer solstice, hundreds of witches gather in a conclave on sacred ground out in the middle of nowhere in western Montana. When the host coven calls the corners, everybody is high on the resonance and naked and *attuned* and it's magical. I mean, of course, it's magical, because there's magic, but I—I was so proud of who I am."

She'd been tired earlier, but now her fatigue ebbed as she spoke of the wonders she'd seen, all so different from the life she'd lived here in Calvert.

"Oh, and any spell you cast in this one place in New Mexico is on overdrive, like the earth is contributing extra energy. I did a protection spell and was damned near invincible."

Leigh made a noncommittal sound—was it disapproval? Joan stared into the fire and kept talking.

"A section of the Las Vegas strip is neutral territory. I mean anyone—even vampires—can walk around and you can't touch them, but they can't touch you, either. I didn't believe it at first, so I went everywhere armed to the teeth, but it was true. It was the first time I saw a vampire up close, though I couldn't do anything about it."

Leigh crossed her arms over her chest as Joan spoke, but didn't say a word.

"I've visited every coven's territory from La Paz to Whitehorse. Met witches from all over the world. One bar in Santa Barbara is bigger than the town square, with wall-to-wall witches from all across the country. They've got a registry kinda like what we've got here at the fire station, and any witch who comes through has to sign in and pledge to do no harm. It was wild."

"That doesn't explain how you became such a badass," Leigh muttered.

"A lot of those places have training halls, or periodic intensives." The next question written on Leigh's face prompted Joan to continue. "Sometimes, in some of those places, like the conclave, there'd be these masters who'd teach fighting techniques. Twice, I trained with masters in the fighting arts. One Tae Kwon Do master up in Canada, believe it or not. Another time, I trained in Kung Fu. Down in Arizona."

"Did you ever think about staying in any of those places?"

127

Joan's excitement waned.

"I thought about it at one point, but I'd have been a hypocrite." Her hands were suddenly interesting, and she trailed her fingers over old scars. "One place I found in northern California, was so much like here with all the trees and open spaces and . . ."

Careful. After all they'd been through, was sharing this too much, too far?

"But if I joined their coven, how was that any different from Calvert? And it might have been a home, but it wasn't this one."

Never mind how homesick the place had made her, how much she'd thought of Leigh. "So, I got back on the road. There were too many places to see, too many different towns to visit."

"Did you stay long in the bigger cities?"

"Only Vegas. And Tijuana, because they had a surprisingly large coven. Thirty-nine witches and the power was unreal. But . . ." Joan sighed and shook her head. "Most of the West Coast cities are under vampire treaty, so I stuck to the smaller towns."

Joan leaned forward, her elbows resting on her knees. "A lot of towns have been completely wiped out. Smaller places where the younger vampires staked a claim, but then got muscled out by the larger guilds."

"How—how many guilds are there?" The distress was back in Leigh's voice.

"About nine or ten across the country. Different guilds have different leaders, but the rules for the most part are pretty much the same. One of them, damned near consistent everywhere I've been, is that no vampire stakes a claim of territory without the guild's knowledge. If Victor is building his own court, it needs to fly with the regional guild. The head of that guild is in Portland."

Elizaveta, First of the Black Rose City guild, who was rumored to be ruthless and intractable.

Leigh's expression turned from thoughtful to tense. Apprehensive.

Joan took Leigh's hand before she thought better of it.

"I'm sorry, babe."

Leigh looked at her in surprise. "For what?"

Light from the fire shimmered in the dark brown of Leigh's irises until they looked like they glowed from within. Her perfect complexion screamed for Joan to cover it in kisses.

"Everything," she whispered, a truth allowed only in the solemn quiet of night.

"Me, too," Leigh said, but with more sadness than relief.

Was everything truly irreparable?

"What do we do now?" Joan asked.

Leigh laughed without sound. "You tell me."

Joan's body answered for her, a familiar visceral, deep tightness that once had only been soothed by Leigh's touch. She opened her mouth to speak, but when she drew breath, Joan tasted Leigh on her tongue—redolent, like earth and desire, with a hint of roses.

It took longer than Joan wanted to rein in the need coursing through her, and to reconcile herself with the truth. Leigh wasn't hers and hadn't been in a long, long time. Even if Leigh's feelings could be returned, fate had already wedged between them.

Joan squeezed her hand and stood.

Leigh banked the coals in the fireplace while Joan checked the locks at each of the windows and sealed a somewhat malevolent ward at the front door.

In the shadows at the base of the stairs, Joan stopped.

"Listen, about earlier . . ." Joan looked at pictures and paintings on the wall, at the door, at the floor, at Leigh's hands—everywhere but into Leigh's eyes, afraid she'd see the hurt, but if she didn't the words would be empty, without weight. "I can't apologize for asking about . . . the things I needed to know, but . . . I'm so sorry for what happened to you. I'm sorry I had to ask about something so painful."

"I understand," Leigh said in a near whisper, "why you had to ask. And I know we need to talk about what comes next, but maybe tonight we could just get some rest."

She didn't look like she actually believed that. In fact, she looked like she was trying to hide her own terror, but there was also resolve.

Joan wanted to chase that terror away.

Leigh's kindness, generosity and gentle nature had always attracted her, but what had captivated Joan most all those years ago was the quiet passion. Out in the world, Leigh had rarely drawn attention to herself. That much probably hadn't changed—not based on anything Joan had seen since she'd come back to Calvert.

But when they had been alone, the two of them face to face like they were now, Leigh held nothing of herself back.

Was that still true?

Joan realized how long the silence had stretched, and how long she had been staring at Leigh's pale lips.

Leigh noticed.

Joan wanted to kiss her. Never mind all the other bullshit going on in her head and in a world growing crazier by the day. She was alone in the dark with Leigh Phan, and she wanted to kiss her and not stop.

Would Leigh push her away?

Leigh answered the question for her by stepping into the rapidly shrinking distance between them. Her cool hands touched Joan's cheeks, and the first brush of Leigh's lips against her own was—

Joan heard nothing but the hum. Everything else was silent.

She thought she remembered how Leigh's lips would feel, but she was wrong. The veiled desire in Leigh's kiss flicked a switch in the back of Joan's head, releasing a kind of madness. Drawn in, Joan pressed her hands to the sides of Leigh's waist, molded her fingers to the curve of her hips, and broke the kiss only to seal them together again.

She tasted Leigh's sigh, breathed in her scent—roses, though

Leigh had always preferred jasmine or sandalwood before.

Then again, what had happened before didn't matter anymore.

Leigh's fingers framed Joan's jaw and pulled her closer. Joan wrapped her arms around Leigh, lifted her up on her toes, pulled Leigh's body against her as she fell back against the hall wall.

Joan didn't want to deepen the kiss. Not yet. If she did, she wouldn't be able to hold herself back, and it was too soon. Leigh wouldn't believe Joan's feelings were real if they tumbled into bed.

And she did feel something. Leigh's confession earlier had blown through whatever walls Joan had erected between them. It freed a part of her she'd kept locked away for years.

The kiss changed.

Leigh's surprisingly strong grip on Joan's shoulders dug into her muscles. An ache that was going to be hard to deny soon swelled between Joan's thighs. She had always been the one to initiate, to urge their passion higher, but now, Leigh slid one hand tight against the back of Joan's neck and pulled her impossibly closer.

When Leigh nipped her lip, then soothed the bite by tracing Joan's lips with her tongue, Joan surprised herself with how quickly she surrendered.

CHAPTER 12

Desire swept through Leigh, dizzying in its intensity, and when she came to her senses, she was in the guest room, straddling Joan on the bed, kissing her full perfect lips.

Though it had been years, Leigh remembered everything. She remembered how Joan liked to be touched and stroked the pads of her thumbs over Joan's breasts. When Joan answered with a thrust of her hips, the strokes turned to precise pinches and they both moaned.

Joan mumbled something Leigh didn't catch, so enraptured was she by Joan's scent—her skin, her sweat, her arousal, all sin and salvation—and the taste of her kiss and the feel of her teeth . . .

The last time Leigh had touched someone had been vastly different.

The thought cooled her passion. This had to stop, now, before it went too far. Before she did something she couldn't undo.

Leigh pulled away but Joan followed her movement. Joan buried her nose in the hollow of Leigh's throat, licking the length of Leigh's neck and squeezing her thighs. Conflicting desires wrestled in Leigh's chest until Joan nipped at her jaw and Leigh was swept away.

Back when they were younger, Leigh had always been content to let Joan lead, to surrender herself to Joan's desire. Now, she couldn't wait that long. She wanted to consume, to claim Joan's joy as her due. Need pulsed low, a hunger that wouldn't be satisfied and wouldn't release her.

Leigh pushed Joan back, flat against the bed, unbuttoned Joan's shirt and loosened her belt. She lowered herself just enough to lick and bite at Joan's exposed umber skin, to suck one nipple with a moan as she inched one hand down Joan's body and into her pants.

Joan cried out when Leigh rose over her and stroked between her thighs. Leigh slowed her touch as Joan's clit swelled, then glided lower and inside, gave in to the urge to nuzzle Joan's neck. Joan pulled herself away, but only long enough to push off her pants.

Leigh thrust deeper, palming Joan's clit while she licked and bit again at Joan's breasts. She wanted it to last, but she couldn't stop, couldn't slow down. Joan moaned and Leigh lengthened her stroke, pushing harder on each pass until it was too much, too good. Joan came with a low guttural moan and Leigh bit her own lip.

When she tasted blood, a sound she didn't recognize burst from her throat, but Joan growled in response and flipped Leigh onto her back.

Joan tried to lift Leigh's shirt, but Leigh tugged it down with the last of her self-preservation. She pulled Joan's head over her still-clothed breast, held her in place until Joan took the hint. Joan bit through the fabric and Leigh cried out.

Joan's hands were at her waist, at her zipper and then Joan's sleek, strong fingers were right where Leigh needed and *stopping* wasn't an option.

Leigh spread her legs wide and pushed herself onto Joan's fingers, begging with her body for Joan to move faster, and Joan held nothing back.

Later, Leigh shivered but she wasn't cold. Joan pulled her closer and drew the quilt that covered the bed over them both.

Leigh needed to escape, but Joan was so close and so delicious, and this might never happen again. She had to leave before the tears started but Joan's hand once again splayed low on her belly, sliding lower, sinking inside Leigh before pulling back to stroke a slow measured beat over Leigh's still-swollen clit.

Joan spoke utter nonsense, half-muttered syllables, soft and hard words. Leigh was desperate for her to keep talking, to keep taking and giving, to keep pushing Leigh higher. She plummeted ever deeper into the sensation, blind though her eyes were open, deaf to everything but Joan and her heartbeat, her head blessedly quiet of voices full of shame and lost hope. The sweeping swell in and between her thighs intensified until it almost hurt.

When she came, neck arched and body clenched, Leigh couldn't make a sound. An ache in her chest swelled and would only be satisfied by her cleaving against Joan until she couldn't hold on, until she sank back to the bed, boneless and heavy.

With a pleased, proud hum, Joan stretched alongside her and pulled Leigh into her arms.

For a brief shining moment, Leigh tucked her head into Joan's shoulder and felt safe and precious. Like she belonged.

She cried when she remembered none of it was true.

Leigh woke as she usually did, before dawn. She froze at the uncommon sensation of another body near hers, but Joan still slept. The even rise and fall of her breathing didn't change when Leigh slipped from the bed.

Panic drove her to complete her morning tasks faster than usual, and Joan hadn't risen by the time she was done. Though she didn't dare make more serum with Joan in the house—even asleep—she could at least make the rosewater.

The Matthews household had two sets of pots and pans, one for food, and the other for the craft. It was an old family superstition to keep the elements of their work from ending up in the food, and from allowing any food to pollute their craft.

Leigh worked as quickly as the process would allow while making Joan breakfast. Once again, the scent of the rosewater mingled with the stench of the bacon and did nothing to calm her unsettled stomach. By the time she got to the eggs, her nervous trembles made everything take longer.

Staying in this house with Joan—no matter how much Leigh wanted to be close to her—wasn't such a good idea. With Nathaniel searching for her, nowhere was safe, but this house was turning out to be more dangerous than she'd anticipated. Now Victor's thralls had increased their attacks on the town—she'd never seen Victor, but she'd seen the horrible acts performed in his name. The mere idea of him made her want to scream herself mad.

It wasn't sound or scent that alerted Leigh to Joan's impending arrival, but a shift in the air currents. A wave of desire passed through her as she thought of Joan's touch, of touching Joan.

Nervous but looking forward to seeing Joan, Leigh turned off the burner beneath the pan of scrambled eggs, but then she noticed her mistake.

She hadn't put away the craftwork tools yet. The other pan and a spatula rested in the dish rack next to the sink.

Joan stepped barefoot into the kitchen, dressed in black jeans and a black long-sleeved, thigh-length tunic.

"Hey," Joan said, eyes warm and inviting.

Leigh resisted, but it was close.

"Just in time," she said, praying Joan didn't notice the drainer. "The eggs are done." She shifted the pan's contents to a nearby plate, trying to hide her dread, and added some of the bacon. She wiped her hands on a towel before turning toward Joan with as warm a smile as she could muster.

Joan held out a hand. "Hold on a sec."

The dread turned into alarm. "Okay. I—if you're not hungry, I can—"

Joan shook her head. "No, it's not about that." She frowned, but she didn't look angry.

Maybe Leigh was reading too much into things.

"I mean, that's great," Joan said. "It's really nice of you. I just think . . . " She paused, as if searching for words.

It was possible Joan regretted last night for her own reasons. Was it because she knew she couldn't stay in Calvert? Was it because Leigh wasn't the same person now?

How surprising it was to know how much that hurt.

Leigh shifted her weight. "Is this about yesterday? I mean, last night? Did you not—"

She couldn't say it. Even though they had no possible future together, she wanted to hold on to what had happened between them for as long as she could.

Joan shook her head to negate Leigh's incomplete question. "No, baby, that was . . . that was wonderful. For me, but I want to make sure that you—"

And then Joan saw the pan in the dish drainer.

Time slowed for Leigh as Joan's expression changed from curiosity to confusion to cold understanding. When her face went blank, Leigh knew, as sure as she knew the food she'd made would go uneaten, they weren't going to talk about last night.

She was both horrified and relieved that Joan would know the truth soon. The air between them filled with an almost electric charge as Leigh waited for the inevitable.

Joan seemed somehow taller when she straightened upright, hands falling to her sides, open yet dangerous.

"What's the rosewater for, Leigh?"

CHAPTER 13

Leigh's eyes widened and then her face went blank, but Joan wasn't having it. Leigh's insistence on keeping some truths to herself wasn't good enough now.

Rosewater had specific uses, none of them a good sign.

"You've never believed in love spells, and you surely don't need to do anything to spell me to you." Joan paced in a half circle around the kitchen, ticking off the count on her fingers. "A peace spell won't affect all this bullshit with the vampires—you know that's just superstition."

She stopped in front of Leigh. "That leaves a glamour."

The blankness of Leigh's expression gave way to fear. So that's what it was. But why would Leigh need to change anything about how she looked? Had her time in the vampire's dungeons disfigured her in some way?

Not that it would make Joan care about Leigh any less.

Joan sighed, and her shoulders sank with the effort. Leigh had kept her clothes on the night before—did she not trust Joan?

"Why are you hiding yourself from me?"

Leigh swallowed with a gulp. "I'm—I'm not. I just—"

Enough. "That fucking vampire wants you tonight and I need to stop him, Leigh. What is so precious that you have to keep lying to me?"

Anger flashed in Leigh's eyes. "I'm not lying to you."

"You're not telling me everything." The headache spiked again, the hum ringing in Joan's ears and pissing her off more. "This is just like that summer. You were always keeping secrets."

"Oh, the summer you talked about nothing but how much you couldn't wait to get out of here?" Leigh shook her head, disdain contorting her face. "What does it matter? You're going to be gone again soon anyway, right? What do you even care when you're going to leave me again?"

Joan was taken aback, since now her truths were in the spotlight. She bit her lip but pressed on. Something important was happening, and she wouldn't back down now, even if she was stunned by the power of Leigh's response. Time was moving too fast, like she had a countdown ticking while she tried to keep two trains from colliding.

"You have to tell me. The truth. All of it."

Anger, fear, and finally loss moved over Leigh's face and through her body. "It'll wear off around noon." She looked at the floor and wouldn't meet Joan's eyes.

Joan wanted to say something then, something to bridge the chasm that had once again formed between them, but she didn't get the chance.

"Maybe you should just leave me alone until then," Leigh said.

She walked away, and it was a long time before Joan moved. To have gone from the night they'd shared to this . . . it stung.

Her cold forgotten breakfast and lost appetite were the least of her concerns.

In the wake of Leigh's exit, the only other thing Joan could do meant tackling the one task she'd been putting off.

If the boundary was receding, someone somewhere knew it was possible. Which meant someone somewhere had written something down about it. If anything involved witchcraft and lived in a book, her father would have a copy in his study. The one room in the house she'd been trying to forget existed.

Set on the first floor at the end of the long hall, Trevon's study was dark and cool. The air was stale, like nothing had moved in there in days, suggesting no one had been in this room since his death.

If her own room had been like walking into her past, this room was a testament to a future denied. The one her father had insisted was her birthright.

The small room held only a large walnut desk, an ancient grandfather clock, and two chairs—one a leather office chair with armrests, worn by age and use, and the other a full recliner set near a narrow fireplace. Floor-to-ceiling oak bookshelves dominated the walls, every available space filled with books and journals and files and stacks of loose paper.

Joan took a deep breath to soothe her nerves and instantly regretted it. The room smelled like her father's pomade, and the memories that came with that scent almost drove her right back into the hall.

Here was where she and her father would retreat when he needed to check a spell's reference. Where he'd taught her the Latin for her binding spells, and drilled her on the uses of every herb and plant on the family plot.

When she committed some infraction, here was where her father had summoned her.

If he wasn't in the fields, he'd been here. She had idolized her father when she was a child, back before her mother got sick. Joan hadn't been as close to her brother Marcus, though his death had spawned her need to become a war witch. Each individual loss squeezed at something inside her, the pain doubling in on itself.

Across from the desk three large portraits, watercolor on hard-to-obtain gesso board, were framed above the fireplace.

Her mother's was top center, ageless eyes in a forever youthful face. Below her, Marcus and Joan, both from the year Joan started high school. They'd all been painted from various photos, because Joan had helped provide them to Leigh. Leigh, whose work had been masterful for one as young as she'd been at the time.

Ashes long cold lay in the fireplace. The farther she got from the desk, the more dust covered everything. The worn carpet could use a vacuuming and the whole room needed airing out.

Or she could close the door once she found what she needed, and leave all this history behind her.

Could she, though? Turn her back on so much of what made her who she was?

The scratch of a branch drew her attention to one of the windows. The tree outside was full of crows, not squawking now but flitting from branch to branch. They were probably foreboding something she didn't want to know about, one more hassle she'd have to deal with. They didn't feel malevolent, but that didn't mean they weren't.

Joan forced herself to task. When she sat in her father's desk chair, the damned hum rumbled low in her bones and in her ears.

Trevon's desk was covered with the work that had filled his final days—a manual about spells to aid natural pesticides, herb stock lists with a plan for next year's planting, a book on vampire lore opened to a chapter about bloodlings, maps of farms in the area and their rotation schedules, all with inserted notes in Trevon's looping scrawl.

The bookshelf directly behind the desk was filled with rows of large leather-bound journals, each from a binding witch who had lived in this house on this land. Where would she begin to look for what she needed?

The full moon ritual. Perhaps by starting with the one spell designed to protect the town she would figure out what Victor was doing to the boundary and stop him.

The large forest green leather-bound volume her father had used time and again held all the details of the ritual. Though she searched back and forth throughout the journal several times, she found no indication of what to do for a receding boundary, or any reference to the possibility itself.

She hadn't expected an easy solution, but such an astounding dead end was a surprise.

Her phone vibrated in her pocket. When she answered, Dayton didn't bother with pleasantries.

"Both the coven and the watch received anonymous messages an hour ago."

Nothing good came from messages no one would claim. Shit—she'd hoped for more time before she'd have to talk to the coven.

"Victor is looking for someone who sounds a lot like Leigh Phan, and don't tell me you didn't know about it." He sounded pissed. It was less of an accusation than it was cold confirmation, but she wasn't going to cave to him or anyone else.

"I'm not giving her up."

"I get it. Really, I do, but you may not have a choice."

"I've still got a few hours—"

"They said we have until sundown, but the coven has already voted."

Fuck. No time at all, then. Of course Gretchen would give Leigh over to the vampires.

But until Leigh told her the whole story, Joan was stuck. "Two hours. That's all I'm asking." It was better than none.

"Joan," he said, and she paused in the action of hanging up. "Don't leave me out of the loop again. I can't help with what I don't know."

He couldn't see her nod, but she disconnected the call without another word.

Maybe Leigh's pending revelation would give Joan something to work with, like giving back whatever Leigh had taken from Nathaniel.

At noon, Joan found Leigh in the garden, standing at the end of one of the raised beds, staring at the herbs flourishing in the weak sunlight. Leigh stroked a blossom on the passionflower planted on a trellis at the end of the bed, though it was late in the year for any to still be alive.

Something about the way Leigh stood, the way she didn't raise her eyes in greeting made it clear Joan should keep her distance, so she stopped several steps away. Oddly, Joan felt exposed back here, as if a threat awaited her in this garden she knew like the back of her hand.

"Does what you're hiding from me have to do with whatever you took from—from them?"

"I've taken nothing." Leigh wore no jacket despite the cold and she warmed her arms with her hands, though it didn't look like it made her feel any better. Joan flashed back to the moment she'd molded her hands to Leigh's hips, the perfect fit of them together.

Would they ever be that close again?

"Nathaniel says otherwise." Joan tried not to make it sound like an accusation. Just a statement of fact. "He says you have something that belongs to him."

"He means me."

Joan scoffed. Then he could wait forever. "Like hell. I don't care what that monster thinks—"

"I'm not worth all this, Joan." Leigh's breath hitched.

Joan didn't know how to ask, but Leigh didn't wait.

"My last day in captivity . . . it was after midnight, but still hours before dawn. One of the human thralls came to pull me from the donor rotation in the—the basement."

Leigh stared across the unseasonably robust plants, her voice a distant monotone. "I was taken upstairs to a bathroom on the main floor. It was the first time I'd been clean in weeks. I wasn't sure what it meant at the time, but I tried to appreciate it for what it was—a brief respite from feeling like a fucking animal."

Joan itched to move closer but stood still, afraid she'd pull Leigh's attention from what she had to say.

"They fed me real food—not gruel, but an actual burger and fries. I tried not to wolf it down, but . . ."

She took a long, slow, deep breath, and exhaled just as slowly as she turned her face towards the sunlight. "I found out I'd been given to a visiting vampire."

The more she spoke, the more matter of fact she sounded.

"For a vampire, she was rather compassionate. She said she was older than Victor but had no house of her own. I guess she was moving here to avoid some guild entanglements back where she'd come from. Honestly, I didn't care. I was too afraid I was about to die.

"She told me she wouldn't kill me. She had not so nice things to say about Victor, but I got the impression she didn't have a choice about being there either. What she did want from me was more than I wanted to provide, but she made me an offer. She had a fetish for—for sex with humans, she said, and in exchange for my willing compliance, she'd help me escape if only to irritate Victor. She thought him pretentious, and she took pity on me being in his clutches.

"It was a simple choice. Had it been one of the other vampires—Nathaniel, for instance—I might have put up more of a fight, but I—I didn't want to die—at least, not then—and freedom was too good a dream to pass up, even if it meant . . ."

Joan's guts seized. This wasn't about scars at all, or disfigurement or whatever else she'd imagined.

Leigh opened tear-filled eyes.

143

"I didn't know what it would do . . . to me. I didn't know the price of . . ." Her body shook as if she were containing sobs. "I didn't know what I would become."

The muscles in Joan's shoulders tightened, as if her body recognized a truth she didn't yet understand. Leigh was suggesting she'd had . . . relations with a vampire, but . . .

"When I was free," Leigh said. "I didn't know where else to go or what to do. The last thing I wanted to do was go back to the same old places where I'd gotten high. I went to Trevon to see if he could—could help me."

Her voice cracked. "I wanted him to help me die, but he wouldn't do it. Instead, he took me in."

Joan wanted to interrupt, to ask why, but stayed silent. She dreaded whatever came next, but she was frozen.

"Trevon treated me like a human being. For all I did to drive you away, he saved my life and helped me with the glamour to keep me safe."

Leigh scrubbed the tears from one side of her face, but they were quickly replaced. "He knew the truth—that I don't want to be—that I'll die before I hurt anyone."

And then the effects of the glamour abruptly faded. For a moment, Leigh appeared to be a shimmering blur, her shoulders rising and falling as Leigh gathered herself and faced Joan.

It wasn't any one feature that changed before Joan's eyes. Leigh was still Leigh, but the youthful fullness faded, and she aged years in seconds. Her cheekbones became more pronounced, her curves hardened ever so slightly, her skin lost some of its luster. She was still beautiful, still stirring—and yet she was a new woman altogether.

Leigh was a leaner, harder version of herself. Scars marked her arms from the inside of her elbow to her wrists—from needles, yes, but also the faint marks of teeth and two wicked parallel scars from a blade.

The irises of her eyes glinted gold, and on her neck, over her carotid artery, were two scarred-over puncture wounds.

Joan gasped and stepped back. She knew logically Leigh would not hurt her, but she itched for the weapons she'd left in the house.

The truth changed what she'd experienced when they'd made love. The strength in Leigh's grip that had held her in place, Leigh refusing to remove any of her clothes. All the facts rearranged themselves, leading Joan to only one conclusion.

Leigh was a bloodling.

"I want to live what little life I have left in peace, because I know someday soon, someone will figure it out and—"

She looked at Joan with a resigned finality. "I am not a monster, and no matter what happens now, I won't let them try to make me one."

Shock kept Joan from moving. She had to get away, but she couldn't leave Leigh—despite her horror at all Leigh had endured, had become.

Her phone rang. Joan couldn't look away from Leigh's newly exposed appearance, but she reached for her phone as Leigh's expression changed to one of sad resolution.

Dayton again—and before the two hours she'd asked for. Joan couldn't handle any more bad news, but that's all she seemed to be getting.

"Dayton." No more words came. What was she going to do? How could she protect Leigh now?

At the sound of Dayton's name, Leigh gasped and bolted towards the house.

Dayton sounded rushed. "Joan, I'm across the road. You've got to come quick. Gretchen Wilson is dead."

CHAPTER 14

Leigh smoothed the quilt over the guest bed with trembling hands. She wouldn't sleep here again.

Once the truth had been revealed, the look on Joan's face had broken something irreparable inside Leigh. Whether it had been disgust or pity wasn't clear, but it didn't matter.

Joan had been horrified. After everything that had happened the night before, Joan thought Leigh was one of the monsters.

The creaking of floorboards warned her that Joan was back in the house, but the sound didn't approach the guest room. When Joan opened and shut the back door behind her, the reverberations vibrated through the house. She'd left without saying goodbye.

Leigh wiped the last of her tears away. She needed to be gone before Joan returned.

She'd never understood how she'd captured Joan's attention. The Matthews family was legendary, and a local celebrity like Joan could have had any lover in town, but she'd picked the quiet granddaughter of the chatty neighbor. For all Joan's faults, including her tendency to lash out when hurt, she also had a way of looking at the world that inspired Leigh to wonder along with her.

Joan had always excelled at everything she set her mind to, and that hadn't changed. Now, she thought she could hold off a vampire lord, his court and his thralls just by willing herself against them, all to protect the people of this town.

It was crazy-making. Victor didn't care about Leigh. She'd never seen him. The one who cared was Nathaniel, and that was only to make an example out of her because she'd escaped.

Escape should have been impossible.

Leigh was only supposed to be a donor to the vampire Sylvia, but donors died all the time when vampires decided to take their fill. The aid Sylvia had offered in exchange for one night in her bed had turned out to be significantly less than advertised. Leigh might have gained a bloodling's strength and speed, but Sylvia had done nothing else to assist her.

The word "regret" wasn't big enough to encapsulate Leigh's shame.

Yet it was bloodling senses that helped her escape, so Sylvia had fulfilled her end of the bargain. Soon after their tryst, Leigh's hearing had allowed her to sense the proximity and location of the guards. Her improved eyesight and sense of smell had guided her through the vineyard. She hadn't grown faster or stronger until days later, but the other improvements had allowed her to free herself.

She wondered what had happened to Sylvia once Leigh's absence was discovered, then decided it didn't matter.

Leigh passed a hand over her face. She'd wasted more time staring into nothing but the past, with no change whatsoever to the outcome. She donned her jacket, zipped her backpack closed and strung one strap over her shoulder.

She slipped out the back of the house, cutting through the garden to the back road behind the property. The Matthews plot of land stretched into the woods but had never been developed past the road.

Leigh forced herself to put one foot in front of the other, to not collapse under the weight of all that had happened. That last eyeful of Joan might have to last her forever, and leaving that house hurt as much as when she'd left her grandmother's home that last time.

Would her life ever be anything but grief?

The wind dried her new tears, and she shoved her hands in her jacket's pockets more from habit than from the cold. She was never cold anymore, not with her new ill-gotten senses. Nothing affected the emptiness inside, but if she walked around in the autumn chill without a coat, people would talk. She drew the hood over her head to hide herself.

The walk to town was a short one, and though she walked on the side of the road, no one stopped to offer her a ride. The times of helping strangers were gone, too, even in the daylight. The dwindling size of the watch meant their street sweeps happened less frequently. When she'd lived on the streets, she had avoided the places most likely to get her ejected from the town. Back then, when Pierce still lived with Trevon, Leigh had done everything she could to escape everyone's attention.

All things considered, she wouldn't accept a ride now even if one were offered.

Less than an hour later, she found herself outside the only church in town offering sanctuary.

The exterior of the church was cracked and faded, but everything in the main area of worship inside was well maintained. All the pews had been polished to a reflective shine, and the stained-glass windows showed not a speck of dust or dirt.

With a glance at the altar, overseen by a peaceful and resolved-looking porcelain savior hanging from a stained walnut cross, Leigh wondered if this was a good idea. She wasn't superstitious enough to believe she could be struck by lightning, but that didn't make her feel any better. All the herb bundles in her bag made her a pretentious heathen in the hall of the Christian god, but Wiccans didn't have churches with basement shelters for homeless people.

She pulled the hood further over her head, hoping to hide the shine of her unnatural eyes.

Leigh saw no one, but faint noise from one of the side halls that led to the basement stairs announced someone's impending arrival. A shadow darkened the doorframe. A moment later, the pastor stepped through and froze when he saw her, but then offered a small smile.

"Good afternoon."

She swallowed her pride to answer his unspoken question with one of her own. "Got a spare bed for a few nights?"

He led her to the basement, where three rows of four cots each sat on one side of the rectangular room. The half-patched ceiling was low, no more than seven feet, and Leigh felt like it was closing in.

She chose a cot tucked against a wall and sat propped on her backpack. If she slept at all, she'd stay in her clothes, keep her shoes on, and use her pack as a pillow—or else something she needed might be gone when she woke up.

Two other people had staked out individual cots in the basement, but the rest were empty. At the other end of the room, a wan older woman worked the buffet line made by two folding tables. She served stew into chipped plastic bowls and handed them out to some of the other residents of the shelter.

Leigh lied and said she wasn't hungry, when the truth was, she just didn't want to eat it. The meat's odor turned her stomach.

So, it had come to this. It wasn't rock bottom—no, that had been when she'd found herself squatting alone in a dilapidated, rat-infested junkie hole less than a year before. This was definitely a step up from that.

Still, that wasn't saying much. She stared for a moment at the bare walls, wondering if this was what her life was going to be now, and if it was worth it.

Two of the shelter's occupants started yelling at each other across the room. Leigh could smell them from where she sat—

one reeked of alcohol and the other of cigarette smoke and stale body odor. The stench of heavy bleach didn't overpower the stink.

One accused another of stealing his shoes, and within seconds, the argument came to blows. By the time the pastor arrived to break up the fight, one of the men had a broken nose. Blood spurted all over his clothes and splattered on the floor.

Leigh fought the urge to gag.

A woman nearby screamed about blood contamination and started ranting about vampires sensing any open wounds and that they were all doomed. The pastor tried to calm her down while dealing with the bleeding man.

In the corner near the emergency exit door, two more men talked to themselves and glanced at Leigh more than once.

Victor and Nathaniel would have spies in town, and where better to hide than here? She was at the mercy of strangers, and anyone might sell her out.

Leigh couldn't stay here either.

She lowered her head and took a deep breath. Hiding had gotten her nowhere. Salvation was a myth, and so was finding a haven. Loathing what she had become had only brought her here, and if she didn't make the choice for Joan, Joan would put herself once again in harm's way.

What happened to Leigh didn't matter now. They could not have Joan.

That left only one course of action—surrender. Leigh couldn't imagine giving Mrs. Wilson the power to decide her fate, but Joan seemed to trust Dayton. Maybe the watch was a better choice.

Assuming they didn't turn her back over to Joan.

Too many puzzle pieces, and not enough time to decide. She'd get to the watch and at least they could use her to bargain for the town's safety.

Leigh waited until the whispering men left before she stood up from her bunk. The emergency exit was near the buffet table and her leaving would attract attention, so she made her way upstairs while the pastor was otherwise engaged.

The entrance where she'd come in was too exposed. Leigh followed the hall running parallel to the nave. There had to be another exit on this side of the building.

When she found it, relief coursed through her. She'd have to walk to the edge of town to turn herself in—and that was if no one stopped her—but at least she'd avoided an altercation here. She opened the door and stepped into the late afternoon light.

A creak and a scuff were her only warning.

"Looks like you're all alone now." A tall man, thin, with a long, bushy beard and thick hair tucked under a trucker's cap, stood outside the rectory door. He stared at her in cold calculation. "No meddling war witch to cover for you."

Leigh's stomach plummeted when she recognized him. She whirled around, desperate to escape, but the two men she'd seen earlier closed in.

CHAPTER 15

Though a few things were different in Gretchen Wilson's living room—a new lamp stood behind one table and the walls were a different color—everything else was the same. The same sage green carpet. Fresh lavender in a small ceramic vase in the center of the coffee table. Four crystal orbs of blue, white, orange, and brown, each a token for an element, in wooden mounts on the mantel above the fireplace.

Gretchen Wilson's home had been another schoolhouse to Joan. She'd practiced incantations in this room, tested her affinity for the elements at the dining room table. This room was as familiar to her as the living room in the Matthews house, but today it seemed smaller and more closed in.

Dayton ended a conversation with the sheriff when Joan arrived.

"She'd taken in a couple of the high school kids whose parents were killed last year. They'd spent last night with friends in town but came home early from school just a little while ago." He nodded in the direction of the dining room table. "They found Gretchen."

A Gretchen-sized shape lay on the floor covered by a white sheet. Joan didn't want to believe what she saw. Gretchen had always seemed like her bones were made of iron, the same as her will. How could she be dead?

"Vampires?" The boundary hadn't receded this far, but Joan couldn't help but wonder if—like the Clarks—someone had killed Gretchen elsewhere and left her body here.

"No," the sheriff said. She was a pale, hatchet-faced woman with piercing world-weary eyes that flicked between Dayton and Joan, and wore a uniform shirt tucked into well-worn jeans. The gun at her side was probably the only weapon she carried. "No, whatever did this, it wasn't a vampire."

"There's not a mark on her, Joan," Dayton said.

The sheriff frowned, which meant she hadn't wanted to reveal that much. Maybe she thought Joan was involved.

If Joan was a suspect, she didn't have time to do anything about that right now. "Maybe it was poison then, which means that someone had to get close enough to her to do it, so she knew who they were."

She thought of the strange dream she'd had, the tall man with his back to the door. She shook her head to dislodge the memory, though it aggravated her endless headache. Joan had never before had any penchant for precognition.

"Have you already talked to the rest of the coven?" she asked.

Dayton spoke while staring at Gretchen's corpse. "They're on their way." It was odd to see him without Willy, but this was no place for the dog.

One by one, the remaining coven members arrived, accompanied by armed members of the watch. Pablo seemed irritated, Ashley sad. Ella and the big man, whose name turned out to be Roy, had the glaze of shock in their eyes.

The sheriff directed her lowered voice at Dayton. "Who had the most to gain from Gretchen's death?"

"I'd say whoever replaces her as head of the coven," Dayton said.

"Wait a minute," Pablo called from across the room, incredulous. "That would be me, but I didn't kill her. I'll admit we didn't get along, and there were times I didn't like her, but the coven needs every witch it has. Forgive me for stating the obvious but killing off the most experienced among us does nothing but put Calvert in more danger."

Halsey arrived, but without a coven member in tow. "I can't find Reed Hill."

Dayton frowned, then contacted the rest of the watch but no one had seen him or Gretchen since the day before. Their earlier vote to give Leigh to the vampires must have been cast by phone.

Joan said what she figured they were all thinking. "You think he did this?"

"More likely he's been taken, like the others." Pablo leaned over as he sat down in a chair and rested his head in his hands. "We've lost another one."

"You don't know that," Ashley said.

Pablo's eyes flashed. "I do, and you do, too." He cursed, and in the silence, near Gretchen's covered body, it seemed that much more obscene.

The sheriff sighed. "Well, frankly, I don't have any other suspects yet."

Ashley approached Joan. "Will you please reconsider joining the coven? Without Gretchen, we're weaker than ever, and you're so powerful, Joan."

Joan couldn't find the words to respond as she watched the sheriff's deputies mark off the area. Death wouldn't stop taking people from Calvert, and Joan felt powerless to stop the tide of loss. She stared at the covered body. Her earlier suspicion about Gretchen made her feel guilty now.

Dayton sidled up to her where she lurked near the front door.

"Where is she?"

In her mind's eye, Joan pictured Leigh and her inhuman eyes. "I need more time." Bloodling or not, Joan wasn't giving Leigh up to the vampires.

"Well, if you've got a plan, hurry it up." He stalked over to the rest of the watch, and Joan couldn't rein him in without drawing attention, even though his presumption pissed her off.

Outside, the crows flocked overhead, constant harbingers of the answers that escaped her.

The coven convened an emergency meeting in their usual room at the library. Unsure of her next action, Joan joined them. Members of the watch had shown up as well, but the coven ejected them, and Dayton and the rest were forced outside.

No one in the coven had the nerve to ask Joan to leave, and she couldn't go back to the house yet. She wasn't ready to face Leigh again.

Joan needed more time—for everything—but she wasn't going to get it.

Around the table, there were more empty seats than there were ones that were occupied. Pablo sat in Gretchen's chair, though the other coven members didn't look happy about it.

Joan leaned against a wall with her arms crossed over her chest.

Ashley was the most vocal in urging Joan to take Gretchen's place until Pablo snapped.

"This is pointless." He slapped his hands on the table. "We are down to four. Four, and the full moon rises in five hours. There's nothing else to discuss unless we want to disband."

The room fell silent. Disbanding was extreme, but a weak coven was worse than none. If word got out, even if they managed to eliminate Victor as a threat, Calvert would be on the hit list of every vampire lord in the region.

He leaned forward in his chair. "Let's settle this once and for all. I will claim the mantle of lead witch in Calvert. All in favor?" He lifted his hand high to lead the vote as he stared at Joan.

Ella's and Roy's hands immediately joined his. Ashley looked at Joan with sorrow but raised her hand as well.

"It's done." Pablo lowered his hand in satisfaction, though

he had the decency not to gloat. "Let's discuss tonight's ritual."

Joan sat quietly while they talked over the details of the ceremony. She wanted to be relieved the coven had made a decision since it meant no one could hound her about assuming her father's job. Though this had been her plan, it didn't sit well.

Mostly, Joan couldn't stop thinking about Leigh. Horrified on Leigh's behalf, she'd been unable to find words when Leigh revealed the truth behind the glamour. Yet knowing Leigh was now a bloodling didn't seem the threat Joan might have thought it would be.

Leigh, whose gentle nature hadn't changed despite what she'd been through. Who stood in the sun and tended to the garden, coaxing passionflowers into bloom.

Leigh, who had gazed at Joan with what looked like love.

"And you," Pablo said to Joan as he stood. "You will surrender Leigh Phan to the watch."

Duty demanded she turn Leigh in. Joan should tell the coven the truth about why Nathaniel wanted Leigh, but the memories of the night they'd shared, the strong but somehow gentle touch as Leigh had loved her, the look in Leigh's eyes—as if she'd known they would only have the one time together . . .

Against all expectations, Joan had once again fallen in love with Leigh, but now this impossible situation would keep them apart.

Joan pushed the pain of the headache aside, submerged herself in the irritation of the merciless hum and drew strength from it instead. She kept her hands free at her sides and stared Pablo down.

He wasn't as powerful as she was, and she could tell he knew it.

Fighting the coven wasn't part of her plan, not that she had much of one. "So this will be the way you lead Calvert? Buying Victor's favor by tossing an innocent woman at his feet?"

She spoke as calmly as she could manage, though she

seethed. "It won't end well for you, I promise."

"You can't hide her forever," he said.

"How about you do your job and I do mine?" After the ritual was performed, Victor might back down like the coward she thought he was. She might hunt him down and kill him anyway.

Pablo dropped his eyes then turned to the rest of the coven. "We begin at sundown."

When he glanced one last time at Joan, his eyes were unreadable.

Back at the house, the guest room was spotless. Leigh was nowhere in the house or the garden.

Joan considered casting a locator spell, but then remembered she'd need a treasured token of Leigh's to make it work.

She had nothing to use to cast the spell, no symbol of Leigh's essence to track her down. Shame and regret washed through Joan before she shoved them aside.

Think. Focus on what she could *use*.

Leigh had been too terrified of Nathaniel to consider sacrificing herself for the town's safety. The roads were still blocked, and Leigh had no way to travel overland except by foot.

Perhaps she'd found somewhere else to stay. But where would she be safe if half the town knew the vampires were looking for her?

Joan walked through the house, trying to form a plan to find Leigh while deciding what she'd take with her when she left Calvert.

Grief seized her chest. Maybe she could take a few of the books, and leave the rest to deal with some other time.

Would she ever come back here?

Leigh's face flashed across her mind again.

None of it felt right. She had to find Leigh. She couldn't

leave Leigh to the monsters.

For the next two hours, Joan searched. She drove to the checkpoints, but none of the watch had seen anything out of the ordinary besides the thralls and bloodlings blocking the roads. The pastor at the church said someone matching her description had shown up earlier that afternoon but had since disappeared.

Where could Leigh have gone? As terrified as Leigh had been, would she really turn herself in? Joan couldn't search every corner of the town by herself, and the more time that passed, the more the headache drove her to near queasiness.

Joan opted to attend the ritual. She'd check in with the watch after and see what she could do about punching a hole in the blockade. One way or another, she'd find Leigh. Somehow.

A half hour before sundown, Joan ate a hasty meal at the house and checked all her weapons. She decided to leave her robes at home. Tonight, she would be just another spectator.

The walk to the hall did nothing to settle her unease, her frustration, or her pain. The air tasted bitter, and the crows seemed as agitated as she was, some of them colliding in small squabbles in midair.

Once again, the hall was full. Though most would normally stay inside after dark, this was a special occasion, and the fate of the town depended on it. Every seat was taken, and people squeezed together to pack more in. Everyone was here to make sure the boundary was reinforced and the new lead witch could protect them.

Leigh wasn't there either, but Joan had only hoped to see her—she hadn't expected Leigh to attend the ritual. The sick feeling in Joan's guts grew.

In the cold air, hope warred with desperation. A drum sounded, its deep tone reverberating from where a few young men and women stood behind large drums. One continued the rhythm, and the others picked it up, pounding in sync. Joan felt each strike in her chest.

From each of the entrances, the members of the coven entered, holding high candles already lit and flickering. Dressed in matching forest green robes, their cowls covered their heads until they reached the circle. Each set the candle at the base of one of the directional points, then took a step back from the circle.

Their diminished number was emphasized by the amount of empty space in the circle. With only four coven members present, most of the circle was open. It frightened Joan to see Calvert so exposed, but hopefully, this ritual would be what helped sustain the territory while the coven rebuilt itself.

Pablo raised his arms and the drums stopped. Beneath his cloak, he wore a black tunic trimmed in thick silver embroidery over matching heavy pants and knee-high tooled black leather boots. Here, dressed as he was, Pablo was more imposing than in his usual farming wear. When his hands were higher than his head, in a clear, resonant voice, he called to the Guardians of the North.

The hum that had been Joan's constant companion for the last few days intensified, and the spike of pain in her head was so strong she had to lock her knees to keep from falling over. She tried not to draw attention to herself, but some of the townsfolk were watching her every move.

And then the shrieking of crows outside grew loud enough that heads turned upward.

Pablo closed his eyes, his brow furrowed in concentration. He began to walk the circle and called each point. Joan expected the resonance she'd experienced before but it didn't come. Was it because Pablo was in the position Joan had once been in? Was Pablo feeling that sensation now?

His tense expression didn't change. All the guardians had been called, and he now stood alone in the center of the room.

The hum in Joan's head rose in pitch, changing from a whining, ringing sound to a pulse in time with her heartbeat.

Though Joan couldn't see it, she felt the moment the moon rose. The dissonant racket of the crows drowned out Pablo's voice; the pain ratcheted higher and made her whimper. Dayton and several others stared at her as the pulsing in Joan's ears intensified throughout her body.

Maybe she'd cried out. She was drawing too much attention.

Pablo glanced at her in disapproval. He made his claim as lead witch on behalf of the coven, then moved on to the part of the ritual that summoned Calvert's land to his protection.

The pain stabbed in her head again, a sharp needle through her skull that then stopped, leaving her gasping in its wake.

She had to get out of here. Every instinct screamed for her to leave, to find relief outside.

With something akin to resignation, Joan quietly stepped to the southern door. Dayton looked alarmed but didn't say anything when she gestured for him to open the door—even though it was against protocol to interrupt the ritual.

She shook her head at Dayton when he tried to follow her. "Lock it back up," she said in a low voice.

He frowned and looked like he was about to argue, but she held up a hand.

"Do it, Dayton."

Whatever he saw on her face made him back up—too slowly, in her opinion, since her head was splitting in half while she waited, but he did what she asked.

Outside the hall, the air no longer pressed against her chest. She could breathe more easily, but the noise from the crows assaulted her ears, drowning out any other sound.

Hundreds of them swarmed overhead, circled her, and dove around her all the way to the ground.

The urge to return to the house was all she could concentrate on, though the familiar streets were impossible to see through the blur of manic birds.

Almost impossible. She squinted in the dark. The birds

thronged in every direction, blocking her view, save the one leading back to the homestead.

The crows guided her through an implausible tunnel of open air in the midst of all the screeching and ever-shifting eddies of flight. Across lawns, between cars, zagging across streets—the crows drove her along the straightest path back to the house.

A copper tang filmed her tongue as she stumbled, the repeated brush of wings keeping her on track. The pulsing was strong enough to ache now, too, and when wetness dripped from her nose across her lips, she wiped it away with her fingers and found her hand painted with blood.

Was she dying?

Not once in all her time as a war witch, or even before when she was apprenticed to her father as a binding witch—never had she felt this bone-deep interference from outside of her. It had to be something external affecting her. She'd been fine until that first fight on the road, and plain shitty since.

She made it to the house, the crows pushing her along the side path to the garden. On her third attempt, she unlocked the latch.

The moment she stepped inside the gate, the wind died down and the cries of the birds lessened as they retreated. Not far. They churned over the garden, the flapping of their wings a susurrant murmur.

She stopped at the end of the first raised bed. Across the garden, a mist formed near the old ancestors' stone monuments. The nebulous cloud billowed along the path between the beds and Joan stared, mesmerized.

The mist coalesced, then morphed from a cloud to an elongated vertical apparition, almost like a man—and a shockingly familiar one.

Ashen and ethereal, a ghostly manifestation of Trevon Matthews shimmered and walked towards her. His ebony skin, once vibrant and rich, had a grayish, bloodless tinge. His hair was matted, like he'd slept on it but hadn't yet combed it out, and he wore his usual cardigan and frayed jeans.

And his face . . .

This wasn't the father she'd argued with before she left Calvert. Nowhere was there any hint of the angry disapproval that filled her memory from the last time she'd seen him.

His eyes were tender, loving, and proud.

The man she'd once believed loved her unconditionally had looked at her like that. The man who'd carried her home after she'd fallen off her dirt bike and broken her arm. The father who'd sat beside her bed and read to her when she'd been so sick with flu that she could barely raise her head.

This was the Trevon she remembered when he'd been present enough to help her through the challenges in her life—not like when her mother died and he'd abandoned her.

The ghost smiled, just like her father had, and her tears were not entirely from the pain racking her body.

Behind him, more patches of mist formed, vaguely human-sized and shaped but with no discernible definition. They flurried around the ancestors' garden, at preternatural speeds beyond her understanding.

The apparition of her father approached her slowly, at normal human speed, his hands up, demonstrating no threat.

Had she finally lost her mind?

He floated overground to hover beside her, facing the garden.

"All that dies," Trevon said.

"Shall be reborn," Joan answered in wonder.

"Sorry to sneak up on you, Pepper," Trevon said in a conversational voice, though it lacked his usual resonance. He'd used his old nickname for her when she'd been a child—the spice of his life, he'd said.

The grief swept through her like a wave, and she sagged where she stood. It was crazy, but he sounded—he sounded like the voice she hadn't heard in eight years.

Trevon raised a ghostly hand but didn't touch her. She wondered what would happen if he did—if his hand would pass right through her. His eyes glinted as if wet. Could ghosts cry?

"Dad? Can—can you hear me?" she whispered at the ghost.

"I was wrong, Joan," he said in answer. "About all of it, but especially about pushing you away. And now Calvert is paying the price."

A spike of agony lanced through her skull, and she couldn't focus on him until it passed.

"And so are you," he said. "It's only going to get worse unless you make a decision."

Whatever was happening to her throbbed in every muscle of her arms and legs—like she'd just finished a serious workout. Each breath ached behind her breasts.

"I'm here to help, Joan. I swear."

"What's happening to me?" She gasped as her chest seized.

He held his hands out, a gesture of helplessness. "There's a lot to explain."

"How are you even here?"

"I'm not supposed to be. None of us are."

"Us?" But then she saw them.

Across the yard, the other swirling clouds solidified—over a dozen of them. Men and women dressed in outfits that spanned the last two centuries. With smiles and fond eyes, they greeted one another before turning to Trevon and Joan.

Trevon raised a ghostly arm. "These are those who came before you and will be here long after you are gone."

The long line of Matthews witches appeared, old faces and young. So much to see, to process, but Joan struggled to stay upright.

"During a full moon," Trevon said, "it's—well, it's easier. We've only got this one chance to try to help you."

How they could hear each other at all was bizarre. How could a ghost make sound?

Some of the crows flew through the space occupied by some of the spirits. Not that the ghosts acknowledged them at all.

"What's with the damned crows?" It was weird enough they were out in full force after dark, much less that there were so many of them, that they had glommed onto her and driven her back here.

"That's one of the things I've got to talk to you about. I wasn't sure at first, but then I thought about it. The combined effects of the supernatural with the natural order—they're so rare but not uncommon in our line."

Trevon spoke in his instructor voice, like she had all night to listen to his explanations. She might be dead by the time he got to the point. It pissed her off.

"Do you always have to sound like you're teaching a class?"

He looked chagrined. "Sorry."

That was new. Trevon never apologized for anything.

"I want to make sure you're listening. Look, this whole thing with the crows . . ."

The thrum was back again. The pulsing drowned him out, but she tried to focus, tried to process through the pain growing stronger with every heartbeat.

"Several generations of Matthews lived on this continent before we moved to Calvert. Most of their journals were lost, but a few remain in my study. One of those ancestors, Agnes Matthews, was known as Agnes of Crows."

The crows must have heard and understood him. Their squawking abruptly quieted, and Joan glanced up at the change in sound. They settled on every surface in the garden—the trees, the power lines, the frames of the raised beds, the ancestors' stones.

"She used them as familiars. Scores of them. They were tied into her power and formed a synergistic loop between her and the elements."

Joan struggled to follow what her father was saying.

164

"She was the most powerful witch in our line. No one since has been able to summon the crows, until now."

"Dad, I'm telling you, I didn't summon shit—"

Moonlight spilled through the trees at the edge of the yard. At the same time, spikes of agony perforated her body. She couldn't isolate one part where it didn't hurt, and she couldn't form the words to ask for help.

Her father knelt beside her, and she realized she'd folded over with her pain.

"You can choose to stay, or you can leave for good."

She looked at him, desperate for his guidance, but he looked sad, though he offered a familiar loving smile.

"I have never been able to make you stay here, Joan, but I should have listened to you. You are so much more powerful than I ever imagined. If you really want to go, to be done with Calvert, I can't say I understand, but I do recognize that it's your choice. Even if it means Calvert will fall."

Shock blocked the pain for a second before it returned.

"What do I . . ." Joan had to breathe in hisses now.

"Our blood is bound to this land so deeply, and you're feeling the call to affirm that bond. The pain will end when you either bind yourself to the land or ask for separation. One of these things you must do this night, or what you feel will only grow worse until it consumes you."

Joan tried to imagine how "worse "might feel. The ghosts moved back as if trying not to influence her decision. She closed her eyes, slowed her breathing.

Would she leave or would she stay forever?

Everyone she had loved was gone. She was alone now, but . . .

Leigh's face filled her mind's eye. Not the Leigh she had known all those years before, or the glamoured Leigh who had greeted her upon her return. The harder, leaner Leigh with the bloodling's face who had looked at Joan with love and fear—fear that Joan would never accept her.

Except Joan knew the truth now, and her heart wouldn't allow her to leave Leigh behind—again.

"I," Joan said, forcing the words over her lips. "Belong here. I will stay here."

The ghosts circled in response.

"Do ... do I have ... do I have to go back to ... to the hall?"

"No," Trevon said. "It will be hard, but ... there's another way."

He moved his legs like he was walking but his otherworldly form floated a few inches above the ground. He walked down a row of the garden. The plants in the bed to one side of him were higher than his head. Trevon drew his ghostly hand through the plants as he passed them.

"Her touch has made its mark on the garden," Trevon said. "These plants are out of season and should be dead already. I knew she was something different, but ... I didn't think she was this tied to the land. What little power she had before has been amplified."

"Who?" Joan asked, but it was a stupid question.

"Everything I've studied only covers those bloodlings with dark intent, ones desperate to join their masters. She is ... she is something else entirely."

Leigh. He was talking about Leigh, who had never had much affinity for the earth before. Perhaps that had changed after ... her ordeal. And Trevon had known it and protected her from discovery.

Later, when Joan could form words, she'd have to ask him why he had chosen to save a bloodling. Then again, hadn't she done the same thing?

She stumbled after her father's ghost, moaning at the throbbing in her legs as she pushed forward.

Across the single lane of gravel road at the end of the garden, hidden in the trees, was a small trail. As much time as Joan had spent as a kid sneaking around places beyond adult attention, she had never seen this path before.

The violent noise of the crows' flight was muted here. The trees were too tall to allow any moonlight to illuminate the trail and overgrown branches pressed against her arms and face. The branches passed through Trevon's . . . *body* . . . as he guided Joan forward, and only the light of her father's ghost penetrated the shadows. She wanted to summon a light spell, but the agony wouldn't let her focus long enough to do anything.

She faltered, collapsing against a tree—the only thing that kept her from falling to the ground. Her father continued as though he hadn't noticed, but the others . . . the other ghosts had followed them.

They stretched their ghostly arms and bid her to continue. A woman with an ancient-looking face smiled her encouragement. A man who looked not much older than she was stretched a hand toward her and beckoned her forward until she stumbled on.

The pain made everything feel like it took forever but they hadn't gone that far—less than half a mile—when the trees abruptly broke into a clearing as large as a baseball infield.

The trail ended here. Low forest brush thinned as the ground rose into a knoll, like something beneath it had pushed up the ground over time. Trevon floated without resistance across the rising ground, but Joan tripped over a root. She sprawled on her hands and knees in the overgrown grass wet with frost.

With a grunt, Joan pushed herself back to her feet.

Trevon hovered at the small peak and pointed to the ground.

"All the earth's power feeds into ley lines where the connection to the land is more potent. Several of them intersect beneath this spot on our land," Trevon said. "Put your hands here."

High on the knoll was a flat patch of clay and earth, not covered by moss or grass, bare to the sky. Joan didn't have to kneel—the pulsing drove her to her knees, and she pressed her hands on the ground. Here, she was just high enough to see through the gaps in the trees at the moon, blood red and full, low over the horizon.

The crows swirled above her, eerily silent but for the flapping of wings. In her peripheral vision, the ghosts of her ancestors formed a circle at the base of the knoll. The spirits of those who had forged the path for her now joined her.

"Breathe deeply and release your expectations," her father said—the beginning of countless meditations guided by his voice. "Breathe slowly, and listen for her call."

Though it had been years, some part of her responded to his entreaty instantly. Images of similar interactions flashed through her mind—the two of them side by side in the hall, or in the dirt of the backyard, or in the quiet of his study.

All of them had begun just like this, with the gentle invitation of his voice.

So many times, she had melded herself with the earth as both a binder and a war witch. Habit helped cut through the pain, and through it, Joan sank into a familiar hyperawareness of the earth below her.

This time, she felt something different, something more. Something ancient, deep—a mourning that made her own grief feel like a faint echo.

Plaintive and sorrowful, the land's cry wasn't audible, but it was no less powerful. The emotion sweeping through Joan wasn't hers, but it tore at her heart, its pain mingling with her own. More tears filled her eyes.

She would have sacrificed all she was to ease the ache she felt in that call.

"Call the true corners, Joan," her father said.

A simple instruction he'd given many times. This was different from the ceremonial way she'd called them at his pyre. At that thought, the memory of his funeral battled with the incongruity of his ghostly presence. She pushed the interruption aside and focused on what he'd instructed.

In the sacred space of the hall, refined by decades of ceremony, the calling was ritualized but no longer as formal as it had once been.

To call the true corners on the land was a deeper connection to the natural order.

Separating herself from the suffering of her ordeal, from the pain of the land, pushing it all from her consciousness so that she could focus, wasn't an option.

Instead, she sank herself into the agony, surrendered to its energy and force, breathed into it, until she and all the pain were one.

"Cus—" The word caught in her throat, and she cried out, slowing her breathing again until she wrestled herself under control.

"*Custodes et speculatores totius lucis et obscuritatis.*" *Guardians and Watchtowers of all that is light and dark.*

A deep note like a subterranean gong reverberated through the earth.

"*Venio in perfecta dilectione et perfecta fiducia, ut me tibi offeram.*" *I come in perfect love and perfect trust to offer myself to you.*

A sob broke through her voice as she spoke the words her father had taught her, Latin words of binding she had never planned to speak herself.

The mourning of his loss and her own suffering conflated in her chest, and squeezed what little air she'd managed to draw in. She stifled her reaction. There would be time for that later.

She hoped.

A rumbling in the ground was the only answer to her invocation. The next step required an offering, but she could barely raise her head, much less reach her knife.

Then she remembered her blood was much closer at hand than usual. She shifted a bit to one side, moaning against the ache in her shoulder when she swiped her palm across her face.

The streak of blood from her nosebleed would have to be enough. She pressed her hand to the ground.

"*Custodes, rogo, iungas aere tuo,*" Joan said through her tears. *Guardians, I ask to join your air.*

On her next breath, a metallic taste, like a chemical residue but unthreatening, coated her tongue. A cold edge, like drinking ice water, seeped into her lungs. She absorbed it, added it to her own nature.

"*Custodes, rogo, iungas ignem tuum.*" *Guardians, I ask to join your fire.*

A crackling hiss, not of active flame, but of the hint of its possibility, rushed her ears. Now the metal on the air tasted of smoke, and heat prickled in her limbs.

"*Custodes, rogo, iungas aquam tuam.*" *Guardians, I ask to join your water.*

A sharp sensation like the shock of static electricity came and went, leaving a peak awareness of every molecule of moisture on her skin and in the air.

With every element, her perception shifted and added a new facet to her senses. She forced herself to adapt.

"*Custodes, rogo, iungas terram tuam.*" *Guardians, I ask to join your earth.*

A rebounding vibration made her arms cramp. The earth's resistance was a rejection—disbelief of her sincerity.

Please. She couldn't speak the word.

Her heartbeat slowed, the organ thumping thickly in her chest.

If she died here, she would at least speak one final truth.

"*In perfecta dilectione et perfecta fiducia,*" she said again, her voice little more than a rasping croak. "*Rogo, iungas terram tuam.*"

She whined at the piercing burst of pain that followed. She lowered her head, pressed her forehead against the back of her hands, desperate to ease the pressure in her skull.

"*Tuo me iudicio offero, et soli tibi servire desidero,*" Joan whispered. *I offer myself to your judgment and seek only to serve you.*

Everything she had left, she surrendered, until her pain became the earth's, and the earth's mingled with her own.

A swelling burgeoned within her until it seemed like it pushed at her skin from the *inside*, stretching beyond her own physical form, like it would burst if she didn't take action *now* —

The elements wrestled and braided with the core of her.

The ground was cold but the sensation that followed was warm—hot as it worked up her arms to her shoulders and chest. It spread through her heart and her diaphragm, swelled into the flesh between her thighs, throughout her body until she raised her head, opened her eyes and *saw*.

Trevon was talking—the urgent hum of his voice registered but she couldn't determine the individual words—and the other ghosts had raised their hands at their waists, palms up in offering.

The rivers of power nestled in the ley lines of the land stretched before Joan, spread out like iridescent blue-white capillaries beneath the surface of the dirt. They wove across the knoll to the larger meadow. To the garden behind the house.

The whole goddamned neighborhood. *The town.*

Not only were they visible, but she could *feel* them. Like a stinging beneath her skin but completely outside of her body.

And then she realized what she felt was the area within the boundary, stretching from where she stood all the way to the original outline of Calvert's territory.

Her land. Her home. Her people—and their fear.

Joan focused on her heartbeat and the new core of her, and pushed her compassion into the land itself. Every inch, every block, every mile—it was all bound to her cells and her will.

She fed her love into the land until she felt something like an exhale.

Her sight changed.

To the south, where she'd fought with the watch, where

the border had receded, the blue-white of the land's power was tainted a putrid green—a gangrenous sickness that assaulted its purity.

Anger, righteous and all-encompassing, surged within her. Joan summoned the collected essence of herself and the elements and pushed the new unity at that infestation with a grunt.

The sick taint of the malevolence of whatever Victor had done cowered before her and faded, slowly at first but then rushing back beyond the boundary line as Joan clenched her fists with the unfamiliar effort.

Power swelled in her, now pulsing from within and pushed *out*, back into the earth, thrumming in the land that was now hers.

The land responded and began to beat in time with her heart, and the cycle fed into a feedback loop, sending energy back to her, filling her with it—more intense than sunlight, than orgasm, than anything, ever, so full, so beautiful and amazing and nothing but pure power.

It seared her until she screamed, until her voice gave out and she gave herself over to it, blind, deaf, senseless, at one with all she had claimed, until finally she could draw breath, could separate herself from the power flowing through her.

But then it grew, and along with it, some extended sense of the land itself. The pulsing grew as well, but it wasn't driving into her now.

The land welcomed her.

She could see and feel those same tendrils of power, those capillaries of light, in the land outside the boundary. They swelled with increasing speed as they grew and expanded, stretching farther as soon as she could understand where they were, pulsing with her heartbeat. Past the river to the east and the mountains to the west, all the way to the ocean.

The expanse felt gray, defeated, but she poured her hope into the places that seemed abandoned.

I am here. Like sifting her true hands through sand, she cast herself across mountains and fields and valleys, like swimming, like *flying.*

To the southeast, the gangrenous entity she'd pushed back followed one of the ley lines away from Calvert, back to a single point.

At its end, a pulsing fist of power the size of a small farm, threatened the greater balance—a fat, globbish neuron of malice lying in wait.

It had to be Victor, but she couldn't spare a thought for him now.

Elsewhere, the energy hit a wall to the north, and her extended senses retreated.

One sensation at a time, she came back to herself.

When she could think again, she was lying on her back on the ground. The thrumming was a distant echo now of her own heartbeat. The headache was gone, in its place a hypersensitive relief and a ringing in her ears—no longer painful but still damned unpleasant. She sat up and opened her eyes, blinking against the residual afterimages of the ley lines and turned to her father.

The sob that racked her chest surprised her.

She was alone, save for the wind through the trees and the silent crows in flight.

Her father and all the Matthews apparitions had disappeared. Maybe they were back at the house, but something told her that they were gone. Her father was gone.

After all he had done to help her, she could not thank him. She couldn't apologize to him for the way she'd left, for doubting him, for leaving, for not coming back before it was too late.

Once again, she had missed the opportunity to tell him— something, anything, about how wrong she'd been.

The moonlight blurred and warm tears dripped down her cheeks to her chin. Maybe it was her father's absence renewed.

Maybe it was the absence of so many others—those long gone, like her mother and brother, and those newly dead, like Gretchen.

Maybe it was the fact that nothing had turned out the way she'd planned or hoped, and there was no one left to help her find answers.

Maybe it was because she didn't know how to save Leigh.

With the boundary restored, Calvert now had a second chance. Power hummed in her veins and limbs, and with it, Joan would protect the town, but what good did it do her if she could do nothing for someone she loved?

Alone on the knoll, with the earth still quivering beneath her, Joan cried for all she'd lost.

CHAPTER 16

Leigh tried not to think about Joan very much. When she did, she couldn't hold back the tears, and tears wouldn't help her now.

Shock warred with her disbelief. Reed Hill from the town coven had been waiting for her outside the church. When she'd first returned to Calvert, she'd hidden herself from everyone, but Reed was someone she'd avoided for years. Since Joan had left town, since the debacle with his nephew, Reed had always looked down on her in disapproval.

Judging by the murderous glares she'd received before they'd covered her head, Reed Hill still bore Leigh nothing but hatred. He hadn't spoken another word to her since the church, where they'd grabbed her and thrown her into a waiting van.

When they chained her to its frame, she realized she'd missed her chance to fight them off. Using her bloodling strength had never occurred to her, and now it was too late. How had they known what she was?

She didn't have her pack with her carefully assembled herbs and tincture. She had nothing, and no one knew where she was, not even Joan.

They'd been driving for almost an hour, far longer than it would have taken to turn her over to the watch or the coven. Was Reed returning her to the vampires himself? Was this on Mrs. Wilson's orders?

Or did he have something far more personal in mind for her? Did he blame her for Pierce's death? It hadn't been her fault that Pierce had been taken, but maybe he held her responsible.

The van finally slowed, then eventually stopped. She listened for clues, but no one spoke. Reed turned off the engine and climbed out. The side door of the van slid open.

Someone removed the hood that had covered Leigh's head since they'd left Calvert. A wave of dread like incipient nausea washed over her the moment she recognized where she was.

Rows of dark, dry vines, stretching as far as she could see.

The vampires' vineyard.

The sun had set, but twilight washed over the landscape, the distant hills purple and pink with the last of the day's sunlight from below the horizon. Leigh wrestled with despair at the sight of the familiar manor house, a place she'd prayed she'd never again see.

Her captors didn't speak as they dragged her toward the pergola-covered courtyard. Thick, leafless bramble wove through its beams, casting thick shadows across the terracotta tile. She scanned the dark for the next threat instead of taking one last glance at the only sunlight she'd likely see again.

Nathaniel waited inside the doorway to the manor, safe from even the threat of daylight, not that any remained. In the time it took to cross a space large enough for four parked cars, Leigh shrank in on herself under his gaze. So many times, she'd wished to avoid his attention, and now all he could see was her.

She whimpered as he glared, his body taut in restrained anger.

"If it isn't the mouse that got away."

Leigh clenched her hands against their trembling, speechless in the face of an unknown but surely pain-filled future. This time, she wouldn't escape.

Nathaniel gestured, and two bloodlings appeared from behind him. They took her from the men who'd grabbed her in town.

"Victor will want to see her," Reed said, though deference tamed his tone.

"Since you failed to deliver the coven you promised, our master has been forced to deal with the boundary himself." Nathaniel stared Reed down, his rank in the pecking order implied. "He awaits your return in the hall."

"Of course, Legate," Reed said.

How was it possible to feel even more shock? Reed Hill was a traitor to the coven—to the town. Calvert was doomed.

Did Joan already know? How long had Reed been working for Victor, and how much danger was Joan in as a result?

Not that Leigh could do anything about it.

The bloodlings tugged her closer to Nathaniel, who waited for Reed and his companions to disappear before he spoke again.

"You were supposed to be my gift to Sylvia. Nothing more than a token to aid my alliance, but now you have attracted Victor's attention, little bloodling." He sounded furious, as if he hadn't wanted Victor to know about her.

Leigh collapsed but the men gripping her arms held her fast. She fought against the knocking in her knees.

"My choice would be to slit your throat," he said. "To make you an example before the rest of the house, but now your master has something else planned to welcome you to the fold."

He said "welcome" like some people said "bloodbath."

"Let us find a nice place for you to wait for your debut, shall we?" He signaled to the other men, then disappeared as they half-dragged her to the basement.

As they descended the stairs, fear accounted for only some of her tears—the stench caused the rest. Her sense of smell had intensified, and the odor of unwashed bodies, vomit and worse drove the horror home.

Everything she'd been through had accomplished nothing.

They passed the donor feeding stations where she'd spent time before her escape, and she was sure they'd toss her back into the horrid cells where drug addicts were forced into sobriety, but then they kept going.

When they reached a corner of the basement and came to a roughly hewn but securely barricaded door, Leigh finally fought against her captors, but it was too late.

Some new hell awaited.

They descended again, this time down rickety stairs that creaked with every step. Deep in a cellar she hadn't known existed, they reached an unmarked door, its shiny steel incongruous with the dirt floor and the smell of cement. One of her captors unlocked it before they threw her into the dark space inside. Behind her, the door closed with a slam and the lock engaged.

Her inhuman eyes adjusted quickly. She stared into the blackness of the tiny room that was her cell.

Square, no more than six feet in any direction, walled by cement bricks. The aged stink in one corner suggested the lack of a toilet, though the dry mustiness meant no one had been captive here in a long time.

Alone, with no hope to keep her upright, Leigh sank to the ground and wrapped her arms around herself. She couldn't hold the sobs back anymore.

If she stayed on the floor, it wasn't that confining, but the dark made the panic worse.

What would Joan have done?

As powerful a witch as she was, Joan would have cast a light spell, but Leigh had never had much affinity for magic. Back when she and Joan had been in high school, huddled together late one night in a gap between the hedges separating their houses, Joan had demonstrated a light-summoning spell.

Leigh had been awestruck. Joan said it weirded her out to have Leigh look at her differently. She insisted on teaching

Leigh the spell, adamant and persistent even when Leigh was certain it couldn't be done.

After weeks of attempts, Leigh had summoned light into the palm of her hand. Joan had been disproportionately proud, insisting they celebrate with a trip to the diner for sundaes.

More tears slipped down Leigh's cheek at the memory. She opened her eyes to the dark again and pledged to pull herself together. Yes, she was going to die, but she didn't have to die mewling before the monsters.

She hadn't tried any deeper meditation in weeks because of the glamour spell. The iron filings dulled her ability to center, leaving her feeling blurred out, a little too foggy to focus. But the last remnants of the glamour had worn off hours ago.

Leigh crisscrossed her legs where she sat on the floor. After a few deep breaths, she began her own centering sequence—the step-by-step meditation of lengthening her torso, setting her shoulders, and drawing from the core of herself. Though she was hungry and thirsty, she was surprisingly clearheaded for the first time in she didn't know how long.

Joan had insisted Leigh craft her own incantation. The words she'd chosen had come easily and quickly to mind—words that still made her think of Joan.

Leigh licked her lips, drew in another deep breath, and pressed one hand flat on the dirt. A cool sensation seeped into her fingers, across her wrist, up her arm.

"*Lux cordis mei, candens et sine fine.*" *Light of my heart, incandescent and endless.*

It took several attempts but then in the center of her other hand, a tiny speck of light the size of a rice kernel appeared.

She smiled and the light dissipated. Her pride faded as she realized she was just brightening up the dark space of her own imminent death, but at least she could make things a little better. The spell took a lot of strength that would only drain her over time, but—

Cold realization hit her.

She was a bloodling now. Human constraints no longer applied.

By the time they came for her, Leigh estimated most of the night and following day had passed. In that time, she had managed to make a ball of fire the size of a walnut. She molded it into different shapes above her palm until muffled voices approached. She expelled it, leaving her once more shrouded in pitch black darkness.

The door opened. Rough hands grabbed her arms and lifted her to her feet. Some survival instinct made her feign weakness, and she collapsed, pretending her legs had given out. As she'd expected they would, they raised her up and then dragged her out of the box.

"Bring the bitch upstairs." A voice she didn't recognize issued the order, and her speechless captors drag-carried her to the bare wooden stairs. "Get her cleaned up. Victor wants her in the hall at moonrise."

Her blood ran cold. Whatever was about to happen, she couldn't count on rescue or mercy. No one was coming for her.

It was too soon to fight back, with so many of them confining her. They stripped her bare and hosed her down with ice cold water in the donor showers upstairs, little more than an animal rinsing station near the back door of the house. After dressing her in a plain white tunic, they left her alone, chained to a wall.

She didn't count the minutes or wonder anymore about what might happen next. Instead, she allowed herself to think about Joan—about the too-brief moments when she'd given in and let herself feel something other than hopelessness or desperation.

With what little time Leigh had left, she wanted to remember how it had felt to be in Joan's arms after so long.

The only place she'd ever felt like she belonged. Joan's kiss, her warmth, her strength, her solid substance offering salvation and safety . . . and love. Even if Joan hadn't felt what Leigh had at the time, what Leigh still felt, it had been more than Leigh thought she'd ever experience again.

Escaping wasn't an option. They'd only attack the town looking for her again. She had to find a way to remove herself from the equation.

Leigh wondered if she could force them to kill her.

Leigh didn't fight as they once again dragged her through the manor house, didn't protest or cry out or offer any resistance. She only thought of Joan, hoping Joan would find a way to defeat Victor and all his court, even against Reed's treachery.

When they stopped, she opened her eyes. Double oak doors stood between her and her fate. Voices and the tinkling of bottles and glasses hinted at some sort of gathering. She would be made a spectacle of, then.

The men at her sides each reached for a door handle, opening them in sync for maximum effect. Sparse applause greeted her, sparking the terror to return to her limbs.

The room was too small to be designated a "hall." Once, this must have been the vineyard's tasting room. Another pair of doors on the opposite end of the room led outside. Stained hardwood floors stretched from wall to wall.

If she hadn't been afraid for her life, she might have laughed at the overly ostentatious decor. The walls were covered in a garish red brocade, and wide crown moldings had been added below the ceiling.

Large, unwieldy chairs of dark wood, with matching low tables set before them, were staged in a semicircle. Instead of seeming stately, it only made the room crowded.

Several vampires filled the room, one in each chair. She didn't see Sylvia, but three of the others were familiar faces. Elder Winslow, once hale and robust, now sallow and grim.

181

Two others, looking blankly at her, were former members of the Calvert coven whose names she couldn't recall in her fear.

They weren't the biggest threat.

Opposite from the bowed semicircle and elevated on a small platform sat a gaudy wood-and-metal chair meant to suggest a throne. It was occupied by someone who could only be Victor.

Leigh's mouth fell open as she was thrown to her knees. She didn't feel anything at hitting the floor so hard but was so shocked, pain might not have registered.

"*You*," she whispered, but the sound carried and someone behind her snickered.

The vampire on the throne was dressed like he'd come from a movie set. He wore a black velvet poet's shirt with long flowing sleeves, open to expose a chest naked of hair, almost adolescent in its lack of definition. His wavy brown hair was combed back from his face but wasn't long enough to fall down his back and kept falling into his eyes. He twitched it back with a tilt of his neck more than once, then took an exaggerated sip from a goblet on the chair's arm.

He made sure everyone in the room was watching before he spoke.

"Leigh Phan. So good to see you again." Victor welcomed her with a suggestive and sinister smile. His voice was contrived—the accent not what she remembered. "I can't tell you how glad I am that you decided to join us."

She thought she'd never seen Victor before, but that was because she hadn't known who Victor truly was. The vampire before her, the lord who had victimized Calvert for months, had once been a resident.

Once, he'd been Trevon's apprentice.

CHAPTER 17

Joan woke with a start, half upright and reaching for her knife. She lay on the guest room bed, still fully dressed. Dried mud from her boots had flaked off the soles and smudged the quilt. The curtains were so thick, she couldn't see out the windows to gauge the time, but the door was open and indirect daylight spilled in from the hall.

Rapid thumping echoed in the room—the sound that had awakened her. Someone was pounding on the front door hard enough to split the wood.

She rose from the bed as tendrils of memory from the night before returned. The visceral high from the ritual on the knoll had faded as she'd lumbered through the woods back to the homestead. Fatigue had slammed into her with a vengeance but she'd somehow made it back to the house, too tired to climb the stairs to her room.

Instead, she'd used the last of her strength to get to what she now thought of as Leigh's room.

Leigh.

How was she going to get Leigh back from Nathaniel and Victor?

The house was cold, Leigh's absence somehow another presence along with all the others who had left their mark, and the emptiness inside Joan swelled. Claiming the land and restoring the boundary hadn't solved everything—the town was likely still blockaded, the thralls at the border still outnumbered the decimated watch, and Leigh . . .

Nebulous points of a plan swirled in Joan's head as she crossed the living room. She muttered a strengthening incantation as she lifted the four-by-four board from its posts, but with her newly acquired power, the push was too hard.

The board flipped to one side so quickly, one end slammed into the floorboards and the other crashed into one of the dining room chairs. She stared at the chair's now broken arm in shock.

How long would it take to get used to this new power?

"Joan?" Dayton called through the door. "Jesus, finally."

She unsealed the ward on the door as she unlocked and opened it.

Late morning warmed the front yard where a few dozen crows danced and flitted across the lawn, the bushes, and the trees. Pablo stood at the base of the porch stairs in full sunlight, his blank expression unreadable.

On the porch, Dayton bristled with energy, like he'd been prepared to kick the door down. Willy nipped and growled at his heels, the two of them agitated in parallel until the dog was distracted by the birds and barked at them instead.

Dayton stared at Joan in bold wonder. "What in bloody hell did you do?"

Pablo climbed the stairs, his hands in his pockets. "You've claimed Calvert, yes? The boundary is restored?"

He seemed relaxed about it. Surprising.

"Yes." Joan might have explained herself, but she was running out of time. She could deal with the coven after she . . . well, after.

All the tension left his frame, as if that had been the only thing he'd cared about. Pablo turned oddly respectful. "Gretchen was always convinced that you would do what was best for Calvert, but she thought . . . well, I'm sure you will."

He nodded at her, almost proud, and then took his leave without saying another word.

Gretchen had certainly not given Joan that impression, but the coven was one less thing to worry about.

Joan stepped onto the porch, tasting the air. Calvert was cleaner now. Not with the rich possibility of her memory, but with something different, something new. She'd have to figure that out later, too. The list was still too damned long.

So much for not taking her father's place.

Joan turned to Dayton, who didn't seem to know what to do with her. Probably smart. "How are the roads?"

Willy greeted her by almost knocking her over, his front paws high on her chest while he tried to lick her chin. She winced at the attention but scratched behind one of his ears.

Dayton frowned. "Still blocked, but no one's tried to raid town since you did . . . whatever you did."

The boundary was holding, but Victor was no doubt regrouping.

"I've got to get to Portland. I need your help to bust through the northern checkpoint."

Dayton stood fast with his mouth hanging open. "You've gotta be kidding me."

"I can't let things stand the way they are." And she couldn't leave Leigh in Victor's clutches. "I just need five minutes with the High Coven."

"You can't just leave after claiming the town."

Joan sighed. "I'm not leaving for good. Just long enough to convince them to help me."

"And what if they don't?" That wasn't a notion worth entertaining. "I mean, is she that important?"

Dayton was a brave man to call her out like that. His wary gaze suggested he knew he was pushing the wrong person, but she had to respect him for speaking his mind when he also knew she could kick his ass.

185

"She is to me." Time to change tactics. "But that's not the only reason. Against their full coven, Victor won't stand a chance. Given enough time to plan, I might be able to wipe him out with the watch in a concentrated attack, but I don't have it to spare."

Of course, taking the watch away from Calvert right now would be stupid, not to mention irresponsible considering how few remained to protect the town.

"I can't take Victor out alone," she said.

"You sure?" Dayton looked at her like she could single-handedly storm a vampire compound. "Forgive me for wondering if you've got a few more tricks up your sleeve than I can imagine."

Joan stared back, but she of all people knew exactly how human she was.

Dayton took a deep breath and let it out with puffed cheeks. "Then I'm coming."

"No, you're not."

"Yes, I am."

If only the gods could send her the patience to deal with overzealous, overprotective men and their damsel in distress bullshit. "I don't need your protection."

"I'm not offering any," Dayton said. "You're damned sure tougher than I am. But I am coming."

"Dayton—"

He lowered his voice. "I promised him I'd help you any way I could if you ever came back. You understand, Joan? Trevon told me that if he wasn't around, I was to make sure you got anything you said you needed, no matter what the coven said."

Dayton had never let on that he'd spent so much time with Trevon, or that her father was comfortable sharing such details with him.

"I worked with him for two years. When I came to Calvert, he welcomed me into this town sooner than anyone else, and he backed me when I took over the watch four months later. I wasn't sure what that promise might mean, but I'll damned sure keep my word. You may not need me, but I'm coming with you."

Joan tried to think of one last argument she might offer, but it was almost noon. If they had to fight their way through the northern blockade—assuming it was still as fortified as it had been—they'd still have to hurry to make it to Portland before sundown.

Arguing with Dayton was burning daylight.

He sensed the change. "I assume you're driving."

"No, you are." She shook her head. As hyped up as she was on new power, she might stomp through the undercarriage if she gave Luther too much gas. "And Willy stays here."

The clash with Victor's thralls at the checkpoint should have been straightforward.

A dozen humans manned the blockade, and the clouds had parted leaving them without bloodling support. The autumn sun slanted from behind Joan and Dayton.

Dayton stepped out of Luther with a loaded crossbow in one hand and a Glock in the other. He shot a bolt into one thrall's shoulder, then used his pistol to shoot out the knees of two more by the time Joan climbed out.

Her first shot with her pistol was wide, her aim off which was . . . different. She wasn't a crack shot, but she could hit a target at thirty feet. Instead, she'd missed this guy completely. With several of them closing in, she switched to spellcraft.

Then shit got weird.

Her battle cantrips—the spells she'd designed herself requiring only gestures, tongue clicks and pops—misfired, either hitting the wrong target or malfunctioning in some way. All her air spells delivered damage to both her targets and herself.

The blowback from one of her fire incantations hit Dayton and burned his forearm before he smacked the flames dead.

Then her targets closed in.

Three attacked her at once, far more skilled than the ones she'd met her first day back in Calvert. One wielded a wicked bat wrapped in razor wire, another a tactical knife. The third knocked her gun from her hand, but she followed up with a kick to the gut that set him back a few paces.

It didn't stop him, and they attacked her again. The thralls were rangy, brutal and fought like maniacs—like they had nothing to lose.

Maybe they didn't.

She gave as good as she got, cursing and spitting and yelling as she parried every blow and got in a few of her own. With her spells not working as expected—her incantations suddenly too powerful with unpredictable range—Joan forced herself to abandon her spells until she could gauge her own power.

She finally managed to take down the idiot with the knife, kicking him into unconsciousness. She turned to finish off the other one when he got a solid swipe along her side with the bat.

She screamed as the razor wire cut into her flesh. The pain fueled her anger—these fuckers were *in her way*—and she moved her knife into her left hand and drew her short sword with her right. A clean slice of her sword across his midsection spilled his guts over his belt. She drew another across his neck until he toppled over, incapacitated enough to lie there and die.

Blades resheathed—no time now to clean them—she retrieved her gun and put some space between herself and the next targets.

She resorted to shooting one in the leg and the other in the head, and then the battle was done. Dayton had dispatched the others.

They had to get out of here quickly, before any reinforcements arrived.

There was no time to tend to the bodies of the fallen and it bothered Joan that she couldn't at least collect them into one communal pyre and free them, if only in gesture.

Dayton gazed at her long and hard while she muttered a protection incantation for their souls, but didn't comment.

Back in Luther, Joan stared ahead while holding some gauze to her side. The wound wasn't too deep, but they'd have to stop at some point so she could bandage it up. Dayton lead-footed the gas, trying to put some distance behind them. Her legs trembled from the ordeal. Still brimming with power, her fingertips and face tingled.

Once they put a few miles behind them, Dayton used one hand to call the watch about dispatching the bodies. No other challenges blocked them as they raced along the rural highways, headed for the main freeway north.

Joan said nothing for the next hour. The closer they got to the city, the more populated the road became and the more attention they attracted. Luther was a sight to behold, so Joan wasn't that surprised, but it seemed to make Dayton uncomfortable.

"What are the chances someone will attack us before we get there?" Dayton said when yet another group of rough-looking humans eyed the vehicle hungrily.

"It's possible," Joan said. "But it'll be the last thing they do."

"What if they shoot out the tires?"

"Enchanted to resist bullets. Still won't stop."

"Flamethrower?"

"It'd suck, but I've made it through one before."

Dayton sounded impressed. "Man, where the hell have you been in this thing?"

Joan had always thought the road from Calvert would take her somewhere far from where she'd begun. But for all her misadventures, all the places she'd been, and all the skills she'd acquired to make sure she could find her place anywhere, she'd discovered most places weren't much different from where she'd come from.

It should have bothered her more to have only come full circle, but then she thought of Leigh, and how she'd felt more satisfied arguing with Leigh in her family home than she'd felt on the road for the last six months.

"All over the place," she answered, and left it at that.

As they approached Portland, Joan's goal to sneak into the city and solicit an audience with the High Coven became an impossibility.

For the last twenty miles, every crow in the area had joined an ever-growing swarm flying in parallel to Joan's path on the highway. It had swelled to several thousand above and behind her as Dayton drove. She could *feel* them, growing in number and sweeping across the afternoon sky, just like she could feel the land's low pulse. A queasiness roiled through her guts.

When she reached the city walls just before sunset, with its daunting mix of cement and metal and fence twelve feet high, her heart sank. The High Coven represented all the witches of the region, a super-coven with hundreds of members and one central council of thirteen witches.

All thirteen stood in full ceremonial dress blocking the city gates, an army of people behind them.

"Looks like they know we're here," Dayton said. He shifted Luther into park though he left the motor running, and exhaled heavily. "Fuck."

She couldn't go through them to get inside before dark, not that it would do her any good since these were the people she'd come to see. She couldn't turn around now and go back—she might be able to protect Calvert but she didn't have any other plan to save Leigh.

But if this was how they were going to welcome her, Joan

wasn't sure they'd listen to her at all.

"If they attack, can you take them?" Dayton asked.

She fought back a scream. "No, I can't take them." One war witch against an entire coven was ludicrous, especially the High Coven of Portland. Any one of them was more powerful than her father. All of them combined could reduce her to ash.

Joan opened her door and stepped out slowly, keeping her hands open and in plain sight. Dayton climbed out as well and flanked her.

"That's far enough." One witch—not the one in the lead—lowered her cowl to reveal a pale shaved head. Her head, neck and face were covered in tattoos so dense it was hard to discern any heritage.

Joan stopped, searching for the words to diffuse the tension. She couldn't lead with asking for a favor, not in front of all these people, even if that was all she'd come for.

The lead witch pulled back her cowl. She was shorter than the others, and long strands of thick, straight black hair fell across her shoulders.

"State your intentions," she said in a clear voice, light like high-pitched wind chimes, with the accent of someone who also spoke Hindi.

"I come in peace with open hands and an open heart," Joan said, loud enough to be heard over the squawking of the crows.

The woman waited a long beat before speaking again. "That remains to be seen."

Joan raised her hands higher. "I'm not here to start anything."

One of the taller witches scoffed. "The spectacle says otherwise." She gestured in a wave at all the crows.

Joan closed her eyes, knowing she couldn't do anything about the damned birds. Yet she couldn't deny them either.

She tried again, some words of the formal request finally pushing to the front of her mind. "I have come from Calvert for an audience with the High Coven."

A murmur rose from the coven and the crowd behind them, but none of the words reached Joan's ears. It grew in volume, parts of it angry, until the lead witch interrupted.

"Enough." She stepped forward, away from the coven and closer to Joan, an arm outstretched to keep her people from following her.

Halfway between the city gates and where Dayton had parked, she stopped. "Let us speak plainly," she said.

Joan met her in the middle of the road, alone, as the dying light of the day slipped behind the western hills. "I'm really not here for trouble. I need your help."

"The High Coven is at no one's beck and call."

Joan shook her head, eager to clear up the confusion. "That's not what I—I mean I humbly ask for your—"

"You can't humbly ask for anything. Not after melding your essence with most of the state without warning, without permission, without telling anyone at all what you planned to do. Yet you wonder why we don't want to receive you in the city."

Of course they knew. They'd felt what she'd done and perceived her as an impending threat. They must think she was trying to seize power of the city as well.

Joan sighed. "That—that was unintentional."

"You'll forgive me if that doesn't make any of us feel any better."

Joan regretted how it had happened, but she didn't regret that it had happened at all and wouldn't apologize for it. Not even to the High Coven.

"If we could just talk about—"

The lead witch slowly shook her head as if speaking to a precocious but dangerous child. "We will not receive you today, Caller of the Crows."

A sensation like running ice water slipped down Joan's spine.

The lead witch continued in a low voice, and Joan felt as if she were being taken to task. "If you truly mean what you say, if you mean no harm and do come in peace, we will speak again, but it will not be this night. And until a formal request is made properly you are not welcome within the city walls."

The clock was ticking. Joan was running out of time. "Please, you have to—"

"We don't have to do anything. Not until you prove your intentions are sincere."

"But someone—people will die if I don't—"

"People die every day, Joan Matthews."

Words died on Joan's tongue at the sound of her name. They knew more about her than she knew about them. Not a good balance.

"Bad things happen," the witch said, not unkindly though still firm. "There is always a crisis. I know this, and I am sorry for your loss. Many of us knew your father."

The witch's tone was compassionate, but her eyes were uncompromising. "I see that whatever need you have is urgent, but we can take no chances until we are certain."

She turned without another word and returned to her coven. Back in place in its center, she called out again. "Send word through the proper channels, and we'll meet on neutral ground."

Joan cast another glance at the city gates. At least two dozen of the well-armed city watch aimed more weapons at her than she could count. The High Coven and the crowd returned through the gates.

Dayton stated the obvious as he turned toward Luther. "We can't stay out here."

Joan beckoned for the keys. "I have a backup plan." Loosely formed, sure, but it didn't matter.

He wasn't going to like it.

Half an hour later, Joan parked Luther in the tiny lot of a worn three-story building near the river. The bricks might have been beige or yellow beneath the streaked grime, but no markings or signs indicated what was inside. Joan's last visit had been months before, and nothing had changed.

Dayton didn't move. "Here or inside?"

"With me. Leave your gear." Though she'd bet money he hid a blade somewhere on his person just like she did.

Dayton climbed out without another word.

They stood in the small landing above the street right in front of the single sturdy door. Joan pushed Dayton out of the view of the camera mounted above the door, then leaned forward into the thin beam of ultraviolet light crossing the entrance.

Joan blinked, then stood straight and arched an eyebrow. "Let me in, Loufield."

After a moment, the door opened. A squat man with splotchy coral skin and a scraggly neckbeard poked his head through the gap. He glared at Joan, and then gave a start when he saw Dayton. "I don't know your friend."

Joan stuck a boot in the door before he could close it again. "Never you mind who he is. I'll vouch for him, and you'll let us in now, thank you very much, or I'll spread the word about what you've got stashed in the attic."

Loufield frowned but since he didn't want word getting out about his private collection of enchanted antiquities—ones he sold to the highest bidder without regard for their intentions—he pushed the door wide. "What do you want here, Joan?"

"I need to talk to the emissary." She ignored Dayton's confusion and held Loufield's gaze.

Loufield grunted. He locked the door and disappeared.

"What is this place?" Dayton muttered.

The surprisingly bright foyer, painted in sun yellow with cream trim, led to a short hall. Voices and music echoed from the far end, and Joan walked toward the noise.

"Safe space on neutral territory," Joan said. "Pub on the

ground floor, rooms for hire upstairs, local heavies in the basement. We steer clear of them, and we shouldn't have any trouble."

The hall ended at a doorway without a door and led to the pub. It smelled of yeasty beer and strong, burnt coffee. According to a chalkboard mounted over the wooden bar, tonight's supper was pasta and meat sauce with garlic bread. Three beers were on offer, but only one wine, and the spirits were limited to gin or whiskey, neither of which had probably been aged very long.

The evening's entertainment was a thin, strung out, clean-shaven white man with long oily hair. He sat in a rickety chair in one corner and sang in a beautiful tenor accompanied by a lone reverb-heavy electric guitar.

A dozen small, heavy tables filled the dimly lit space, half of them full. Joan took a table along the wood-paneled wall and sat with an eye-line to the door.

Joan had no intention of drinking, but she ordered a round of beers to blend in. Dayton watched a couple of people walk through the room, having arrived mere minutes after they did, then turned his attention back to their table. "We gonna hole up here, head back to Calvert at first light?"

"No." Joan wasn't going back empty-handed, and first light was too far away. Something told her they didn't have that kind of time.

"How the fuck did that get in here?" Dayton reached for his knife.

A lone vampire stood in the space dividing the pub from the hall and appraised the room with cool interest. The guitarist stopped, and everyone else froze. He might have been mistaken for a sun-starved tax attorney, as unassuming as he seemed in a dress shirt and slacks, but for the inch-long talons at the ends of his fingers. He wore aviators, silver ones, indoors. At night.

Ugh. Pretentious vampires.

"Leave it," Joan said.

The vampire actually smiled at them. After a beat, he navigated to their table.

Joan didn't draw her knife from its sheath, but her arm ached from *not* drawing it.

After turning his head in Dayton's direction, he shifted toward Joan.

To her surprise, he offered a small bow—just a tilt from the waist. "I am Bartholomew."

Of course he was.

Joan didn't like her backup plan, but that wouldn't stop her from executing it. "I am Joan Matthews of the Calvert coven. I request an audience with Elizaveta."

Dayton choked down a cough but said nothing—nor did anyone else. A pin could have dropped in the next room and everyone would have heard it.

The vampire answered with a nod, then quietly left. In his wake, the guitarist restarted his song, and slowly, conversation around them resumed.

Finally, Joan glanced at Dayton, who stared back in disapproval.

"How does a woman like you walk around with such large bronze balls between your legs?"

"I've tried our best option. Now, I'm trying our worst."

When the vampire returned, the room didn't come to a screeching halt, but it was suddenly tense. The performer stopped singing but still strummed his guitar.

"Elizaveta extends her welcome to you, Joan Matthews," Bartholomew said with another bow. "She invites you alone to Gaden House one hour after moonrise. I will provide safe passage to and from Black Rose City should you accept her invitation."

Not much longer then, and there would be no meeting on neutral territory. Dayton was already seething at being excluded, but she couldn't think of any other way to stop Victor.

It was her own idea and she wished she could take it back, but instead she offered a cool nod.

He walked across the room and took a seat at another wall-side table. He, too, selected a chair with its back to the wall.

"This is insane," Dayton scoffed.

Joan resisted the urge to laugh. Of course it was insane, but what other choice did she have?

"If I'm not back in four hours, wait until first light and then take Luther back to Calvert." The vampires here would abide by guild rules, and she had to believe she'd survive the night, but if she didn't return, Dayton could make it back, assuming he didn't run into any opposition.

He gaped at her. She wanted to tell him to trust her, but she had no idea what she was walking into.

Bartholomew led Joan on a short walk to the riverside, part of the border around Portland established by the river.

As she walked, trying to keep her eyes on the vampire and her surroundings in equal measure, she noted how many dwellings were built in this neutral area.

People lived here. Though not within the city walls, they still gained some level of protection by proximity, and tiny walled communities of apartment buildings and fortified multi-home compounds populated the area.

With a shock, Joan realized she could feel the earth here—a tired wariness and unease. The ritual had bound her to this land, and while she could probably navigate Calvert with her eyes closed, this no man's land was nowhere near as familiar. She knew the roads and a few of the buildings, but nothing else.

Every community had a leader, even if that leadership was distributed across a council or a coven. Yet she had no idea who controlled each territory, and how many practitioners might be aware of what she'd done. How many of them were angry or afraid? How many of them would she hear from when this was all over?

So many questions, and none of them had answers within easy reach.

And now she was going into another unknown, on the small chance that this greater devil could help defeat the smaller one. This was the stupidest thing she'd ever done, and she wouldn't be surprised if she got herself killed. Obviously, she was out of her damned mind, but every time she thought of turning back, the next thought was of Leigh.

Joan followed the vampire, Bartholomew.

Finally, they reached the clearing above the dock. Down the ramp they strode, toward the only boat tied off on this side of the river. Bartholomew approached it casually and she faced her last chance to back out.

This reeked of a trap, but logically, she couldn't find a reason for this to be an elaborate scheme to kill her. Even if they considered Joan an unknown power, the vampires might try to test her. She couldn't fight off endless reinforcements in vampire territory.

The vampire noticed her hesitation.

"Let me remind you that Elizaveta has assured your safety. You will be returned to this spot unharmed once your . . . conversation . . . has concluded."

If Joan left now, she had nothing but her own resources to bring against Victor, and that might not be enough to save Leigh. If she spoke to Elizaveta, there was the tiniest chance the First vampire would want to swat the bastard herself.

Bartholomew untied the ropes securing the boat to the dock while Joan checked all her weapons. Had she ever done anything as stupid, as reckless as this?

Nothing came to mind.

Feigning confidence she didn't exactly feel, Joan joined

Bartholomew on the boat. It was small, little more than a simple fishing boat with room for four people.

She hoped she wouldn't have to swim back to shore, and seated herself as he started the engine.

There were no lights on the boat. Normally, she'd think it unsafe, but she guessed that he could see well enough in the dark—even with the ridiculous sunglasses—to avoid any hazards or traffic.

Then again, there was no other traffic on the river tonight. Black water stretched far to the right and left of the boat, scattered lights reflecting near the shoreline. Off to the south, she saw a tall, glorious green-bronze bridge stretching across the river, parallel to their path, but she guessed that was under the supervision of the High Coven.

The calls of birds above her drew her attention to the sky. The flicker of faint moonlight on wings moving in and out of her vision indicated the crows had followed her here as well, despite the darkness.

Now that the hum was gone, the driving pain dispelled, an odd itch irritated the base of her skull. Some instinct told her the crows were responsible. A loud whisper of alternate consciousness tugged at her, and she shook her head to dispel it.

She didn't know what to do with the crows yet, but no one else knew that. And if an appearance of power was enough to save her life here in the den of the beast, then . . .

Facing forward, Bartholomew drove the boat slowly across the river, leaving but a small wake.

Joan stared at his back as she took long, slow deep breaths and centered herself in her seat. Finally, she closed her eyes.

This was the first time she'd made a conscious attempt to connect in some way with the birds.

She tried to focus on the sounds of them first, to sink into their calls and see if that could provide some sort of connective baseline. The crows were inconsistent, though, as they flew closer then away again. She couldn't pick any one call out, and the cacophony was too uneven to match her calm.

Perhaps a different approach would work. With her eyes still closed, she tried to envision seeing as they saw, their view from above. She pictured herself in the boat as she might be viewed by the birds in flight, but it was too weird, and took so much focus she kept having to relax her shoulders from the mounting anxiety.

Nothing. No disjointed images like in her dreams, no seemingly split vision, no sensation to indicate that she had connected with the crows at all. Only an odd queasiness that might very well have been because of the damned boat. She opened her eyes with a sigh. Bartholomew still faced ahead, and the boat still slowly slid across the water.

The lights of Black Rose City loomed before her as more details of the dock came into view.

Several docks, in fact, as a dozen more boats like this one were revealed, all moored along the river. A few workers—humans, she'd imagine—bustled about the dock. One saw them approaching and ran to meet them.

Bartholomew said nothing to the new arrival as he tossed a rope towards the dock. The thrall caught it, secured the boat, then stood back while they disembarked.

Bartholomew extended an arm towards the city. "This way."

They walked along a four-lane central street in a heavily trafficked area. Unlike in Calvert, the night life thrived. Businesses lined the street, all of them open, the windows and storefronts free of graffiti, not a barricade in sight. At first, a few people attempted to approach them but one gesture from Bartholomew and they fell back or scattered altogether.

Evidently, this particular vampire was more than just a messenger.

Though no one approached them again, some of the braver passersby called out to her, taunting her for being human.

"Such a pretty donor," one called.

She tried to stare them down, but so many of them gathered on the streets as they passed. Dozens of vampires—until she was so outnumbered, she could no longer keep track.

"Maybe when the boss is done, she'll share," another laughed.

The more they shouted, the higher she held her head and the more she pulled into herself, summoning her own power and presence. If any one of them tried anything, she'd make them pay for it before the rest of them killed her.

A seething anger prickled in her veins, but if this was what stood between her and saving Leigh . . .

This time, she felt the crows when they approached.

When they passed a giant storefront, its front wall mostly glass, she caught her reflection in her peripheral vision. In her wake, lit by streetlights and shop signs and the mostly full and golden moon itself, hundreds of crows swarmed in formation, landing on buildings, streetlights, and power lines.

The vampires on the street stilled now as she approached, and the catcalling stopped.

She guessed the vampires didn't know what to make of her either.

She wanted to move faster. Every minute that passed was another where she didn't know what had happened to Leigh.

Six blocks later the storefronts gave way to large houses, followed by a park perhaps four square blocks in size. Amber streetlights yellowed every surface, and monstrous oaks and cedars towered over a children's playground in the park's center. Two vampires laughed and smoked like malevolent fairies near the children's play structures. One of them, a gangly man dressed all in black, was swinging back and forth on the swing set. The other, a woman in an out-of-place red cocktail dress, called out to Bartholomew, then quieted once she saw Joan.

The swinging stopped but they both stayed where they were. Across the street from the park, an imposing three-story stone and lumber manor house stood, backlit by the moon. Bartholomew led her between the two lampposts up the cobblestone path. Above the door, a bleached elk skull with huge eight-point antlers had been mounted, its base set into the stone. Torches flickered in the faint breeze on either side of the door—pure theater considering the recessed lighting.

Bartholomew let himself inside and gestured for her to follow.

Joan took a deep bracing breath, though she tried not to make it too obvious.

The foyer was well-lit, but she didn't notice much of the furnishings besides the fact that it was all dark wood. She was too busy looking for threats.

Bartholomew stepped to one side and opened a door to a small closet. Inside, there was nothing but empty shelves.

"Your weapons," he said. It wasn't a request.

Panic washed through her before logic dominated.

If they wanted her dead, she'd be dead. She removed her weapons and stashed them all on one shelf. While she was at it, she took off her jacket—slowly, so as not to reveal the stiffness from her injury. Her arms were free now in case she had to call out the heavier spells. The greater range would be helpful.

Joan clenched and unclenched her fists. She hadn't felt this . . . aware, this dependent on only her powers to protect her, in a long time.

It wasn't an altogether unwelcome feeling, not with new power coursing through her, but she prayed none of that was necessary.

If she expected some grand theatrics, she was disappointed. The house was mostly empty. From somewhere, she heard the strains of classical music—some rather tinny harpsichord nonsense that grated on her nerves. She saw a human or two, but they looked like servants and glared at her in suspicion. The house was cool but not cold, and some of the halls and rooms were dark. The sharp scent of antiseptic failed to mask the odor of old death.

Finally, Bartholomew stopped before double doors. After a muffled acknowledgment from inside, he opened one of them and gestured her forward. He didn't follow.

Bartholomew closed the door behind her once she'd crossed the threshold and stepped into the room.

It was a study.

As large as the entire main floor of Joan's house in Calvert, this was more of a library with wall-to-wall bookshelves. An oak desk, some eight feet wide, stood at the far end of the room, and four tables—two on each side—created an aisle down the middle of the space.

There were no windows, and a small fireplace provided little warmth. Books covered every surface—the shelves, the tables, the chairs. There were even stacks on the floor.

At the end of one table, before the only chair not occupied by endless volumes, stood the room's only other occupant.

However Joan might have imagined a First vampire might look, Elizaveta was the opposite of it.

She was tall for a woman—taller than Joan. Pale-skinned, she had a sharp, masculine jaw, broad shoulders and long black hair tied in an immaculate bun at her nape. She wore tailored slacks with a matching vest over a masculine dress shirt—all in shades of dark gray—and gloves to match.

Odd to wear them indoors. Vampires didn't feel cold. Maybe her talons kept tearing into the pages.

Elizaveta didn't move, but after a long moment, she spoke. "So, you're the new power that has everyone in an uproar."

Joan didn't know quite what to say to that, though she found it alarming that people she didn't know were talking about her at all.

The silence stretched on, and Joan twitched to take action. When was the last time she had been this close to so many vampires without killing anyone?

Elizaveta arched an eyebrow, more rakish than threatening.

"I must say it is my preference to ignore a request such as yours, but I wanted to get a look at you myself, and since the High Coven wasn't going to let you in the front door . . . She gestured lazily toward the direction Joan had traveled from.

Joan wanted to deny that she deserved any attention at all. "I didn't mean to . . . that wasn't the goal."

"If your intention was to remain anonymous, why come to the High Coven at all?"

Normally, Joan wouldn't even consider sharing practitioner business with a vampire like Elizaveta, but her other concerns made the point moot.

"There's a vampire lord blockading my town in blatant disregard of guild practices."

"And you thought the coven would help you?"

Her flippant tone was irritating. Perhaps these issues were trivial to someone of Elizaveta's age and stature, but they damned sure mattered to Joan.

"He's killing my people, and I need help to put him down."

She winced internally at her own phrasing. Telling a vampire about killing another vampire might not have been the best move.

"Well, best of luck." Elizaveta focused on the papers before her, as if the matter was resolved.

"It's not just that. I think he poses a greater threat to someone like you."

The vampire frowned. "And why should I concern myself with a fly like Victor?"

If Elizaveta knew who he was, Victor was probably a little more than an irritating insect.

Joan conjured every argument she could think of, but nothing seemed substantial enough to make her case. She tread carefully. What would motivate a First?

"Because people might get the idea that guild power is slipping. If word gets out that vampires like Victor and Nathaniel are left alone, more of the young ones will strike out on their own and disregard the guilds. Without the guilds . . ."

Joan shrugged, implying the loss of membership and less control of information—which meant at best the loss of leverage and power, and at worst open war with the covens.

Without that leverage, Firsts like Elizaveta would be swatting more gnats than they could count with fewer resources to do it.

They stared at each other. Was Joan's restlessness her own, or coming from the crows outside?

Elizaveta squinted. "I want to be clear about this so that there are no misunderstandings. I might be willing to assist in this Victor problem, but I'll expect a favor in return."

The thought of doing anything at the behest of a vampire seized Joan's guts. These creatures were monsters, parasites on humanity, nothing but ill will and malevolence, despite how they presented themselves.

Owing a favor to someone as powerful as Elizaveta was foolish, not to mention insane.

On the other hand, if it got her what she wanted . . . no matter how distasteful it might be, she had to consider it.

"What favor?"

Elizaveta stepped closer. Joan twitched, expecting an attack, but Elizaveta arched her eyebrow again in wry disapproval.

That she'd almost lost her own composure pissed Joan off even more.

"One to be decided at a later date," Elizaveta said.

An unknown future favor was worse, but Joan nodded. She had no other choice.

Elizaveta's lips parted, fangs clearly visible in her wicked smile.

CHAPTER 18

Sprawled on her hands and knees on the polished hardwood floor, Leigh closed her eyes and pictured Joan, proud and tall. The image gave her strength.

Leigh hadn't seen Pierce in years. She'd avoided him after the severe fallout of their brief nearly nonexistent tryst—Joan leaving, Trevon ostracizing her, Pierce bitter at her rejection. She had been sad when he was taken, but only because no one deserved this fate.

He had obviously adapted.

Now he held court over more vampires than she'd ever seen in one place, and even without considering their history, she was doomed.

To entertain their master, the attending vampires suggested ways Leigh might be punished for trying to save her own damned life. Gruesome and grisly, the tortures described nearly broke her, but she kept her tears in check and tried to tune them out.

Until Nathaniel spoke. "May I offer a suggestion, my liege?"

His liege. Had any of them ever been to a royal court in their lives? Everything they emulated probably came from old movies or bad television. Still, these cretins held her life in their hands. Let them play their games if it meant she got five more minutes without pain and stayed her own execution a little while longer.

Even if they turned her into a vampire, it would still mean her death. If they changed her, Leigh would no longer be herself.

If there were a way to spell herself to death, she'd have done it long ago.

"Well, dear Nathaniel," Victor said, lifting a goblet in salute. If it weren't so terrifying and tragic, it would be laughable. "I'm not sure I should let you suggest anything, since you're the one who lost her in the first place."

Someone snickered.

"Still, I am merciful, and you have learned from your mistake with Sylvia. Make your suggestion."

Nathaniel's expression changed from one of reluctant deference for Victor to pure hatred when he looked at Leigh. She might have dropped her own gaze in some measure of self-protection—anything to keep from aggravating him further—but she couldn't look away.

"The very worst thing you could do to her," he said. "The most despicable and horrible fate that she could imagine, would also be the most nefarious blow to your new nemesis."

Victor squinted. Cold anger mingled with something indecipherable and warped his expression. "I'll raze that war witch's claim from the earth no matter what, but a distraction won't hurt."

Joan had claimed Calvert?

"You're right, of course. Perhaps once little Leigh joins this court she'll finally have the attention she so craves." Victor—Pierce—had deciphered Nathaniel's meaning himself. "But first, let's have a little opening entertainment, shall we? Bring in one of the donors."

Leigh sobbed in horror.

Two vampires lifted her to her feet and held her fast, and sooner than Leigh could have imagined, a young woman was brought before her. Barely twenty, with vacant brown eyes and long auburn hair, the woman looked ravaged by withdrawal. Her lips were split and dry, her ochre skin pocked and blemished. Circles beneath her eyes sunk into her cheeks, and she stared at the floor.

Someone had taken the liberty of sinking bites into her neck and the insides of her arms.

Leigh groaned in discomfort. The woman was sickly and unclean, but her blood smelled sweet. Leigh's stomach twisted but her mouth watered for the taste of what she would not let herself have.

Once, she had been this girl. No matter how hungry Leigh was, this reflection was too much to endure.

Victor and his entourage taunted her for what seemed like forever, laughing as the girl was pressed against Leigh's chest, but still Leigh resisted. One of the vampires holding her dipped a finger in the girl's blood and tried to swipe it across Leigh's lips, but she turned her head. She fought the urge to dart her tongue out against her cheek, to taste it just once, but she spit on the floor instead.

Victor stopped laughing.

"I'm tired of this game. Tie her down and pour some down her gullet," Victor said, cold as his eyes. "That ought to inspire her to join us."

Leigh screamed as she was lifted from the ground.

A humming vibration swelled, rumbling through the floor and rattling the windowpanes. The deep thump of a helicopter in flight suddenly drowned her out.

Whoever was in that helicopter wasn't expected, because Victor's attention was no longer on Leigh. The rumbling intensified as the helicopter flew directly overhead, and then the rhythmic beat began to slow. It had landed nearby—right outside if the slowing whine of spinning blades was any indication. When the engine stopped altogether, the room fell silent.

Victor snapped his fingers at the guards at the far end of the room. "Well?"

Three men made haste in leaving. Leigh's chest heaved as she tried to catch her breath.

The sound of boots on tile and indeterminate shouts echoed back before silence fell.

One of the guards reappeared. A human thrall, he had short, shaggy brown hair and broad shoulders, and appeared to be unarmed.

"Master, it's that war witch, the one who fought back when we tried to take Calvert, but . . ." He paused, confused and scared.

Joan was here? A different terror seized Leigh. Her own death was a foregone conclusion, but . . . how could she help Joan?

Victor's faux grace collapsed. "Spit it out, you idiot."

The guard gulped before he spoke again. "She's here with another vampire."

The tone of the party changed, and Leigh struggled to understand what was happening. What was Joan doing with a vampire? Did she know Leigh was here? A restless murmur rose from the attendees, and the vampires holding her let her fall to her feet.

Victor tapped a fingertip on the arm of his chair. "How interesting." He glanced at Nathaniel and flicked his hand in a brushing-away gesture in Leigh's direction. "Let's save the surprise."

Before Leigh could process his movement or attempt to free herself, or even warn Joan of the danger awaiting her, Nathaniel wrapped one arm around her waist and tugged her against his chest, his other hand covering her mouth.

He pulled Leigh into an adjoining room, where two chairs and a small table sat before an empty, long unused fireplace. Floor-length drapes covered what must be a window. On the other side of the chairs was another closed door.

Once inside, he kicked the door shut behind them, though she could still hear the voices on the other side. He tugged her to one side of the door where a tinted pane of stained glass allowed him—and Leigh—to see the new arrivals.

"Well, well," Victor said, his voice muffled by the glass. He crossed his legs in artificial elegance. "If it isn't the prodigal daughter."

Joan stood as steadfast and intimidating as usual, clad in black with her hands at her sides. She most likely had weapons stashed on her person, but only the sword hilt at her waist was visible through the glass.

The vampire with her frowned when Victor didn't speak to him first. He was shorter than Joan, and wore a dress shirt opened at the collar and dark gray slacks. He looked like a corporate attorney, except he wore aviators. Under different circumstances, that might have been comical.

Joan laughed without humor.

"Pierce Hill," Joan said, her eyes cold and calculating. "And here I'd heard you died."

Leigh recognized that look. It meant Joan was about to do something dramatic. Hopefully it wouldn't get her killed. Leigh must have twitched because Nathaniel tightened his grip.

"Sit tight, little bloodling." His whisper in her ear made her cringe. "Looks like your beloved is going to fix what you ruined and take care of my problems for me. I don't have to kill that neophyte if she does it for me, and then I can use you to keep her in line."

What the hell was he talking about?

In the other room, Victor smiled, but he didn't seem happy to hear his previous name. "Nobody calls me that anymore."

"Asshole works, too. Where's Leigh?"

Leigh's jaw would have dropped if Nathaniel hadn't held it in place. Joy and hope mingled with the fear in her chest, and she fought to catch her breath.

Nathaniel tightened his grip around her arms. "Don't get too excited."

"She's mine for good now, Joanie." Victor's grin was biting. "She had some difficulty getting back where she belonged, but Uncle Reed was more than happy to offer his assistance."

At least that had been revealed, not that it made Joan any safer. Reed Hill stepped into view and stood behind his nephew, for once tall and domineering instead of obsequious and servile, and glared at Joan with malice. Leigh didn't know what his beef with Joan was, but she was more concerned with getting out of Nathaniel's clutches.

"And who is your friend?" Victor asked, his tone losing its feigned disinterest as he stared at Joan's . . . ally? What was she doing here with a vampire?

"I am Bartholomew," the new vampire said. "I come as an emissary of the Ruby Court guild in Black Rose City." Bartholomew didn't yell, but his voice carried, nonetheless. "Your claim on this territory has been deemed invalid and declared an unsanctioned encroachment."

The murmur rose.

Victor leaned forward from his pretend throne. "Your guild is archaic. Completely out of step with the times, and my coven doesn't require guidance." He sneered on the word as he stood. "Calvert was promised to me, and I will claim every inch if I have to bleed the entire town."

"The hell you will." Joan took a step forward, but the vampire with her stretched an arm to block her path, though he didn't touch her.

He removed his glasses. His eyes—sclera and pupils both— were a milky white. Whoever he was, this vampire was old, ancient compared to those in the room.

"I am one of the Firsts, Legate to Elizaveta by oath, not siring." Bartholomew's voice was lower now, each word enunciated crisp and terse. "I was here before the horde of your barbaric ancestors swept across this land like a plague.

"Whether you have use of it or not, young one, the guild's

211

laws and Elizaveta's oversight still apply to you. You will be held to account, and any who align themselves with you will be censured."

Nathaniel gasped. The penalty for being censured must have been severe.

The murmur grew to a buzz, the other vampires talking among themselves. Two of them stood and left.

Had Victor noticed? He spoke louder, an obvious attempt to hold the floor.

"There are no laws here, only what I want and what I have no use for. You fall into the latter category." At his gesture, four vampires jumped to surround Bartholomew.

"Remove him while I deal with this witch and my new pet."

Bartholomew didn't struggle as they seized him, but his face twisted into a grimace that suggested incontrovertible doom. "I didn't think you slow-witted. Perhaps it is already too late for you to learn your lesson."

"Yes, yes, I'm sure Elizaveta will no doubt summon a conclave so they can discuss how I'm to be spanked, but by then, Calvert will be mine. And you won't be there to see it."

Furniture toppled, voices rose, and bodies blurred in movement. Who started the brawl wasn't clear from where Leigh stood, but she heard Joan cursing and fighting with the rest.

Joan was outnumbered, even if she had some strange vampire as an ally. Leigh had to help.

"Now, now, little bloodling, you stay here." Nathaniel gave her a jarring shake. "You have ruined enough of my plans. I think perhaps this little melee is the perfect distraction. I'll find another way to bend your war witch to my will."

He was going to kill her.

Leigh could not let her fear hold her back anymore. If she was dead, she couldn't help Joan.

Then again, if she was dead but she took Nathaniel with her ...

She took a deep breath, and closed her eyes. She pictured a large flame, like the end of a torch, visualized a shield around it, a field of sparkling energy—one of protection, of rejecting anything contrary to one's self, designed to push away the essence of malevolence in close quarters.

"*Contra omnes mina.*" *Against all threats.*

Nathaniel's grip slipped, then tightened again. Had the spell worked, or was it just a coincidence?

His lips brushed her ear as he spoke, cold and dry. "You are too weak to join the court I'll build once Victor is dead. Perhaps I will make Joan my legate and she will serve me instead."

The thought of Joan in Nathaniel's clutches was enough to spur Leigh into action, but before she could break free, Nathaniel held her fast.

"I see there's some fight in you after all." As the fight in the next room intensified, Nathaniel removed the hand over her mouth and quickly bit into his own wrist. He raised his arm before her, and though she avoided it by twisting her head from side to side, his other arm still pinned her in place.

"Join me, then. Together, we will build a greater house than Victor could imagine, as I am far more powerful than he could ever be."

To her horror, his blood smelled even sweeter than the donor's. Base and obscene, but delectable. As much as she hated him, the scent of him wasn't as repulsive as she wished it to be.

Her mouth watered. She closed her eyes, desperate to stave off the attraction to his blood. She wouldn't become a monster.

Leigh pushed from her mind the sounds of the fight on the other side of the door and ignored her instincts to drink from Nathaniel's wrist. She forced herself to lean back, to press her body against his. Before she lost her courage, she spoke the incantation again, channeled her desire and fear and powerlessness and hope and every shred of love she felt for Joan into the spell.

He gasped and let her go. She whirled to face him.

Nathaniel's mouth fell agape as he reassessed her. She had to act quickly, or he would overpower her again.

Leigh spoke the incantation for a tiny flame to appear over her palm and coaxed it into a fist-sized ball. She cast it at his clothes. They caught fire, and he grunted when they burned against his skin. Distracted, he swatted at the fire, movements awkward as he avoided using his bare hands on the flame.

Leigh lifted a nearby chair and smashed it against the wall. The leg in her hand split from the frame, its wood splintered and sharp. Nathaniel raised his hand and moved his fingers in an arcing counterspell. Desperate to stop him, Leigh cried out as she stabbed the jagged wood into his chest.

It was nowhere near his heart.

Nathaniel fell to his knees, grabbing at her, closing his huge hands around one of her arms. He squeezed tightly enough that he'd break bone if she didn't stop him.

She pulled the thick stick out and stabbed him in the eye.

His hand loosened.

Nathaniel tumbled onto his side, into the curtains covering a boarded-over window. The flame of his clothes leapt to the drapes, while he cried out, the chair leg jutting from his eye socket.

He yelled something in a language she didn't recognize and the air in the room turned acrid. Droplets of water appeared in midair and streamed towards him, spattering with increasing speed against the fire on his clothes, but the flames spread over his skin like plasma. He screamed and lurched toward the other door.

Though Nathaniel fled and left her behind, Leigh wasn't safe yet.

Fire engulfed the drapes as she lurched back into the main hall.

The fight had moved into the courtyard. Joan and her ally

were gone, and so was Victor, as well as all of his guards and court members. Several vampires lay unmoving on the floor.

Reed Hill stood in the courtyard doorway, his back to Leigh, oblivious to her presence as he watched the battle.

Outside, a scream pierced the night. One of the human thralls ran past the enormous viewing window, illuminated by the outdoor lights. Three crows pecked at his head. One had already gotten to his eye, and blood ran down his face. Behind him, a shower of crows descended upon the yard.

Leigh shivered in recognition.

The crows had joined the fight.

CHAPTER 19

Pierce—*Victor*—talked too damned much.

"Once you're dead, Calvert will be all mine," he said, stepping gingerly in a half circle as he taunted her. "With Gretchen out of the way, what's left of the coven will fall to me. When I'm done, they'll wish they'd given up sooner."

Joan spat blood on the courtyard's cobblestones. Once all hell had broken loose, several of the human thralls had tried to take her down. One of the guards had landed a kick to her jaw before she killed him. She'd wounded another before the others got smart and left her to stronger foes.

Like this maniac. His movie-villain dialogue was over the top. "The boundary has been restored, you prick. Calvert will never be yours."

The ginger-stepping stopped. He planted his feet and propped his hands on his hips. "I'm not talking about the fucking boundary. Once I had enough mages, breaking it was child's play, and I can do it again. Trevon was so worried you'd never come back, he was stupid enough to show me how it was built. No Matthews around to pass on the family legacy to, so I got *all* the secrets, Joanie."

Guilt and grief threatened her concentration before she squashed them. She added this information to the endless fucking list of things she needed to research later, assuming she made it out of this alive.

"Gretchen was supposed to get all his land for me, but it doesn't matter. I will take everything he promised me. No place for you, Joanie." He arced his hands in the air, his middle fingers touching his thumbs. "*Aeris fuga.*"

Take flight. A concrete bench flew across the courtyard at her.

Joan clicked her tongue against her teeth and raised her hand to arc her index finger in a fist-sized circle. She moved her lips as her cantrip rejected his attack. A body-sized block of air countered the bench, but instead of bouncing back as she expected, it shattered to dust.

Her new power had intensified the effect of the spell.

"Your head always was too big," she said. He'd always resented her for being stronger, more powerful. Though he was a vampire now, maybe he'd succumb to his old egotistical human emotions and make a mistake. "Not that it made you any brighter."

He flipped her off. Time to turn up the heat.

"*Mille acus aegis,*" Joan said. *A thousand needles of air.*

Focused spikes of condensed air thronged Victor, puncturing his clothes and his skin, but part of the spell backfired. Joan hissed as some of the spikes stabbed at her legs.

Pinprick spots of blood peppered Victor's face and hands. He growled before dissipating the spell. "I will gorge myself on your blood."

She shrugged, forcing nonchalance. "You won't see another moonrise. I can't believe you thought you could set up shop in Calvert."

Joan thought of Leigh, and all she had been through in this very place. "No more donors for you."

"You're a fool," Victor said. "I can get blood anywhere. If it weren't for the ley lines, I'd have erased that place from the map."

She almost tripped in surprise. Victor knew about the place

Trevon had showed her—which meant he knew about its power.

He spread his arms wide and then clapped his hands. "*Aeris murus.*"

Wall of air. Though the wall itself was invisible, debris moved in a line on the floor, racing toward her.

Joan muttered an incantation and sliced her arm vertically. The wall split and moved past her.

He kept talking. "With that power, I can claim the whole valley, everything between the great rivers and the mountain ranges. Coven boundaries won't matter anymore, not when I control the elements."

More important details she had no time to focus on now. She shifted to one side, more concerned with Victor than the others still fighting nearby. Victor shifted with her and she realized he was trying to keep her between him and the others.

She glanced behind her. At the edge of the courtyard, Bartholomew had killed another vampire by punching his whole fist—talons first—through his victim's chest. Few of Victor's court remained, perhaps because Bartholomew had dispatched three of the four who had tried to restrain him. One would spend the rest of his long undead life without an arm. Another had attempted to stab him in the heart.

Bartholomew had knocked the man to his knees and torn his head from his shoulders.

When the third found a slim stiletto driven into her eye, the fourth had disappeared.

When Bartholomew had been sent to join her against Victor, Joan had thought the unassuming messenger a weak trade for the favor Elizaveta had demanded of her. She still reeled with the knowledge that the vampire who had escorted her to Elizaveta and shepherded her here must have been nearly a thousand years old.

Now, Bartholomew turned toward the last opponent—a lone bloodling, but Joan looked back at her own target.

Victor had her attention.

"Looks like you've lost your backup," she taunted.

Something moved in her peripheral vision. Reed Hill, lurking in the doorway, watching them.

Her quarry followed her line of sight. "I only rely on family."

Fucker. Enough of this bullshit. Time to find what she'd come for.

"Where's Leigh?"

He wiggled his eyebrows, a gauche gloat that didn't match the arrogant elitist image he seemed to want to project. "Dead. I slit her chickenshit throat."

He meant for it to break her, and for a split second, the heartbreak threatening her felt like a physical crack in her chest. Then relief washed over her when he glanced at his uncle for confirmation.

"You were always a shitty liar, *Pierce.*"

"Fuck you, Joan."

No more talking.

She was so focused on Victor, she didn't pay any attention to the itching sensation on the back of her neck. When it intensified into something like a burn, when a swelling *something* inside her felt like it might burst through her skin, she wondered if it was the power itself, eating her alive.

Even the sounds didn't register until a few shadows flew between her and Victor. Then the strange sensation at the edge of her consciousness had form.

Dozens of crows thronged the courtyard. Victor noticed a few moments after she did. Eyes wide, he stepped back with slowly increasing speed until he turned and ran back into the manor house.

Letting him escape wasn't part of her plan. Joan followed.

The room where Victor held his court had filled with smoke. Flames licked at the inner manor house walls. Across from the entrance, Reed pushed aside a chair and tried to move an overturned table that blocked another exit. If he didn't clear it, the door they'd come through was the only way out.

No one else remained.

He turned to face her, fear and rage twisting his face. She guessed he'd done the math—this was a zero-sum game. Either she'd kill them both, or she'd die in this room.

Here in the manor house, calling earth magic was more difficult. Air spells were more reliable—at least when she wasn't wrestling with unpredictable power surges—but Victor nearly matched her on that front.

Every spell she cast, he countered. Every spell of his, she blocked with increasing effort. As a human, he had been most adept with air, and had only grown more so as a vampire. If she could catch a moment's break, she might find a way to draw him back outside and find some earth nearby to use against him, but Victor was relentless.

She was tired, flagging. Too much spell work in too short a time with very little recovery, and the wound on her side from the checkpoint screamed every time she raised her arms. If she didn't end this soon, overtaxed resources would deplete her, her fine motor skills would decay and squander her attention.

Meanwhile, Victor looked fresh for someone who was already dead, and his spells were coming too fast for her to mount an offense.

The burning sensation on the back of Joan's neck made her wince. Instinct compelled her to *push* the feeling at him, as if the sensation in her body could be passed through the air *at* Victor. When it left her body, her shoulders sagged a bit in relief, but she drew herself up, pushed herself back into the fight.

Crows threw themselves at the window, their blood streaking the glass as they fell, and still they came. Something the size of a small melon hit left of center and cracked the glass, weakening it, and with half a dozen more collisions like it, the glass broke.

The crows streamed in while the smoke poured out and the

flames grew. When the crows attacked Victor, he fought off the first dozen with magic, but soon there were too many. He screamed his frustration as he resumed his attack on Joan.

She coughed and couldn't stop, the smoke stealing her breath. Now the power of air waned, and she had nothing left to draw from but fire, an element she'd never successfully wielded—

Power.

Victor had said the power of the land granted control of all four elements. He knew as well as she did that spells needed proximity to the element to be effective. Maybe *control* meant she didn't have to be close enough to the element to summon its use.

The crows around him tripled, several pecking at his face, distracting him from his next attack on Joan, but it gave her a moment to consider something impossible.

She had this one chance, and if it failed and he fought off the birds, she was fucked.

Go for broke and pray it is enough.

Joan summoned earth, air, fire, and water all at once. "*Terra, aer, ignis, aqua. Mecum in remissione coniunge.*" *Earth, air, fire, water. Join me in release.*

One bloodshot eye widened in response and understanding as Victor, the vampire who had once been her father's apprentice, recognized the spell and saw his own doom.

She raised one hand from her waist palm up, then pointed her index finger at him as she called to water. She no longer needed to speak—the power flowed through her, cells stretched to their limits as her body acted as its conduit.

He spoke the beginning of an incantation, a counterspell, but a coughing fit interrupted him. He choked and vomited water, a flood flowing from his nose and mouth.

Joan raised her other hand to match the first, and summoned fire. Flames around the room formed lines that crawled inexorably toward Victor, and he shook his head in denial, still choking on the flow of water coming from his own body.

She called to the earth and the floor began to shake. The stones in the floor split, their mortar crumbling as the earth pushed through, pushed up and heaped at his legs, freezing him in place.

With Joan's final gesture—a flick of her wrist and flare of her fingers—a tiny yet forceful tornado of air swept the flames over his body and consumed him.

Joan didn't leave though the smoke thickened. She wanted to see him burn.

By the time his blackened corpse fell to the floor, Joan had been driven to her knees by the smoke. Fatigue crashed into her and knocked her to the ground. She tried to push herself up but couldn't. The power had waned.

Exhausted, she rolled onto her side. She had no energy left to push the fire away, to thin the smoke so she could breathe.

She hoped Leigh wasn't here, that she'd made it out alive. She hoped Nathaniel had died with the others and couldn't hunt Leigh anymore.

Joan hoped Leigh would find somewhere safe, like she deserved.

The air was too thick for Joan to cry very hard.

One of the inside walls crumbled, smoke and ash and fiery debris crashing to the ground. Through the smoke and fire, Reed Hill screamed from where he was pinned by blazing debris. The screaming suddenly stopped, and Joan lamented a lost opportunity. She'd wanted to kill that traitorous shit-heel herself.

Now the only sounds were the crackling of the flames and the screeching of crows. They prodded her, poking her limbs. Idly, she wondered if enough of them together might be able to carry her to freedom, but the coughing kept her from laughing.

Eventually, after several of them dropped dead, even the crows surrendered and left her alone. She didn't have the strength to shove their corpses off her. Glamorous, for her to kill the monsters but die filthy and alone, covered in dead birds for her trouble. No good deed . . .

Another section of the ceiling collapsed to the floor, blocking the only way out.

Around her, the flames roared.

Joan closed her eyes.

CHAPTER 20

Leigh had never seen the manor house as empty as it was now. The guards were nowhere to be seen, Nathaniel had disappeared, and the few humans she saw were scrambling for the exits like she was.

The smoke from the fire followed her through the corridors and side rooms until she found her way outside. She had to get to Joan.

She rushed around the manor, through the long-dead side gardens and past the carport, until finally, Leigh crouched behind a stone retaining wall and watched the battle below.

Two clusters fought in the courtyard—the old vampire against Victor's henchmen, and Joan against Pierce. The distance between the clusters increased until Joan and Pierce were alone while the other fight moved off toward the vineyard. Then Joan chased Pierce back into the manor house.

Somewhere out of sight, glass exploded and a new stream of black smoke leapt for the sky.

Human thralls raced from the far side of the manor house, no longer held captive. They ran to the roads, the lanes of the vineyard—any available path away from Victor's collapsing influence, and the same way she'd once escaped herself. More flames appeared in the glass-less windows, the smoke thickening as first light turned the black sky indigo.

The old vampire chased someone Leigh couldn't see around the building. Whoever he was, he was terrifying and Leigh didn't want to be anywhere near him.

Joan hadn't come back out of the manor house. She was somewhere inside that fiery hell.

When a small flock of crows burst from the smoke with still no sign of Joan, Leigh couldn't hold herself back anymore.

Barefoot, she ignored the bite of the carport's gravel and the courtyard's cobblestone and rushed to the manor house door.

Leigh paused at the edge of the room. The smoke made it difficult to see, but the flames cast flickering light, revealing debris and reflecting off shattered glass. Reed Hill was nowhere in sight, and neither was Victor, but . . .

Joan lay motionless on her side, a handful of dead crows strewn across her body and another dozen around her on the floor.

A flaming wall of debris separated Leigh from Joan, but it didn't matter. Leigh cleared the pile in one jump, rushed to Joan's side and shoved the birds away.

"Joan." Leigh shook Joan's shoulder but nothing changed. The sweet scent of blood made her salivate, but then worry eclipsed the sensation. The presence of blood meant Joan was wounded. She pressed her fingers to Joan's neck, sobbing in relief when she felt a pulse.

Leigh stood awkwardly, lifting Joan in her arms, her deadweight and height difference complicating the motion. Rational thought returned, and she shifted Joan's body onto one shoulder. She peered through the thickening cloud. The only escape was the way she'd come in.

The acrid odor of burnt flesh hit her halfway to the gap. Someone else had burned to death nearby.

Leigh prayed it had been Nathaniel. Maybe it had been Pierce—but it didn't matter right now. She had to get Joan out of here.

Another set of beams collapsed in front of her. The flames blocked her view of the exit.

They were trapped.

She screamed at her own powerlessness. After all this, was she meant to die in this place that had only ever been hell to her? To have come so close to escaping doom, to have found Joan, only to have fate once again seal her in darkness?

No.

She might deserve it, but Joan wouldn't die here.

Leigh shifted Joan's weight on her shoulder, holding her fast with one hand. With her other, she reached out to grab a flaming beam and tossed it aside with a cry. She thrust ahead, smothering the flames that had caught on Joan's clothes with her free hand, oblivious to any pain. She was probably too full of adrenaline to feel anything.

Once the way was half clear, she stepped across the remaining obstacles, weaving her way through the destruction and unmoving bodies until she crossed the courtyard. She carried Joan past the wall, through another garden of dead flowers to the grassy hill beyond it.

Finally clear, Leigh set Joan down on the ground and checked once again to make sure she was breathing.

She suppressed the urge to lick the blood from Joan's cheek.

Leigh sat beside Joan, taking a moment to breathe before she figured out what to do next. She looked down, expecting to see burns, hoping they weren't too awful.

Instead, her hands were smudged with ash and charcoal, but the skin was otherwise unblemished.

What did that mean? Was she too strong to get burned now?

Joan coughed, brackish and body-wrenching, and then pushed herself upright. She glanced at the madness surrounding them until her eyes fell on Leigh. Her lips parted with her smile. Even covered in ash, soot and blood, while reeking to high heaven, Joan Matthews was a beautiful woman.

"Fancy meeting you here," Joan croaked, her gaze warm despite their circumstances.

As always, it seemed like Joan could see into the soul of her. For a brief moment, Leigh's heart ached with the knowledge that Joan would never look at her so lovingly if she knew the truth.

Then she remembered her glamour was long gone, and Joan saw her as she was. Leigh burst into tears and squeezed Joan so tightly, Joan started coughing again.

Soft footsteps on the grass came closer. The old vampire—Bartholomew. She froze when his milky white eyes assessed her, but he spoke only to Joan.

"I am pleased and not surprised to see you alive, Joan Matthews."

Joan grunted. "What happened to the others?" She pushed herself to her feet. Leigh joined her.

"Dead or dispersed."

"Any chance one will try to take his place?"

The vampire shrugged a shoulder, but the move was too wooden to be fluid. An affectation, not a habit. "I will remember every face I saw this night. They will all be censured."

"Censured?" Leigh asked, but then wished she hadn't spoken. His gaze was too keen on her. Was there some punishment for being a bloodling, some price he'd expect her to pay?

"Eternal banishment. Forever sounds like a blessing until they realize they will have no peace or sanctuary for the rest of their lives."

A chill passed over Leigh's skin despite the heat. Joan squeezed her shoulder, a gesture of protection and support.

He looked back at Joan. "Is this the reason you were in such a hurry?"

Joan flinched. Leigh pulled away, suspecting she wasn't welcome, but Joan clung to her arm.

Around them, chaos reigned. The crack and thunderous fall of more of the house as it gave in to the flames rumbled through the earth. Another scream from within the building sounded, cut off as someone was consumed by the fire.

Leigh hoped Nathaniel's corpse burned to ash.

"I must go," Bartholomew said.

Joan dropped her arms and turned toward Bartholomew, daunting even as her chest heaved with visibly painful breaths. "I won't forget that you got me here in time, but that doesn't mean I won't kill you if I ever see you again."

"I understand." The vampire smiled, one of genuine amusement that revealed the length of his fangs.

He glanced at the sky, which grew lighter with every passing moment. He nodded at them, and after one last weighted glance at Leigh, he left without another word.

Moments later, the helicopter started up, its blades picking up speed. Bartholomew wasted no time and ascended only high enough to clear the trees. He turned north and disappeared in less than a minute.

Then, the roar of the flames was the only sound.

Leigh sniffled, blinking against the smoke. "I'd ask why you're here, how the hell you got here, but I don't care." At least, she didn't right now.

"I couldn't let them keep you," Joan said, her voice catching.

Leigh embraced her again. This time, Joan didn't seem to mind the squeezing so much.

They rounded the house from a distance as the heat grew unbearable. Hand in hand, they walked toward the vineyard's parking lot and the remaining cars—their owners had fled or died in the raging inferno behind them.

Leigh pointed. "That one." It was Reed Hill's van.

"Blah blah, something about begging and choosing," Joan muttered, then busied herself with hot-wiring it before they climbed inside.

The van's old engine roared, its exhaust steaming in the cold.

Victor was dead, but they were alive, and the terrors that he'd wreaked upon Calvert had come to an end.

In the passenger seat, Leigh looked back once. The fire had spread to the vineyard, its dormant vines ablaze.

Joan guided the van to the road back to town.

The sign on the side of the road displayed the seven miles remaining to Calvert. Neither of them had spoken a word in a long while when Leigh finally broke the silence.

"What are we going to tell the watch . . . and the coven?" Leigh asked. She clasped Joan's hand in both of her own on her lap.

As far as the town was concerned, the vampires had held Calvert hostage to force Leigh's surrender. What would they say when she returned? Even though Victor and Nathaniel were dead, someone was bound to have some questions about why they'd wanted Leigh in the first place.

Joan shrugged, the gesture slow with her fatigue, and she squeezed Leigh's hands in reassurance. "Obviously, I'll tell them about Reed and Pierce, but I don't know what to say about Bartholomew."

Leigh had forgotten about the other vampire. She'd have to get that whole story from Joan later, but now she had more pressing concerns.

"I mean about me," Leigh said. She tried to pull her hand away, but Joan squeezed tighter.

"It doesn't matter what they say," Joan said. "Calvert is your home, and I won't let them take it away from you."

"You may not have a choice. Against the whole coven? Joan, you can't do that." If they found out Leigh was a bloodling, they'd never let her stay.

229

Sheepishly, Joan glanced at Leigh and then back at the road. "There are some things I've got to tell you," Joan began, but Leigh mustered the courage to interrupt.

"We don't have to tell them anything," Leigh said, her voice almost a whisper.

Sunlight broke through the trees and flooded the car. Joan stared into Leigh's eyes and seemed to understand.

"You want to keep the glamour."

"Yeah." Leigh released Joan's hand and stared at her own palms for a moment. "I'm the one who has to live with it."

"Baby, I don't want anything between us. Not ever again."

Leigh turned in her seat towards Joan. "Not for you, love," she said. "For them. They'll never let me stay. I'm one of the monsters."

"You're not."

Joan had to know Leigh was right, but it took her another mile to admit it.

"We'll tell them Nathaniel and Pierce are dead," Joan said. "We'll tell them about Reed's treachery. But that's it."

Relieved, Leigh pondered the possibilities of having more time. She was still a bloodling, but the only person who mattered accepted her.

For the first time in what felt like forever, Leigh considered the prospect of hope.

Joan's tired and wry smile was a balm to every ache in Leigh's chest.

CHAPTER 21

Dayton waited at the border like the day Joan had arrived in Calvert. This time, he sat in the chair. Willy lay beside him on the asphalt.

How it had been less than a week was beyond Joan.

She slowed the van, the squeaking brakes loud in the otherwise quiet air. Leigh had found a blanket and pretended to be asleep, her head sagged against the passenger side door and her legs tucked under her on the seat. Bare feet blackened by soot and dirt poked from under the blanket.

When Joan rolled down the window, Willy leapt up and tried to climb through it, his paws scratching the paint. He sneezed and snarled, and Joan had seconds to ward him off.

"Guess I killed enough vampires tonight that I reek of them," Joan said in greeting, but she had one hand on her pistol.

"Back up, Willy," Dayton said. The dog sneezed again and backed off, then heeled by Dayton's side with a whine.

One confrontation down, one to go. Then the meaning behind Dayton's solitude sank in. "What happened to the blockade?" Joan asked.

"Funny thing," he said, his fatigue bleeding into his tone. "I got back about an hour ago, just in time to see them light out of here like they were on fire. The checkpoints all reported that the roads are clear. We've still gotta clear out the treefall, but . . ."

She was too tense to show how relieved she was. Too much remained at stake.

Dayton didn't wait for her to respond. "Visiting a First alone? What the fuck, Joan?"

He barely acknowledged Leigh, which was good.

"I didn't have a lot of choice." Joan had to give him something before the questions started in earnest. "Here are the highlights. Victor and Nathaniel are dead. Reed Hill was the mole, and he's dead, too. The vineyard is burning and there was no one alive when we left." There had been no point in waiting for the fire to burn out to confirm the body count.

Dayton's eyebrows conveyed his shock. "You are definitely better than advertised. Luther's in your driveway, before you ask." He reached into his pocket and tugged out her keys.

He didn't know the half of it. Probably never would.

She sighed, the fatigue dragging her body down deeper in the uncomfortable seat and tearing at the scabbed-over wound on her side. "We've got to talk, but right now, I just want a fucking bed."

He looked at the passenger seat. "You vouching for her?"

Joan forced herself not to glance at Leigh. "Yeah."

"Good enough for me," he said, and backed away from the van to wave them through.

That was a problem for another day. She squeezed the cracked vinyl of the steering wheel and pretended all this deception wouldn't come back to bite them both in the ass.

Sunlight brightened the tops of the pines as Joan took the back roads to the house. She didn't want to drive Main Street in Reed Hill's van. Someone was bound to flag her down, and explaining how it came to be in her possession wouldn't be a short conversation. She needed time, to rest and to regroup before she dealt with all the people who would want something from her.

These outer roads were her favorites—the transition from

232

the civilization of town to the open farmlands and surrounding woods and hills. Joan exhaled, relaxing her shoulders as she drove, calm for once. Leigh was safe beside her, the latest battle won. So much work remained, but with Leigh by her side, the coven that she'd pledged to lead, Dayton and the watch—maybe she could make Calvert better. Not what it had been, because those times were gone, but maybe something different.

Was that what her father had tried to tell her?

She still had to tell Leigh about his ghost.

The crows came in slow, sweeping flights across the sun's path. Fewer of them now, a hundred or so, but they'd followed her where she'd needed to go, and aided her in ways she'd never imagined. She couldn't have killed Victor without them.

Caller of the crows. She'd have to find those answers soon.

"Can you be happy here, Joan?"

Leigh shifted again as the words tumbled out. She untucked her legs and sat upright. Leigh's hand was gentle against Joan's. "Don't stay just for me. You'll only resent me in the end, and I can't live with that."

As Joan turned onto the road behind the homestead where her father had lived his whole life, she searched for words. She only had this one chance to make Leigh understand or the tenuous bond between them might break before it could strengthen.

She pulled into the carport next to the shed on the back of the property and turned off the van. The clicks and pings of the old engine filled the cab as she leaned back.

"Calvert is a part of me, and I'm bound to it now. But even if I did stay for you, you're reason enough to do anything."

Maybe Joan never should have left all those years ago, but if she hadn't, she wouldn't have been strong or capable enough for what she'd done in the last few days.

"My place is wherever you are, but I want us to be here, in this house, and I don't want you to ever leave. Nowhere else has ever felt like home."

No *one* else, either, but she left that unsaid.

Leigh stared at her. Joan stared back, trying to pull into herself whatever strength or power might show Leigh who she was now, and how much she meant what she said, but she was too tired. She wondered how long she'd be able to rest before the coven came knocking. Or Dayton.

Jesus. What the hell had she signed up for?

Joan eased herself upright. It should have felt heavier, this responsibility, but now, all she cared about was the fact that she was alive, and so was Leigh. All she could do was be herself and hope that was enough. She didn't have anything else to give.

Whatever Leigh saw on Joan's face must have convinced her.

Joan wanted to kiss her, but not in this horrible van. They climbed out and cut through the hedges to the backyard. Leigh pulled up short and tugged Joan closer, her hands clasping Joan's jacket. She smelled like smoke, like fire, but her lips were cool, and they tasted like Leigh. That was all Joan cared about.

Leigh leaned away first. "I heard you, and I love you, too."

Joan offered a tired smile. "You gonna take me to bed or what?"

Leigh laughed and it made Joan's heart sing.

Joan took Leigh's hand and led her through the garden rows.

EPILOGUE
SEVEN MONTHS LATER

Joan set the small pack she'd brought at the base of a tree at the edge of the ley line clearing, then removed a flannel blanket to spread over the relatively flat stretch of grass and clover. She kicked off her boots with relief. After the day's heat, losing every last stitch of her clothes sounded like the best idea ever. She dumped her shirt, jeans, and underwear in a pile nearby.

Naked on the blanket and propped against the tree under the warm golden light of the glorious high-summer moon, Joan allowed herself the luxury of a wide smile.

A few bold crow caws warned her before someone shuffled through the woods, a courtesy on their part, but she wasn't surprised to have company.

Leigh ducked under the last low branch blocking the trail and smiled when she saw Joan. Unglamoured and dressed in a thigh-length plain linen tunic with centered buttons from neck to hem, she held two wine glasses in one hand and a dark green bottle in the other.

Joan's heart raced in welcome. "Right on time," she said.

"Witches." Leigh shook her head in mock disapproval at Joan's nudity despite the half smile twisting her lips as she walked across the grass. "Any excuse to get naked."

"Blessed be," Joan said with a smirk, and spread her legs, unashamed.

Leigh snickered as she set the glasses on the grass next to the blanket and pulled the cork from the already opened bottle.

"Come here. Three days felt like forever." Joan had returned not an hour ago from another one of her envoy missions with Dayton.

They'd spent the last few months extending an olive branch of sorts to some of the neighboring covens. As she'd expected, some folks were polite but wary while others were openly hostile, though they hadn't raised weapons or made any threats. Still no word had come from Black Rose City, and the threat of Elizaveta's owed favor lurked in the back of Joan's mind.

Right now, though, she wanted her hands on Leigh as soon as possible.

Leigh fanned herself with one hand as she sat down on the blanket. "It's too hot for flannel."

Joan had some ideas to distract her from the warm fabric—none of them cooling.

"Why don't you let me help you?" She bit back a smile at the effect her voice had on Leigh, whose gold-tinged pupils dilated.

Leigh sat between Joan's legs, her back to Joan's chest, and sank against her. Joan unbuttoned her dress and splayed her hands across Leigh's exposed skin.

"I love you," Joan whispered, nipping at one delicate earlobe.

Leigh gasped and wrapped one hand up and behind Joan's head. With her other hand, she guided Joan between her thighs, and Joan moaned at the warm wet against her fingers.

"You miss me?" Joan asked.

Leigh hummed. "And eager to welcome you home." She pushed Joan's fingers inside herself.

Joan hissed. All that mattered was Leigh, and all she wanted to do was please her.

She lost herself for a while, until Leigh's cries filled her ears.

Later, with the loving between them paused, Joan took a swig from the bottle of red wine before handing it to Leigh.

"We could have used the glasses, you know," Leigh said, her voice lower than usual, a sign her body was replete, at least for now.

"Nah," Joan said, reclaiming the bottle for another drink.

They sat in warm companionable silence until conversation resumed in bits and pieces. Joan was happy to listen as Leigh relayed what had happened while she was gone. One tense altercation had risen between the watch and a supply caravan of former human thralls.

Which led Leigh to bring up something Joan didn't want to discuss. Again.

"I need to learn how to fight, like you do," Leigh said. "And I understand why you don't want to teach me yourself, but that doesn't mean I won't find someone who will."

Joan didn't want any harm to come to Leigh from any quarter—she'd kill anyone who tried to hurt her. Leigh was strong enough to fight and only needed skill, but Joan didn't want her exposed.

Still, she felt too good right now to argue, and if she said one more time she'd prefer otherwise, Leigh would probably punch her. Leigh lacked finesse, but a bloodling's strike would still hurt.

So far, they'd managed to keep Leigh's secret, but sooner or later . . .

Joan squeezed her lover and nuzzled her neck, a peace offering of sorts. Leigh grasped her back.

"Sooner or later, Joan, someone's going to come knocking on our door who's as bad as Victor." Leigh looked at her, her dark eyes troubled despite her relaxed state. "Or worse."

As if hinting at future trouble, the crows rustled in the nearby trees, ever present when Joan was outdoors. Still, nothing threatened them right this second, and for now, she was right where she wanted to be. Leigh was safe and in her arms.

"Let them come," Joan said.

As long as they were together, they'd find a way through.

The flutter of wings murmured in the warm night. Joan kissed Leigh's warm and waiting lips, then pulled away to rest her head against her lover's. She brushed her lips against the side of Leigh's head again.

Joan could never seem to stop herself.

ACKNOWLEDGEMENTS

By the Laws of Debut Novels, I'm to thank my publisher, my editor, and my wife, though not necessarily in that order. With love and respect to them all, I've made some adjustments and additions.

To every butch black lesbian war witch I've ever met: I see you, sister. Keep fighting the good fight because we are absolutely winning.

I am eternally thankful Stefani Deoul took me by the hand to personally introduce me to Salem West and Ann McMan, and by extension to Bywater Books. Stefani insisted my work had value and was certain we'd all get along famously. I should probably never argue with Stefani about anything, since her proven prescience is now publicly established by the existence of this book.

Anna Burke is the only person who has ever said "Virginia, you can do better" in a way that made me want to immediately improve, skipping my usual hackles-up reaction. As the primary editor of this manuscript, she pushed me to dig deeper. Thanks, Anna. I hope to one day (cough) return the favor.

Everything I write—short story, fan fic, novel, flash—first lands in Quinn Clarkson's inbox. Her commentary falls into two categories: "nice bones" means the piece needs work, while "hurry up with the next part" means I'm on the right track. (This story got both, so here we are.) Thanks for all the hot-or-not checks, the morning-after responses to my nightly NaNoWriMo emails, and the random chats about plot development. Fear not—I've got more coming your way.

Heather Flournoy, editor extraordinaire, has been an instrumental resource for my story development for the last four years. Before I even thought about submitting this story for publication consideration, I sent it to Heather to ensure it was worth shopping any further. Thanks for helping me strengthen Leigh's voice.

Thanks to Bruce Wyman and Kate Dilworth, who helped me reach the finish line on-time(-ish), both offering help before I asked.

Special thanks to the folks at Moving On Media, Christa Morris, KT Jorgensen, and Jess Harris-DiStefano, for enduring my bi-weekly "yeah, I'm behind on that; still working on the novel" updates. As for Christa and KT, thank you for your patience during every brunch moment where I stared into space while ignoring the conversation. For two decades, you have supported my every creative endeavor. This book is as much your achievement as it is mine. (KT, you can scratch this one off the monster list.)

A separate and distinct word for Ann McMan, who designed the utterly gobsmacking cover. Believe me when I tell you it brought tears to my eyes. I still don't understand how she was able to encapsulate the core of the story in an image—particularly one that didn't include either of the main characters—but she did. I told her I'd probably make it a tattoo. She may be horrified to know I was serious.

Terri Furuya and Shawn Marie Bryan were often my accountability partners during this book's journey, and I'm grateful for their support and encouragement.

To my family, natural and chosen, my sisters, brothers, and cousins; to family extended by love and marriage; to those living and dead who have encouraged me; to those who have inspired me (yes, Tylor and Micaya, this means you); to those who know me by other names and other lives but have supported me just the same; to those I've loved who will never see or hold this book—to all of you, thank you.

I've likely forgotten someone, perhaps more than one. Kelly Barnhill once wrote "an acknowledgements page is, by its nature, incomplete." Please know the omission is inadvertent and thank you for helping to bring this book into the world.

Thank you to my mother, Rosemary, for always accepting me as I am. Please lie to me and tell me you skipped Chapter 12.

Thank you to Chase, the elder, though you left us decades ago. You would have loved this, even if you'd never read a word.

Thank you to Chase, the younger, for being as excited as I was about this book's publication, even if it ain't your cup of tea, and even if being psyched about something your mama did is not in any way cool.

I offer my endless thanks to my wife, Kate, who never protests when I say I need to write, and always understands me in those moments when I can't find the words at all.

ABOUT THE AUTHOR

Virginia Black likes strong whiskey, loud music, and writing, though not necessarily in that order. When not penning dark speculative fiction, she is almost always reading. Born in California—where even green is brown—Virginia escaped to the rain showers and vibrant hues of the Pacific Northwest. She lives with her wife of twenty years and their savagely witty teenage daughter.

Learn more at virginiablackwrites.com.

And follow her at:

Twitter: @virginiablk517
Facebook: www.facebook.com//virginia.black.779642
Instagram: www.instagram.com/virginiablk517/

At Bywater Books, we're committed to bringing the best of contemporary literature to an expanding community of readers. Our editorial team is dedicated to finding and developing outstanding writers who create books you won't want to put down.

For more information about Bywater Books, our authors, and our titles, please visit our website.

www.bywaterbooks.com

CPSIA information can be obtained
at www.ICGtesting.com
Printed in the USA
JSHW011447050223
37298JS00004B/9